To Janet
Hopp
a.t.

It's all about ME!

Carolyn Swann

This book is published by BITE Publishing, Cardiff.

A copy of this book is available at
the National Library of Wales and the British Library.

Print ISBN 978-0-9928509-6-8
Ebook ISBN 978-0-9928509-5-1

Cover design and typesetting by Ritchie Craven
(ritchiecraven@gmail.com)

To the Madeleine in us all.

Today (Saturday, 18th October) 7.20a.m.

A flash of livid red hurtled towards the steamroller. With no hint of a reduction in speed, the car bounced in and out of a deep pothole spitting gravel and dust in its wake, and disappeared.

Lacking the ability to perform any kind of emergency stop and not entirely convinced he hadn't rolled the speeding car into the driveway, the man at the wheel of the trundling machine peered back over his shoulder. To his relief, the car was not neatly embossed in the gravel.

'Blimey,' muttered the man. 'So, the nail varnish didn't match after all then!'

Monday, June 3rd, 8.55a.m. Two years earlier

Hayden Elliot sat down on his trusty swivel chair and sighed. It was one of those shoulder-slumping sighs that said, 'Oh bollocks, I knew that was coming!'

A searching glance at the letter hanging limp in his hand betrayed his impotent hope that it might have changed its message during the relatively short walk from kitchen to study. But, one floor up and overlooking the rumpled waters of Landsmere Bay, the view on this wet Wednesday in early June was as joyless as the message conveyed in those stubbornly unchanged words:

Dear Hayden

I've met someone else and I'm moving out – actually I've already moved out (as you will see if you look in my dressing room).

I doubt that you've noticed but I haven't been happy for quite some time and the debacle at this year's Champagne Lunch really was the last straw – I will never forgive Dennis Peters for what he said about my lovely new teeth, or you for laughing.

You can have Landsmere – it's falling down and I've always hated the freezing British sea anyway.

I will of course be keeping the villa and if you have any heart at all you will not begrudge me this one indulgence – let's call it my going away present!

You will have to find your own lawyer as I have already briefed Raymond – if you really must contact me, go through him. You and I both know that Raymond will make sure I get what I'm due!

Sorry to do this in a letter but my plane leaves in an hour. I would say I've enjoyed the last fourteen years with you but I'd be lying.

Have a nice life.

Carla

P.S.   I'm keeping the clothes – after all there's no guarantee my replacement will be a Size 10 FF

P.P.S.   Thanks for the boobs, Fabio loves them! X

Monday, June 3rd, 9.10a.m.

Madeleine Edwards swept into her office, slid her overtly expensive briefcase onto her desk and ran her perfectly manicured fingers across the letters M.E. elegantly engraved across the brass fastening. She smiled at the reflection of her bronzed face in the mirror on the opposite wall. After two weeks in Amalfi lying by a pool she felt ready for anything.

Half a dozen unopened envelopes were stacked in her in-tray. The top one looked plump with promise; the rest, she guessed by their brown flatness, were not. So, making a mental note to get her assistant, Tanya, to go through them later, Madeleine picked up the bulging pack that had first caught her eye. It bore her name in thick, black felt pen in the stylish scrawl of Josh, the brilliantly talented graphic designer from Davies Hart Design; Madeleine was pleased that Josh, a fairly recent discovery, was already proving to be the perfect complement to her own significant marketing skills. And the pack, she guessed with the smug excitement of a job she knew she had done well, would be the product shots from the launch of the DV16 that she had orchestrated just before her holiday. Madeleine grimaced briefly as she recalled the vision of the model's face when the poor girl caught her pubic hair in the fan (it was her own fault – a short skirt and a thong is a recipe for disaster in anyone's book!) before pushing the image easily from her mind.

Kicking off her shoes, Madeleine made a second mental note, this time to book a bikini wax. Then, tapping the remaining envelopes into a neat wad, she stood sideways to admire the view in her office window and nodded appreciatively; other than a bit of a pasta bulge-ette, she really did look great for forty-five. And her bum looked tiny in her new tailored white linen trousers.

The phone rang. Her boss's number flashed up on the LED. She let it ring while she sat down and crossed her bare feet up on the desk.

'John! Hi!'

'Madeleine, you're in!'

'Looks like!' She beamed at her reflection again. 'Not late for a meeting, am I? The time difference has thrown me completely. Haven't had two minutes to look at my emails. Mountain of post to get through and no sign of Tanya yet. I swear, if that girl's going to slip into her old ways again. You know what I said, John – your niece or not, if she can't perform she just can't stay. God knows we've got no room for dead wood, not in this financial climate!'

A slightly strained voice cut in. 'Madeleine, er, you haven't opened your post yet, have you?'

'No – well – yes. Some of it,' Madeleine lied. She flicked through the envelopes again quickly and continued to chat. 'Was the press coverage OK, John? My flight was so early. Didn't see any British papers. And once I got to Amalfi..., oh, you know what it's like. I was absolutely exhausted. Just had to put it all out of my mind until I got back.'

The large manila pack dropped to the floor, together with a white envelope Madeleine hadn't noticed earlier. Again, her name was handwritten on the front, this time in small neat capitals. As she made a grab for it the button on her trousers pinged to freedom.

'Ooh, my, my! What have I got here?' She waved the envelope at the phone while trying to retrieve the escape button with her bare toes. 'Not the bonus I've been laying heavy hints about for the past month, is it?'

With the receiver wedged under her chin she slid a pen into the corner of the envelope and carried on chatting.

'My God, John, you haven't finally realised that I really am worth my...'

She stopped. There was no cheque.

'Madeleine? Are you still there?' John's disembodied voice floundered. 'Well... er, I guess... er... Oh, for Chrissake, Maddy, haven't you seen *any* news? You announce the biggest advance in surgical equipment since the... the scalpel, as far as the rest of the world could tell, and then bugger off out of the country for a fortnight and don't think to look at a paper – *or take your phone!*'

'But I was on holiday– '

'I don't give a shit, Maddy! It didn't work! If you'd just waited that extra week – like Technical said. And that model threatened to sue – you know, the one who caught her... where the hell did you get her from anyway? Don't tell me, another brilliant idea from Davies Hart! You do not want to know what I've had to deal with since you skipped off for your *well-earned break*!' After a shaky start, John was now under full steam. But as he vented the frustrations of the past fortnight, the words of the letter in front of Madeleine extinguished the sound of his shouting:

Dear Ms Edwards

As you are aware Rowland and Finch are a relatively small company and the newly created post of Marketing Director was dependent upon the company's successful entry into the cardio-vascular surgery market. Following the premature and disastrous launch of the DV16 earlier this month, the Board have taken the decision to terminate your employment as Marketing Director of this company with immediate effect.

As our Terms of Employment clearly state, owing to the highly competitive nature of this industry we are unable to allow you to remain on the premises to work out any period of notice. I therefore request that you clear your desk of any personal effects immediately and report to HR in order that they can confirm you have not removed any confidential or sensitive items belonging to this company. Once this check has been carried out you will be escorted from the building by a member of the security team who will inspect your company vehicle and ensure that all keys are returned to Rowland and Finch on your departure.

I would like to take this opportunity to thank you for all the hard work that you have put into your role since joining us last autumn and wish you every success in your future career.

Yours sincerely
John Bradshaw
Chief Executive

Madeleine looked down at the signature. The letter was signed by John's PA.

Monday, June 3rd, 10.30a.m.

Madeleine sipped her cappuccino and licked chocolaty froth from her upper lip. Outside the otherwise deserted coffee bar, a woman in a red jersey dress locked her car and strode towards the café from the other side of the street. She was hardly through the door before she started speaking.

'Oh, God, Maddy, are you OK?' The woman greeted her friend with a theatrical hug and a tumble of questions. 'How could they do this after all you did? I came as soon as I could. Are you OK? What did they say – the bastards? You said the launch was great. Do you think my car'll be OK over there? Would you like me to read the letter? No? OK, that's fine. Are you sure you haven't misunderstood it?

'No, Nia, it's pretty clear.' Madeleine handed over the letter, which Nia scanned briefly.

'Hmm, not much doubt about the meaning there, I'm afraid. Look, I'm going to get a coffee. You want another?'

'Oh, yes, that would be lovely,' said Madeleine with a weak smile. She gulped down the one in front of her and handed over the warm cup. 'Cappuccino, thanks. Tell Travis it's for me – he'll add extra topping. Were you busy? I just didn't know what to do when they took my car. I tried Josh first but he's in a meeting.'

'Fairly. Yet another tender. God, I hate them – the curse of the self-employed! Let's hope this one's worth the effort!' Nia said from the counter. A young man bustled out from the kitchen and

Nia ordered the coffees – a cappuccino for Madeleine (Travis glanced over at Madeleine who gave him a coquettish wave) and a black coffee for her. Madeleine talked across the deserted bar.

'I thought we could have lunch. I've brought a copy of my CV. I need to update it before I start sending it off.'

'Sorry, Maddy. Bit busy, I'm afraid. The deadline for the tender's three-thirty tomorrow.'

Nia returned. Two sheets of A4 now lay on her side of the table. Madeleine drew the fresh cappuccino towards her, dipped her finger onto the coca-covered frothy topping and cast a critical glance around the table.

'No bikkies?' she said with a pout and licked her finger. 'People who are in shock should be given sugar, you know. And I'm in deep shock, Nia.'

Nia patiently retraced her steps and returned with four home-baked shortbreads neatly arranged on a crisp white square side-plate.

'Bon appétit,' she said as Madeleine helped herself.

'Mmm. Thank God for Horton's,' said Madeleine, casting an indulgent eye of approval at the low wooden tables that nestled fashionably between dark brown leather settees. 'Coming here always makes me feel better.'

Nia sipped her coffee and scrutinised the CV.

'I didn't know you had a degree in marketing, Maddy. Weren't you doing some professional qualification instead?'

'Well, technically I should have it by now but I failed the last exam – only just, though. I'll pass next time. It's so much easier to say I got my degree in marketing at university ages ago – see, 1984.' Just in case Nia had trouble locating it, Madeleine pointed to the date over the top of the paper.

'Yes, but saying you've got a 2.1! A bit *risqué*, don't you think?'

'No one ever checks. Anyway, it's what I've done since that really counts!'

Nia changed tack.

'So, any ideas about where you're going to send it? I'm not sure who's recruiting just now – difficult times, as they say,' she said without raising her eyes from the ~~work of fiction~~ CV.

'I've already done some ringing around – just now,' replied Madeleine. 'Dom Campbell, you know, at the Chamber? Always had a bit of a thing for me. He's promised to put the word out. I won't be looking long – that's the one good thing about only being at Rowland and Finch for such a short time; people still remember me from Broadhurst and Dunst.'

'Did you hear that they're really struggling now?' said Nia, with her pen poised over one of the sheets. 'Just issued another profits warning.'

'Yeah, I heard. Serves them right for making me redundant three days before my birthday!'

Madeleine took a gulp of coffee. On the table, her phone bleeped. She read the screen and brightened immediately.

'Oh great, it's Josh. He's only just got my text.' She talked as she typed, pressed send then reached for the remaining biscuit.

Nia glanced at her watch. 'Look, is it OK if I look at this tonight?'

Madeleine's phone bleeped again. She grabbed it up immediately.

'Oh, er, yeah… Yes… fab. Look, Nia, it was lovely to see you but Josh is going to take me to lunch. He's on his way. I'm going to ask him if they need anyone at Red Hot. I'll give you a call tomorrow. Have a think about who I should target.'

As she spoke Madeleine scooped up her handbag and briefcase, and headed for the door.

'Thanks for the coffee,' she shouted over her shoulder.

Outside a midnight blue Volvo pulled up. Madeleine swung

the door open and tossed her things onto the back seat before jumping into the front.

On the table, Madeleine's half-eaten biscuit and cooling cappuccino sat abandoned. Nia drained her own coffee and, with a polite smile towards Travis, carefully folded her friend's CV and retrieved her wallet from her own bag. Only as she walked back to her car did she spy a parking ticket neatly tucked under her wiper blade.

Tuesday, June 11th, 1.10p.m.

Madeleine spotted Beth Franklyn from across the street just after Beth had noticed her, making it too late to duck out of sight into John Lewis. Madeleine had been out of work for three weeks now and with no positive news she was in no mood to talk to an ex-work colleague who had left Broadhurst and Dunst for a fabulous new job only two months before Madeleine had received her post-Amalfi dismissal letter from Rowland and Finch.

'Madeleine – Maddy – hi!' Beth advanced, beaming broadly. Madeleine couldn't help noticing that Beth had put on a few pounds – and, ooh, that lime was definitely not Beth's colour.

'Gosh, Beth. What a lovely surprise! Life must be treating you well, you look fab! Love the jacket – that colour's great on you!'

'Aye, thanks. I've just had a wee break actually – went back up to Scotland to see my mum. Och, sad, isn't it? I'm thirty-two next month and I still miss my mum!' Beth grinned. 'How're you? Such a shame about Broadhurst – bastards! You're at Rowland and Finch, now aren't you?'

For a second Madeleine toyed with lying but Beth had gone to work for Deart Solutions, a go-getting marketing agency that had offices in three major cities – there were rumours of a fourth in the pipe-line.

'No actually. Just my luck. They've been hit by the downturn in the market and being last in–'

'Och no, Maddy, not again!' interrupted Beth. In fairness, Madeleine noted, she did have the decency to look genuinely shocked. 'That's awful bad luck. When?'

Madeleine blinked.

'Two months ago – April,' she said, putting a bit of distance between her and the DV16 debacle.

'Och, at least it wasn't your birthday this time! Actually...' Beth pursed her lips and dropped her gaze for a second, thinking. Madeleine tried not to look like she was holding her breath.

'Our Business Relationship Manager's up in court tomorrow – drink driving,' said Beth eventually, her voice suddenly a conspiratorial whisper. 'He'll lose his licence for sure, which means he's gonna lose his job, too.'

'Oh dear,' breathed Madeleine.

'Nah, not at all – he's a bastard,' frowned Beth. 'Maybe I could put a word in for you, if you like?'

'Gosh, that would be very kind, Beth,' said Madeleine, feeling brighter by the minute.

Beth delved into her bag and drew out her phone. From the buckle, Madeleine could see it was a Fendi – not her favourite designer bag and somewhat last season but she could see how the classic peek-a-boo style and the bright-young-thing pink lining might appeal to Beth.

'Look, why don't you give me y'number and I'll speak to the boss? She's OK with me. I'll give you a call if anything comes of it,' said Beth.

Madeleine rummaged in her not-nearly-as-designer handbag. 'Tell you what – I'll email my CV over. We could meet up for lunch tomorrow.'

'Och, I don't know that I'll have any news that quickly,' replied Beth with a look that made Madeleine think of a rabbit, a dark road and her brand new viper-green VW Beetle (even with her optimistic budget, she hadn't quite been able to run to the convertible model).

'No, of course! But let's have lunch anyway. It would be lovely to catch-up,' pressed Madeleine, phone poised. 'What's your mobile number? We could meet at Horton's.'

They exchanged air kisses and with Beth's mobile number safely stored in her phone Madeleine breezed into John Lewis.

Thursday, July 11th 10.15a.m.

The clock on the wall said ten-fifteen a.m. The coffee was cold; there were no biscuits and the eight a.m. team meeting was life-sapping. Madeleine pretended to read the sheaf of papers in front of her and let her mind drift. She had joined Deart Solutions two weeks ago and things had worked out rather well; not only had she got the salary she'd asked for, but as Business & Marketing Manager (with specific responsibility for new business development) she was also Beth's boss and, being well aware of Beth's weaknesses as well as her strengths from their brief time together at Broadhurst and Dunst, Madeleine had already decided which she would play to.

Madeleine studied Dart's MD as she listened, drew lines through reports and made notes. Oh yes, Madeleine could see that

Sally Mansfield, a well-groomed, intelligent woman, was definitely a go-getting individual. At Madeleine's interview Sally had made no bones about her intention to open four new city-based satellite offices (including, to Madeleine's delight, one in Paris and one in Madrid) and increase turnover to £15 million (from the current £5 million) within five years. Madeleine had come out of the interview immensely impressed and convinced she and Sally would get on brilliantly (although an invitation to Sally's much-publicised cocktail party the previous weekend had not materialised – an oversight, Madeleine was sure).

'…and Madeleine, what do you think about that?' Sally fixed Madeleine a steely gaze over the top of her Donna Karan glasses.

Madeleine was suddenly aware that six sets of eyes around the boardroom table were awaiting her response to… what? She had absolutely no idea.

She tapped her lip with her pen as if deep in thought and then said, 'Hmm, of course, being the new girl on the block, I don't think it would be appropriate for me to make any sweeping judgements at this stage. I'd prefer to put some proper thought into that one and report back with more a considered suggestion, if that's OK?'

She flashed a wide, confident smile around the table. Sally's eyebrows rose behind her Donna Karans.

'Mmm, I'm struggling to see what value a *considered* response will add to the cost-saving proposal to buy toilet rolls in the local Aldi – am I alone here?' She flashed a glance around the rest of the management team without the merest hint of a smile. Simon, Sales Manager (Existing Business) coughed and took a gulp of his undoubtedly stone-cold coffee.

Madeleine, however, didn't miss a beat.

'Well, no, on the face of it, it doesn't. But as a marketing professional I think it important to look at all cost realignment

13

opportunities across the piece for the true benefit to have an impact – especially in this challenging fiscal climate.'

The shadow of a smile crossed Sally's face.

'A fair point, Madeleine, and I'm sure Purchasing can follow up on that suggestion – OK with that, Janet? On my desk by end of play next Friday.'

At the far end of the table a stick-thin girl with mousy blonde hair scribbled diligently on a notepad and nodded without looking up.

'Thanks for that, Madeleine,' said Sally, also scribbling a note on the papers in front of her before consulting the agenda. 'Right, Item five – Growing the business. Madeleine, where are we with that?'

Taking her cue, Madeleine began (although in reality she had nothing significant to suggest at that stage) and was waxing lyrical about brand reinforcement and customer relationship optimisation when Sally cut in.

'Yes, that's all fine, Madeleine. But what about *new* business? Your remit is very specific; I'm sure the rest of us can look after the business we've already got!'

Heads, like nodding dogs, bobbed around the table.

'I need your recommendations on my desk by end of play tomorrow, Madeleine. You've had two weeks to fanny around. I want to know how you intend to help me grow this business – not how we can save money on loo roll and hand-wash!'

Madeleine smarted through the rest of the meeting which went on well into lunchtime, and then phoned Josh for a quick moan before grabbing a sandwich from the local café.

Twenty hours later she presented Sally with her completed business plan – including bar graphs that perfectly matched the colours of the Deart Solutions logo (Madeleine was very pleased with the result).

'Thanks,' said Sally, flicking though the first few pages before chucking the document into her in-tray. 'I'm off to Belgium tomorrow so I'll read it next week.'

'Oh, but… er, OK,' said Madeleine, dragging her face into an overly bright smile. Sally leafed through pages of her cluttered diary and carried on talking.

'I'm off to Monaco on Tuesday. There's a golf event in Turnberry next weekend. Hate the game myself but it could be useful to us, so I've booked you to go. Penny'll sort your flight up to Glasgow and the car hire – you're there two nights. You do play golf, don't you? It's on your CV.'

Thursday, 11th July, 5.05p.m.

'Yes, Josh, golf! Haven't played since I was about twenty, with my Mum! And Turnberry's one of the most famous golfing hotels in Scotland – I need your help to brush up on my game.'

Madeleine listened to Josh's reply from the other end of the phone while she marched across from the office to her car.

'Oh, I'm sure Emily won't mind – you play all the time anyway, so why not play with me? I'm going to have to get in as many games as I can over the next two weeks. And anyway, I'm getting on really well with the MD so you never know where it might lead for you.'

Up ahead her viper-green Beetle unlocked on her approach. She interrupted Josh's reply.

'Ooh! But you can go shopping anytime, Josh,' Madeleine said, all but stamping her feet. 'I really need to get some practice in. I don't suppose you've got some clubs I can borrow?'

She held the phone almost to her ear and scanned the event

information that Sally had handed over only minutes earlier. The hotel really did look beautiful and the views across to the Isle of Arran were spectacular. She'd have to get her hair done… and her nails. The brochure shots of Pringle-clad golfers alone justified new golf gear… a set of clubs, certainly. On the other end of the phone Josh had stopped speaking. Madeleine had no idea what he had just said, although she did catch 'Sunday' as he did so

'No, Saturday's much better for me,' she said with a shake of her head. 'Pick me up at two. That way we'll finish at a respectable time for a gin and tonic.'

Wednesday, July 24^{th,} 5.55p.m.

'Yeah, it was good,' said Madeleine in that matter-of-fact way normally best heard coming from the very rich and not easily impressed. But then she added, 'The golf was fab and the guys were a hoot. We finished the last game with a bottle of Bolly on the eighteenth. There's another one in September – Gleneagles. I'll be going, of course.'

'September? Isn't Scotland full of midges in September?' asked Nia. It had not been a good Monday and in an attempt to relax she had intended to go to her yoga class after work as she hadn't been for weeks but Madeleine had insisted on meeting up at Horton's.

'Och no, not on that side,' said Madeleine, sounding marginally more knowledgeable than she did Scottish.

'So did you make any contacts?' asked Nia, a glass of red wine held to her lips.

'Oh, yes. Spent ages talking to a guy from a new footwear

company – Stewart something – I've got his card somewhere. They make the soles of their shoes from old tyres or bottle tops or something.'

'My guess would be tyres, Maddy. But don't quote me on that one. Anyway, at least you sound like you're doing OK. I didn't get that tender, by the way. The letter came this morning.'

Madeleine picked up her glass of white wine. 'Sally's really pleased anyway – had lunch today. We've got some things coming up that you might be able to get involved with. I'll have a word.'

'Oh, that would be great, Maddy. Anything in particular?'

Madeleine was sniffing her wine and frowning. 'Mmm, not sure about this wine. Which one is it?'

'Haven't a clue. I just asked Travis for your usual – Chardonnay, I'm guessing,' Nia replied, squinting towards the bar as if it might offer up a clue.

Madeleine took a sip and wrinkled her nose.

'Must have just got used to better,' she said. 'We had Chateaux La Fayette on the last night.'

Her voice was overly loud in the quiet bar. Nia frowned.

'Don't you mean Chateau Laffite?'

'Yes, it was red. Stewart – the shoe guy – said it was over two thousand pounds a bottle.'

Nia raised a sceptical eyebrow but said nothing. Madeleine took a larger sip of her Chardonnay and continued.

'I think it was tyres. Anyway, he's sending me a pair of their boots. God knows how we're going to make them look good, mind! Must speak to Josh. I'm trying to get him into Dart – bring in some new blood. Our head designer is just God-awful!'

'Bugger Josh, just remember your needy friends!' Nia drained her glass and grinned. 'Look, I'm going to have another small one then I'd better be off.'

Madeleine's glass was still half full.

17

'Oh, right, I'll have another, too.' Madeleine threw back the mystery wine in one gulp.

Nia went to the bar.

Left alone, Madeleine sent a text to Josh:

> Hope you well. Fab time in Scotland.
> Golf this W/E? Me x

'Oh, I must tell you my news,' she said when Nia returned with the drinks. 'I'm buying a house! Took Josh to see it last week. It's small and needs loads done but he said that with my taste I can't go wrong. He's such a sweetie.'

'Wow, Maddy, a house! Are you sure it's the right time?' Nia asked, her expression betraying her genuine surprise.

Madeleine gave one of her fixed jaw, definite nods.

'Can't rent forever. For Chrissake Nia, I'm forty-five, never been married and never owned my own house! At least I can do something about the latter!'

'But house prices are very high at the moment. Perhaps you should wait?'

'No. The guy's accepted my offer as long as I can complete in four weeks. Can't see a problem with that,' said Madeleine with a look of steely determination. Nia conceded.

'In that case, well done you. A new job and a new home!' She raised her glass. 'And where is Chez Madeleine?'

'Amrose Street – about three minutes from here – ideal!' said Madeleine. 'It's–'

Her phone vibrated loudly on the wooden table.

'Oh good. That'll be Josh – we're playing golf again on Saturday.'

Holding the phone at arm's length, she peered at the text.

'Oh, sod it! Apparently Emily needs help with something – changing the loo roll probably!'

She tapped out a hasty reply with her expertly manicured nails then absently sipped her wine and watched the phone as if commanding it to answer. Seconds later it obliged with a loud buzz. Madeleine read the message, smiled and then picked up the conversation exactly where she had temporarily abandoned it.

'Yes. The owners bought it to do up, but they're getting divorced. Need a quick sale so I went in way under the asking price and they went for it.'

'So how much work are you going to have to do?'

'New windows and decorating throughout – oh, and central heating… and carpets.'

'My God, Maddy!'

'I've got enough for the windows and the central heating from what Tom *eventually* gave me after Dad died. I'll just do the rest bit by bit.'

'Hmm, busy and poor for a while then!' observed Nia.

'Nah, it'll be fine,' replied Madeleine. 'It'll be like being at home again after Dad left Mum for Tom. We had absolutely no money then and we survived.'

'Well, on Sunday let's go look at furniture,' suggested Nia. 'Can't afford any luxuries myself at the mo but I'm more than happy to help spend someone else's money – besides, I could do with something to cheer me up.'

Madeleine downed the last of her drink.

'Sorry, playing golf.'

'Oh, I though Josh was otherwise engaged?'

'Not Sunday!' Madeleine tossed her phone into her handbag. 'I need to keep my game up for Gleneagles! Look, I've gotta go. Having supper with Dom Campbell – need to press him for leads. Sally's starting to nag. I'll give you a call next week.'

With barely a touch of lips on cheeks Madeleine was gone. Nia glanced at her watch – six-thirty p.m. Too late for yoga.

'She's gone then?' Travis picked up the empty glasses. 'You'll be picking up the tab again then?'

'Mmm,' answered Nia.

Travis gave her a pursed lip grin.

'Tell you what, I'll get you another glass of red – on the house.' He turned to the bar and said over his shoulder, 'Won't be Chateaux Laffite, mind!'

Thursday, 29th August 6.30 a.m.

From the window of his study, Hayden watched a tiny fishing boat skip easily over the gloriously blue sea of Landsmere Bay. He'd seen the busy little boat every morning that week at six-thirty a.m. when he got up to walk Morris, his elderly and exceptionally faithful Irish Wolfhound. At this time of year Hayden always made an effort to rise and walk a little earlier because Morris didn't cope well in the heat of the summer – even late summer – and anyway, just now Hayden was grateful for a reason to get up. He wasn't sleeping too well just now, although he certainly wasn't missing Carla.

Morris, on the other hand, had absolutely no trouble sleeping. In fact at that moment he was snoring loudly at Hayden's feet, making the most of the final minutes of his pre-walk nap. Hayden watched the boat disappear around the headland towards Little Landscombe and resolved to wander down to the harbour there to find out what they'd been catching. He hoped it might be mackerel.

Hayden was rather partial to mackerel. It was a simple fish – far too meagre for Carla, of course. She had always tutted loudly when he ordered it in restaurants and, to make a point, he knew, she would go on to order the most expensive thing on the menu – usually lobster – even though she hated the sight of food that looked back at her. But as Carla was Hayden's very soon to be *ex*-wife, the taste of fresh mackerel was even better – especially when it came stiff and glistening from one of the few remaining fishing boats that still sailed out of Little Landscombe. Filling the kitchen with the smell of the sea, pan-fried mackerel on the bone with fresh bread and butter was, as far as Hayden was concerned, truly the perfect breakfast.

With his mouth now positively watering, Hayden was just about to wake Morris from his contented slumber to pursue his investigation when his computer pinged. He had mail.

Two messages flashed-up from his stockbroker, Neville Savage of Savage & Backs; one contained news about the price of some gold Neville had advised Hayden to buy the previous day (inflation on the rise – a good time to buy, Neville had insisted), and the other was to invite Hayden to join him at the club that evening for a gin – or, knowing Neville, several gins. Hayden was pondering Neville's invitation when another message popped up – this time from Hayden's daughter, Saffy, from halfway across the world.

Hayden had always struggled with Saffy's move to Hong Kong. On the one hand, she had married a very bright, highly successful bloke who seemed to make her happy; on the other, Hayden missed her every day. Her mother, Hayden's first wife Georgina, had been killed in a tragic skiing accident just before Saffy's seventeenth birthday. Carla had appeared on the scene only eighteen months later and although Saffy had tried to hide her disapproval, Hayden had always known that his daughter and his new, and much younger wife, were never going to be best friends. But, back then, Saffy was off to university, and Hayden couldn't picture himself rattling around in a six-bedroom house with just a part-time housekeeper for company.

He smiled sadly at the photograph on his desk – it had been taken the day of Saffy's graduation, exactly one year before she met Alistair (by crashing into his BMW), and two years before their wedding.

He clicked 'Open':

Hi Dad,

Hope you're OK? Alistair's taken Ben to the park so I thought I'd drop you a line. They've taken the tricycle you sent over – Ben loves it – thank you. I can't believe he's three already! He's so tall now – definitely takes after our side of the family!

It's been very hot here today but at least it's stopped raining!!! I bet Landsmere looks gorgeous just now – especially the woods. I do miss it. Is Mrs Bosworth's fruit cake still as good as I remember it? Alistair has promised we'll come and visit soon but you know what he's like – working fourteen hours a day at the moment on some big merger so goodness knows when he'll get any real time off!

Oh, I can hear Ben crying – knew the peace wouldn't last! Better go.

Love to Carla.

Hugs – miss you… and Morris!

Saffy

XXXXXXXXXXXXXXXXXXXXXXXXXXXXXXXXX

Hayden read the email three times, relishing the words as if Saffy was there speaking each one to him. The time difference meant that phone calls were a major logistical operation – especially now Ben was growing up and wanted to speak to *Baba Britain* – or *"Ba Ritten"* as his grandson would say.

"Love to Carla," Saffy had written. He read the line with a twinge of guilt. The decree nisi, dated three days earlier, lay under the electricity bill on his desk.

The papers passing ownership of the villa in Calabria over to Carla, where she was now living – with Fabio, apparently – had been signed a week ago. But to date, none of Hayden's weekly emails to his daughter carried any news of the failure of his second marriage; maybe that was why he wasn't sleeping?

He re-read the email once more and tapped Morris gently on the bottom with his toe. Morris opened his eyes, looked around as if trying to remember where he was, hauled his huge frame stiffly to a sitting position and yawned. Hayden rubbed the hound's soft ear fondly.

'Come on, old man; let's see if we can buy some mackerel for breakfast.'

Monday, 2nd September 9.55a.m.

'Look, I'm sorry, Beth, but someone's got to follow up these leads and I simply don't have the time,' insisted Madeleine. With as little commitment as possible, she was holding between two beautifully manicured fingers a piece of paper with over twenty names scribbled down in the large capitals and swirling tails of Sally's distinctive hand.

'Yes, but I've never done sales, Maddy. I write copy and book advertising space, remember?' said Beth, failing to hide her frustration. 'You've already asked me to do the copy for that boots brochure, so when would *I* have time?'

'Mmm, yes, Beth, but try to look on this as a chance to broaden your skills-base… you know, prove that you're not just a one-trick pony. I'll do the copy for the boots brochure to free-up your time. Stewart's expecting a really good job anyway and I don't want to let him down.'

'Oh, so you're saying that I wouldn't do a good job, then?' challenged Beth, her wide eyes suggesting she was very close to tears.

Madeleine held her other hand palms up and smiled.

'Oh, Beth, of course I'm not saying that!' she said gently. 'Look, I'm just giving you an opportunity to show Sally what you're really made of. Just give these guys a call. If there's any mileage in any of them let me know and I'll take it from there. Just think of it as part of the learning curve – something to put on your CV.'

'So it's just the initial calls?' said Beth, defeated.

'Oh, absolutely!' Madeleine nodded. 'Any leads – just pass them straight to me. I'll make sure that Sally knows too, so you can share the credit when I get the business.'

Madeleine slid the list of names and numbers onto Beth's desk and, with the same beautifully manicured fingers, teased a buff file from Beth's in-tray.

'I'll take Stewart's file now. He's coming down Monday and I want to be sure we've got something really great to show him.'

Madeleine strode back into her own office and closed the door.

Beth snatched up her pencil and shut her eyes. With a brief swirl of her wrist she stabbed the pencil onto the sheet and squinted at the speared number. Then, with a deep breath, she picked up the phone and dialled.

Tuesday, 3rd September 8.32 a.m.

Nia opened the door of her office and clipped her post with her toe, sending envelopes skittering across the laminate. Her watch said eight thirty-two a.m. – the postman had been early for a change.

Among the usual bills was an envelope bearing a cheque. Nia scrutinised it with a relieved smile. The message light was also flashing on her office phone – like the appearance of a cheque, it was a rare occurrence in her office these days. She pressed play and fished in her bag for her mobile – there were three missed calls, all from Madeleine's number.

'Nia, hi!' chirped Madeleine's voice from the answer phone. 'Look, Josh is going to a christening on Sunday. Apparently Emily *forgot* to tell him! So, needless to say, I've been let down for golf, so we can go shopping. We could go to that new designer place with the little café on the second floor – Hobson's Choice. The cappuccino is fab. Josh and I went last week. Anyway – I'll try your mobile. Bye!'

Nia pressed the number on her phone – Madeleine sang down the phone in two rings.

'Hi-i…'

'Maddy?'

'Oh… Nia. I thought it was Josh again – spoke to him this morning. Apparently the christening's not 'til four, so we're playing in the morning.'

'Oh, that's OK,' said Nia. 'I can't make Sunday now anyway. I'm having brunch with Ros. I've hardly seen her since I stopped playing badminton – but the membership fee is just impossible to justify at the moment. Funnily enough we're rendezvousing at Hobson's Choice! I met someone there for a meeting last Tuesday – got some work out of it, too!'

'Oh, right – ah! There's another call coming in – it's Josh, gotta go. Love to Ros. Bye.'

Saturday, 14th September 7.35p.m.

Nia stepped over the threshold into Madeleine's very new home. 'Wow, what a fantastic smell! Did you manage to get hold of Ros?'

'Yes…, she's bringing Ivy,' said Madeleine, with a slightly less than enthusiastic smile. 'I invited Paolo and Tony, too, but Paolo called earlier to cancel.'

Nia frowned. 'Hmm, *tout n'est pas parfait* there, I fear.'

She presented Madeleine with a bottle of Chateaux Laffite and a condensation-coated bottle of Moet & Chandon.

'Oh, champagne – lovely!' said Madeleine with barely a glance at the red wine. She added both bottles to a neat little hall table that was already crowded with a very large bunch of peach carnations. The bell chimed again.

Nia removed herself to the front room to make space in the tiny hall. Sliding her arms out of her coat, she surveyed the room. Madeleine had achieved so much in only a few weeks – but then, when Madeleine wanted something… the original offensively pink walls that Nia had only seen in hastily taken photographs on

Madeleine's phone, had been replaced with a soft cream that, with the newly varnished pine floor, gave the room a reassuringly simple cottage feel on this warm autumn evening. Above the mantelpiece a huge, vivid abstract painting dominated the chimney breast.

Nia had just positioned herself between a pair of pale leather settees to admire it when Ros entered, laden with bags.

'Oh, hi, Nia. How are you? Am I late? I tried to text but I've got a new phone – hate it.' She offered up her handbag and grimaced – she was clutching her mobile phone in the same hand.

'Oh, it's like mine,' said Nia, after a sympathetic glance. 'Don't worry, you'll get used to it. You can have different ring tones for different people – I found a great one for my Mum – *The Entertainer*. Makes me smile every time she phones.'

Madeleine reappeared. Ros offered up the bag in her other hand – a simple brown paper affair bearing the *Hobson's Choice* logo.

'I saw this and thought it would look lovely on that table in your hall – I was so pleased that you took my advice to buy it. It really is lovely – it is oak, isn't it?' Ros looked slightly nervous. 'You haven't got something already, have you?'

Madeleine took the offered gift and unwrapped a beautifully simple crystal vase.

'Oh, Ros, it's perfect. I'll use it now – Josh dropped flowers round earlier. Emily was cooking supper so he couldn't stay.'

Nia looked past Ros.

'I could've sworn I saw Ivy behind you?'

Ros did a very good impression of a startled animal caught in headlights. Madeleine answered for her.

'Yes, you did. She's nipped to the loo. Did you pick her up from the flat, Ros?' Madeleine asked Ros pointedly.

'Well, no,' answered Ros, equally pointedly.

'Ah,' said Nia, catching up rapidly. 'So we could be in for an entertaining evening then.'

Before anyone could say anything else, Ivy swayed into the lounge.

'What a nice house,' she said her smile overly bright. 'You're so lucky to be able to afford it! It'll be lovely when it's decorated.'

'This room is decorated, Ivy!' said Madeleine. She took Nia and Ros's coats. Ivy opened her mouth to speak again but Nia cut in.

'Right, Maddy, where can I find glasses? That champagne will have lost its chill if we leave it there much longer!'

Ivy brightened.

'Oh, champagne – lovely! I'll get the glasses. Where's the kitchen?' She headed in the direction of the delicious smell of cooking.

Nia threw Ros a questioning look and mouthed, 'The Bear?'

'Need you ask?' said Ros, looking genuinely mortified. 'I'm so sorry, Madeleine. I'd arranged to pick her up from her flat. But half an hour ago she called to say she was "in town".' She made inverted comma signs with her fingers.

'I thought you were going to have "a word", Nia?' said Madeleine, mirroring the inverted comma fingers. 'After all, you've known her the longest.'

'I know. I… I'm waiting for the right moment, that's all.'

'Right moment for what?' asked Ivy loudly, stalking back into the room clutching one very full glass.

'Oh, to tell Paolo that I don't think Tony's the one for him,' answered Nia, her face suddenly full of concern; Ros's expression suggested she'd missed something but Nia continued. 'Paolo thinks he's failed because things aren't working out.'

'Oh, that's just silly!' Ivy announced to no one in particular.

'I'll have a word with that Tony next time I see him! He's no right to make Paolo feel like that!'

Madeleine glanced at Ros's concerned expression and mouthed, 'She won't remember!'

Wednesday, 18th September 10.35a.m.

'So Ivy was up to her usual tricks,' sniffed Paolo. He and Nia had been talking on the phone for almost half an hour. He took a deep, shuddering breath – close to tears again.

'Yes, 'fraid so. You know how she can be,' Nia answered with an unseen nod.

'Yer, challenging and difficult – I've seen it too many times now, Nia. I could have died last week. We met her in Bar Mojo. As it was, Tony was in a foul mood. She did her usual disappearing act at about nine-thirty, thank God. But we still ended up… having… a b-blazing row… and… he s-slept in the spare room!' Paolo burst into tears again. Nia waited. After half a dozen choking sobs he blew his nose loudly and took another shuddering breath.

'Sorry, Nia, it's all a bit raw. I just can't believe it's over – *again!*'

'I know, Paolo, but… well, maybe it's for the best,' Nia said gently. She'd lost count of how many times they'd had this conversation – love 'em and get left by 'em, that seemed to be Paolo's way in life. Paolo sniffed again.

'I know. I'm just a sucker for a pretty face, I guess.' Nia could hear a brave smile in his voice. 'So Ivy managed to ruin another night out then?'

'Well, it was a bit awkward, let's just say.' Nia was grateful for the change of subject. 'I did feel sorry for Madeleine; she'd gone to a lot of trouble.'

'Oh, don't you worry about her – as long as you and Ros said all the right things about her house and her food. Goes to a lot of trouble to make herself look good, does Madeleine Edwards!' Paolo said and then, with a bitchy laugh, added, 'It's no coincidence her initials are M.E.!'

'Paolo! *Un peu de sympathie, s'il te plaît!* She's always nice to you.'

'Only when she can't find anyone else to get drunk with!' Paolo retorted. 'It's a nightmare now she's working down the road from the theatre! Honestly, Nia, I don't mind going for a quick drink after work, as you know, but I can't sing with a hangover and what's more, nine times out of ten, I end up paying! Can you believe that – the world's biggest collection of handbags and none of them hold any money… apparently?'

'I think things are a bit tight now she's got the new house,' said Nia, loyal as ever. 'She'll be better when things have calmed down a bit. I must say, that painting you found for her looks wonderful in her lounge.'

'Mmm, well maybe you could remind her she still hasn't paid for it! Tony put it on his credit card and now he's hassling *me* for the money – it was three hundred quid, Nia!'

'Oh, I'm sure she'll remember. She's just busy. Oh, that reminds me. I need two tickets for the show – any good seats left? Don't worry about the cost – I'm taking a client. I really need to impress him. Thought tickets for La Trav would be ideal.'

'Yer. For you, no probs,' said Paolo. 'I get two free tickets for the last night anyway and Tony's hardly going to use them now, so you're welcome to them – next Saturday OK?'

'Oh, you're a sweetie. Are you sure you won't need them?'

'Nah… So, does mystery client have a name… and are we talking short skirt and no knickers?'

'God, Paolo, you're such a tart! It's Jackson Tranter, MD of Trevor Maylard. And I certainly will be wearing knickers. This is purely business.'

'Well, never heard of them, darling. But if you're pleased, I'm pleased!' Paolo sounded slightly bored now sex gossip was off the agenda. 'Tickets'll be at the box office for you on the night. Ros and Ivy are coming on Friday. Ooh, it'll be like having my own private fan club!'

'I don't suppose you could wangle an intro with Emma Jenkins? You know, quick chat with the lead soprano after the show – bound to impress.'

'God, darling, I'm far too lowly for that! Perks for the chorus go as far as two freebies, I'm afraid. Formal intros to the stars start much further up the food chain!' laughed Paolo. 'Ooh, look, hun, just noticed the time! I'd better get a shimmy on. Rehearsal's in an hour and I've got three days' stubble to groom.'

Tuesday, 24th September 10.30a.m

'…and so I said, well, why don't you place the order now?' recounted Beth, her eyes shining with excitement. 'And do you know what he said, Maddy? He *actually* said yes! Can you believe it? I've just got a twenty grand order! Sally is so pleased.'

'What?' said Madeleine, paling under her fake tan. 'You told Sally before you reported to me?'

Beth's sparkle faltered. 'Well, yes. You… you were at a meeting and… Och, I just had to tell someone. Sally asked me to do the follow-ups after I got a lead last week – Sally followed one up, too… I think. I did tell you but, well, you've been so busy on the branding stuff for Stewart. Och, it was so exciting, Maddy. I never thought I'd–'

'For God's sake, Beth,' said Madeleine, interrupting again. 'Stop throwing your arms around like that! You're going to have someone's eye out with that pen! So how many of those companies have you called? When did I give you that list?'

'Three weeks ago,' said Beth, suddenly looking guilty. 'I've been working through it when I've had time. But what with everything else… God, some of those receptionists are real dragons. D'you think Hatty's like that when sales people call here? She always sounds so nice when I phone in.' Beth handed Madeleine the original list, which now had notes, times and dates scrawled all over it. To Madeleine's alarm, some of the names also had pound signs and numbers next to them – big numbers ending in noughts… before the decimal point!

'They're trained to deflect sales calls, Beth – it's part of their job!' she said waspishly.

'Oh, right,' said Beth. 'Well anyway, I just kept calling everyone and in the end… well, I think some of them just felt sorry for me and put me through. One woman was really rude but the rest were lovely. Another one wants a meeting. Sally's going and guess what, she's asked me to go with her – it's in Edinburgh! She said I can have a few days off afterwards to see my mum, too. How great is that!'

'Look, Beth, I'm really pleased that you've had this modicum of success but I wouldn't start packing yet. I'll go and see Sally – sales meetings with prospective clients really are my field of expertise – after all, it *is* my job!'

Before her next breath filled her lungs, Madeleine was out of the office and down two flights of stairs. She rapped her knuckle on Sally's door and entered without waiting for an answer. Sally was talking to Simon, the Sales Manager (Existing Business). On his lap sat a sheaf of papers. Sally stopped talking. They both looked up.

Madeleine closed the door behind her. 'Oh, good, I'm glad I've caught you both; it'll save two conversations,' she began, taking the seat next to Simon. 'As you might know, my assistant, Beth Franklyn's been chasing up a few leads for me as part of her skills development. And it seems she has had some modest success– '

'Yes, funnily enough, that's what Simon and I were just talking about. Come in by the way, Madeleine,' said Sally with a chilling smile. 'Although a twenty thousand pound contract is, arguably, a little more than "modest success".' The tips of her neat fingers made the merest hint of a movement towards inverted commas. Madeleine leapt in.

'Oh, I suspect there's a bit of exaggeration there, Sally. I mean, you can't really blame Beth, bless her, for letting her enthusiasm gild the facts. But I'm pretty sure I'll have a bit more work to do before that one's in the bag.' Her nod towards Simon was not returned. 'And as for the meeting in Edinburgh; well, obviously it'll be far more appropriate for me to go.'

Simon shifted in his chair. The top sheet from the papers slid off his lap and lazily drifted to the floor under Madeleine's seat. She bent to retrieve it and caught sight of the words *Pro-Forma Invoice*. Then her gaze was drawn to the amount of £20,000 at the bottom of the sheet. Madeleine was robbed of speech.

Gently tugging the invoice from Madeleine's frozen fingers, Simon got to his feet. 'Right, well, er, I've got to make a quick phone call, Sally. So maybe we can catch up after lunch, OK?'

Sally studied her diary for far longer than Madeleine felt was necessary.

'Hmm, better make it three o'clock, Simon. I've got a conference call at two,' she said eventually without lifting her eyes from the page. 'Another one of Beth Franklyn's modest successes.'

Tuesday, 24th September 12.30p.m.

> ...and give Ben a big hug from Ba Ritten.
> love Dad
> xxx

Hayden re-read the email – keeping his finger well away from the 'send' button. That crucial bit of information was still missing. But try as he might, he just couldn't find the right words. He let his finger settle on the delete button instead and watched the cursor gobble up news of late ripening tomatoes and roses still in full bloom. Then he looked down at Morris, who was as usual doing an exceptionally good impression of an unkempt rug.

'The trouble is, I don't know what to say. I mean, it's not as if they really got on,' Hayden confessed. 'In fact, I'm pretty sure Saffy didn't even like Carla. And I know for certain how Carla felt about Saffy.' Morris fixed his master with a pair of unnervingly human eyes; his shaggy eyebrows twitched as he seemed to make a valiant attempt to understand what he was being told. 'I didn't think Saffy was spoilt,' Hayden continued. 'OK, I did let her get away with some stuff but, for goodness sake, her mother had just died! She was entitled to get a little bit wild – and anyway, it all came right... in the end.'

Morris's efforts to understand while also trying to remain awake had clearly proved too demanding. By the time Hayden had finished speaking the great hound's eyes were firmly closed once more.

Hayden grinned and hit 'Exit'– the computer politely asked him if he wanted to save the changes to 'Saffy 23 Sept'. Outside, Landsmere Bay was mill-pond calm. A tiny boat laden with lobster pots was motoring steadily across to Oxmore Head where, no doubt, the pots would be sunk. In the morning, Hayden knew, the same pots would be hauled back aboard bearing a catch for kings – well, kings now that Carla was no longer around! He turned back to the computer and hit 'No'; news of the demise of his second marriage could wait for another day.

In the time Hayden had been failing to email his daughter, more emails had arrived; among a number of adverts for Viagra and something very dubiously entitled, 'Fun Girls' (where they got his address from he would never know!) was a message from Jackson Tranter. Hayden opened the email.

> Hayden, invited to opera this Saturday. Not really my thing
> but can't say no. Nia Griffin – remember her from the
> Board? Nice legs. She's fishing for work. Might be useful.
> Got two extra tickets – I will tell her to bring a friend. Brian
> will bring the car around at 6.30. Jack

Hayden re-read the message knowing there was little point in trying to decline – he'd known Jackson Tranter for far too long.

***

Tuesday 24th September, 4p.m.

'I just can't believe she could have done that to me, Nia!' sniffed Madeleine. 'Since I started at Deart I've only ever tried to be fair to that girl.'

Travis delivered two cappuccinos, each bearing a copious sprinkling of chocolate in the shape of a love heart. Nia mouthed a silent thank you. Madeleine barely paused for breath.

'Honestly, Nia, I only asked her to make a couple of bloody warm up calls – I didn't expect the little cow to hijack my job in the process!'

'I'm sure she didn't do it deliberately, Maddy. You said they've made your post redundant – and they have given you a month's pay, which was pretty decent – they didn't have to,' said Nia fairly. 'It's just that kind of time – everyone's looking for ways to cut costs. Beth is, after all, cheaper than you.'

'Thank God they aren't making me work my notice! Well, Little Miss Sales of the Month will fall flat on her face, you'll see. It was just beginner's luck.'

She paused, unwrapped an amaretto biscuit and then went on.

'D'you know what Sally said? After all those hours I spent doing that marketing plan… *and* the time I've spent on that bloody footwear brochure for those God-awful boots. Do you know what she said?' Madeleine demanded but didn't wait for Nia to say what she knew.

'She asked me if I understood what my job was!'

'My God! What did you say?'

'I told her that finding new business was all very well but, in my opinion, the company needs someone to lead a far more holistic marketing effort,' Madeleine replied, drowning the biscuit in her cappuccino.

'Oh. And what did she say to that?' asked Nia, her expression neutral.

'Told me that *she* was in charge of marketing! Well, Nia, honestly, I nearly laughed. From what *I've* seen, she doesn't know the first thing about marketing!'

'Yes, but she also owns the company, Maddy – and it is incredibly successful,' said Nia, safe in the knowledge that Madeleine wasn't listening.

'I mean, I wasn't even out the door when they announced that Simon's now in charge of a new sales team!' She did the finger quotation marks with her free hand. 'You met him at the barbecue, Simpering Simon, I call him. Looks like an overgrown teddy bear – hairy and fat. Well, I can tell you, that's just not going to work!' Madeleine was now positively vitriolic. 'To be honest, Nia, I always thought Dart were a bunch of amateurs – and *that* just proves my point!'

'Look,' said Nia, grabbing the opportunity to change the subject. 'I'm going to see Paolo in La Traviata on Saturday. I've invited Jackson Tranter – you know, Trevor Maylard, big nautical engineering firm based in the old docks building? He's accepted but apparently he already had two tickets so he's asked Hayden Elliot. Remember him from the board? One of the exec engineers. Got hold of a parachute just before the Broadhurst and Dunst plane started to nosedive. He's chair of Tranter's company now among other things, from what I gather. Oh, please come, it'll be fun and you never know, there might be an opportunity somewhere for you!'

Madeleine wrinkled her nose.

'Oh, Nia, you know I hate opera. Couldn't you have got tickets for Coldplay? They're in the stadium on Saturday.'

'Yes, but Paolo isn't in Coldplay and he's having such a miserable time again. He needs our support... and *I* like opera, as you well know,' said Nia. She waited. Madeleine pursed her lips and remained silent. 'Look, if you really don't want to come I'll ask Ros. La Trav is one of her favourites – been already, said it was brilliant. I'm sure she'd go again… especially if she knew an eligible bachelor was going.' Nia took a lingering sip of her coffee…

'Oh, I'll go, of course,' said Madeleine, on cue. 'I'll have to get something new to wear though. Oh well, guess that money from Dart'll come in handy then! Don't remember an Adam Elliot though. What's he like?'

'Hayden,' corrected Nia. 'Oh, he's a real sweetie. But now I think about it, I'm pretty sure he left before you came upstairs. Structural engineer, consultant – a real gentleman. I'm pretty sure he's semi-retired now. Keeps busy though. Non-exec director of a couple of small companies. Set up a charity called Cornerstone – children's literacy – does the fund raising mostly, I think.' Madeleine dunked a large shortbread biscuit into her coffee, only half-listening. Nia ploughed on. 'Heading for an OBE, most likely. Wife number one died. She was lovely. Wife number two was quite a bit younger than him, apparently, but I never met her – left him earlier this year… He lives up at Landsmere Grange.' Nia waited.

Madeleine stopped dunking – the soggy biscuit disintegrated with a messy plop into her coffee.

'What? That huge house overlooking the bay? The one with the turret?'

Nia nodded, chomping on the last biscuit.

Madeleine abandoned the remains of her shortbread and retrieved a leather lipstick case from her handbag. Flicking it open, she held the little case at arm's length, turned her head from side to side and squinted into a tiny mirror on the lid.

'Can I use your phone?'

'Course,' said Nia with a frown. 'But what's happened to that new iPhone you had last week?'

'It was Deart's. Made me give it back. I'm going to ask Adam to fit me in this afternoon,' said Madeleine tapping numbers as she spoke. 'I thought it was a bit mean actually. Oh, hi, Madeleine here. Can Adam cut my hair this afternoon?' She listened. 'No, Madeleine Edwards... Oh, but surely he could fit *me* in?' She looked at Nia and cast her eyes heavenwards. 'No, dear, Monday is not good. Look, can you put Adam on, please?' She put her hand over the phone. 'Can you order me another coffee?'

Nia looked at her watch. It was four-fifteen p.m. The Maylard pitch was sitting on her desk where she had abandoned it when she got Madeleine's plaintive phone call but, as Madeleine now had her phone, there was little chance of escape. So, with a resigned sigh, she nodded to Travis and pointed towards their cups.

Madeleine suddenly straightened and threw her shoulders back – the effect on her boobs was quite impressive. 'Adam, hi,' she said, smile wide... Her smile stiffened. 'No, Madeleine *Edwards*. Soft auburn, no highlights?' Then she nodded slowly. 'Yes, Beth's friend... oh, she's fine. Anyway, Adam, be a darling and squeeze me in this afternoon. I've got a really important meeting in the morning and–'

'...' She listened.

'Yes, unusual on a Saturday but that's business for you at my level.' Her smile returned. 'Oh, you're a treasure. See you in fifteen; I'm only round the corner. Bye.'

'Success?' asked Nia.

'Of course,' said Madeleine handing the phone back to Nia. 'Honestly, that girl on reception – I don't know why he keeps her. Absolutely half-baked! Right.' She gathered up her things. 'He's going to squeeze me in now, so I'd better run. Oh, what time tomorrow?'

'Can you meet us at the theatre at seven?'

'Oh, no lift,' said Madeleine with a pout.

'Oh, I was going to... oh, never mind, I'll pick you up at six-thirty then. We're meeting Jackson and Hayden there.'

'Oh, you're a love. Are you sure? I'll pay the parking. See you tomorrow then.' And with that Madeleine downed the dregs of her coffee and was gone.

Travis appeared with a cup of black coffee in one hand and a hand-held card payment machine in the other. He stopped two steps short of the table.

'Thought that was going to happen when I heard her on the phone.' He offered up the coffee. 'That's why I did you a plain black one. I'll drink it if you don't want it; it's my break now anyway. I'm guessing you're picking up the tab?'

Nia threw him a grateful grin.

'You are an angel,' she said and handed over her credit card.

Saturday, 28th September 6.30p.m.

'This new?' asked Hayden, nodding to the man holding open the rear door of a very sleek, shining black car for him.

'Picked it up two weeks ago,' answered Jackson with a hint of the Glasgow he had long ago left but never forgotten. 'It's only the usual Jag. Couldn't give a fuck really, as long as Brian gets me from A to B without being late.'

Brian pushed the door closed.

'So what did it set us back then?' Hayden asked, undoing the buttons on his old, faithful cashmere jacket – living alone, he had no one to nag him about eating too much and with an endless supply of Mrs Bosworth's cottage pie and whisky-soaked fruit cake it was beginning to show.

'Fifty odd grand, I think,' answered Jackson. He leant forward. 'What is it again, Brian?'

Brian, now back in the driver's seat, pushed the seatbelt into its receiver.

'XJ three litre diesel luxury,' answered Brian via the rear view mirror.

'Nice,' nodded Hayden.

'Like I said,' said Jackson. 'Couldn't give a fuck. It goes. Girls like the leather and I haven't missed any flights yet, so it'll do for now.'

Hayden grinned and shook his head. That was Jackson Tranter all over. Straight talking, totally committed to the business and a complete rake – Jackson's idea of a long term relationship was a second date!

'So, you do remember Nia Griffin then?' Jackson asked as the car swung down the rutted lane that served as the drive to Landsmere Grange.

'Just about. Nice girl, I seem to remember – competent. Did that new solar panel launch just before I went,' said Hayden. He was good at remembering people, especially good people; you just never knew when they might be useful again. 'Not your type at all, mind, Jack. Too old by about twenty-five years!'

'I know,' said Jackson, without a glimmer of guilt. 'Looked at her website.' He wiped the window needlessly with the back of his index finger. 'You had chance to look at the Boston job yet? Eighty-four grand – they're having a fucking laugh!'

'Had a quick look this morning. How many engineers are you looking to send?'

'For that money, three... max two weeks... and they'll have to travel fucking economy!'

Hayden shook his head and laughed. That was why Tranter was CEO of Maylard; he was a hard bastard who knew how to make money, it was in his blood. A highly accomplished structural engineer in his day, Hayden had been chairman of Trevor Maylard for the past seven years and, thanks to Jackson Tranter, he was now a very wealthy man.

Saturday, 28th September, 7.15p.m.

'Yes, but it would have been just a bit more helpful if you'd remembered your contact lenses before we got to the lights,' said Nia testily. 'That junction's a complete nightmare!' She scraped the gearstick into reverse and aimed her Mini Cooper for the only parking space they had come across in the last half hour. She was not happy.

'How was I to know that the entire Coldplay audience would bring their cars!' retorted Madeleine.

The past thirty minutes, trying in vain to find somewhere to park, had been somewhat tense. They were now late and Nia had been counting on a glass of red to calm her nerves, having spent almost the entire previous night preparing; she could recite all eleven countries in which Trevor Maylard had offices. She knew turnover, profits and marketing expenditure for the past five years and, by four o'clock that morning, she could recite the name of every building, dock and jetty they had ever built or repaired including port and post... or zip code. Maylard's were clearly going places and Nia desperately wanted – needed – to get in on the action; the arrival of yet another credit card bill that morning had added a dark shadow to the crabby tiredness she was already feeling.

And now, thanks to Madeleine, they were running fifteen

minutes late – thirty minutes later than Nia would have been, had she come on the train as she had originally planned.

Madeleine remained in the passenger seat, examining her eyelashes in the visor mirror. Nia took a deep breath.

'Right, I'll just get a ticket. You OK to get out there?'

Madeleine cast a sideways glance at the car next to them, eyebrow pencil poised.

'Just about. I'll be there now. Adam did my eyelashes yesterday. I love the colour – got him to throw in an eyebrow wax, too – really shows off the natural arch of my eyebrows, don't you think?'

For a millisecond, Nia found herself wishing she had a razor.

'Ooh, please,' said Madeleine, meeting Hayden Elliot's offer of a drink with a sparkling smile. 'G and T would be fab.'

The theatre lobby was crammed. Wall-to-wall silk and faux fur jostled for space at the bar, or jostled to find drinks ordered pre-performance. The cacophony of fervent opera buffs exchanging ignored opinions was close to deafening.

'So, what do you think so far, Jackson?' asked Nia, returning from the loo where, as evidence would suggest, she had unwittingly gathered up the hem of her skirt in her tights. Jackson nodded in answer to Nia's question while he patted his jacket pocket.

'Really good... Great seats, too.' He waved a miniature cigar and a lighter with an almost guilty look. 'Just going to have a quick puff. Won't be long.'

Jackson headed for the exit. Hayden handed him a large scotch before making his way back through the throng clutching a tiny wine bottle with an upturned plastic tumbler over the neck and two plastic tumblers of gin and tonic.

'Sorry, no ice and they don't give out glasses at these events – health and safety, apparently!'

Madeleine grimaced and took the offered tumbler. Hayden grinned. 'Warm but wet,' he said and held his glass to Nia in toast. But whatever he said next was drowned by the Tannoy announcement that the performance would recommence in two minutes. Nia cast an anxious glance around the bar.

'Oh, I hope Jackson hasn't got himself lost.'

'I wouldn't worry.' Hayden took a large gulp of his own drink. 'What do you think of the performance so far, ladies?'

Nia opened her mouth but Madeleine sprang into life.

'Oh, it's fab! I absolutely love opera – La Triv is one of my all-time favourites!'

'Oh,' said Hayden, without a blink. 'Yes, one of mine, too. Emma Jenkins is in fine voice tonight, isn't she?'

The Tannoy counted out another minute. Jackson waded back against the tide of the emptying bar depositing his glass on a passing tray. As the crowd around them cleared, Jackson raised an eyebrow and looked down pointedly at Nia's still exposed knickers.

'Gosh, Ms Griffin, I know you're out to impress tonight but there's really no need to show me your drawers!'

Trying not to drown on the merlot she had just inhaled; Nia dropped her hand to drag her skirt free. The look she gave Madeleine should have turned her companion's gin and tonic to vinegar.

'You could have said something!'

Vinegar or not, Madeleine finished her drink in a gulp.

'Thought you knew,' she said casually and turned to follow Jackson and Hayden back into the auditorium.

***

Wednesday, 2nd October, 10.45a.m.

'Gosh, Madeleine! It sounds like you two really hit it off,' said Ros. A waitress arrived to take their order. 'I'll have a filter coffee, please. Oh, and a Danish pastry – can I have one with apricot jam? It is apricot jam, isn't it? Not marmalade? Not keen on marmalade.' She peered over the top of her glasses towards a plate on the counter that was piled high with icing-coated pastry swirls: some dotted cherry-red. Others glistened gold.

The waitress smiled.

'No, it's apricot. And was the filter coffee with milk?'

'Oh, good. Yes, filter, no milk – must make an effort somewhere.' said Ros, with a mischievous grin. 'With Nia not playing badminton I'm short of partners – everyone else is far too good! Although with my hip, it's probably time for me to hang up my shuttlecock anyway, after all, I've retired from almost everything else. Thank God for books!'

Madeleine ordered the same as Ros and then changed her mind and ordered a cappuccino and toast instead – with marmalade.

Ros leant across the table; her eyes were hungry for news.

'So you're getting on well then? How many times have you been out since the opera?'

'Only the once – last Sunday. We went to The Old Plough out in Sageston for lunch, then went back to the Grange to walk the dog.' She grimaced.

'Dog? What kind of a dog is it?' said Ros, suddenly alarmed. 'I'm afraid any love I may have nurtured for animals was extinguished at a very young age when my brother put his pet rat into my bed – scared me half to death. I had nightmares for weeks!'

'Yes,' said Madeleine, not really listening. 'Irish wolf-thing. Huge, smelly and scruffy!'

'Does it have a name? How big is this dog?' asked Ros.

'Maurice… Horace? Something like that.' Madeleine grimaced again. Her phone bleeped. 'Oh, that'll be Josh.' She glanced at the illuminated screen. 'He's hoping for an intro into Maylard's. I'll call him later.'

'So what's Hayden like then?' pressed Ros.

'Oh, the house, Landsmere Grange, is fab – well, it could be… needs a bit of work. It's huge – six bedrooms! There's a music room that would make a lovely study – the one he uses now is tiny – on the first floor, can't think why! The kitchen's OK but a bit old fashioned. Not really my taste. And it's got a wine cellar absolutely crammed with wine – red and white! Some of it's really old – worth a fortune apparently. His car's nice – he's got a Saab that he drives himself – smart but a bit boring, and a battered old Land Rover for the dog.' She rolled her eyes skywards but then became animated again. 'And there's the Jag – bit low key, but at least he's got a driver.' She paused while the waitress set down the two coffees.

'And Hayden?' prompted Ros. 'You know… hair – has he got any? Eyes – what colour? Sense of humour…? Does he like any other music as well as opera?'

Madeleine applied a liberal coating of butter and marmalade to her toast before answering.

'Oh, he's fab. Grey hair. Brown eyes, I think. Yeah… nice.' She shrugged her shoulders and bit into her toast.

Ros pressed on.

'So, are you going to see him again? Are you going to invite him over to your house for a meal?'

Madeleine stopped mid-chew. The look of abject horror on her face suggested not.

'God, no! After Landsmere Grange, my house is a hovel! No, no. If we're going out again I shall insist we go somewhere nice!'

Thursday, 24th October, 9.05p.m.

Hi Dad

Gosh, what a lot of news to take-in in one email!

I mean, it's not as if I was that keen on Carla as I'm sure you guessed (but always hid well, bless you). You must have been very hurt… but not to tell me until now – I would hardly have tried to talk her round!

Seriously though, Dad, are you sure you're not jumping into something new a bit too quickly? Your new lady sounds nice but are you ready to start 'dating' again? (I can't believe I'm having this conversation with my own father!!).

Look, I'll try to give you a call on Saturday night – it'll be about midnight your time – is that OK? We can have a proper chat then.

Take care of yourself and don't do anything rash!

Love as always

Saffy

XXXXXXXXXXXXXXXXX

PS Ben sends hugs OOO

Saturday, 30th October, 11.55p.m.

Hayden sank into an armchair, phone in hand. It was eleven fifty-five p.m. and Saffy was due to call any moment.

He had just spent a very enjoyable evening in the company of Madeleine Edwards – the third this week – although the previous two had progressed satisfyingly through to toast and coffee-sharing experiences at about nine o'clock the following morning. As, however, his daughter was going to call this evening all the way from Hong Kong, Hayden had gently suggested that Madeleine catch up on some sleep in her own bed tonight. Madeleine had resisted (actually she'd made it patently obvious that going home was not her preferred option) but she had eventually departed once Hayden had promised to take her somewhere 'lovely' tomorrow for breakfast; fortunately Madeleine's idea of 'breakfast' was brunch at about eleven-thirty a.m., which would give Hayden plenty of time to walk Morris, collect the paper in the morning and catch up on emails and phone calls.

The phone sprang into life.

'Dad, hi!'

'Darling, it's so good to hear your voice. How are you?'

'Oh, fine, fine. Ben's here. He's not going to leave me alone until I let him speak to you... Is that OK?'

Hayden grinned. There was a moment of muffled negotiation on the other end of the phone, a brief scream and then a little voice shouted, 'HEWO, ITH THAT BA WITTEN?'

Hayden jerked the phone a foot away from his ear; from the other end he could hear Saffy trying to explain to his grandson that he didn't need to shout, as Ba Ritten could hear even 'little voices'.

'Yeth, but he'th vewy far waway,' objected Ben.

'It's alright Ben, I can hear you,' said Hayden, in a slightly louder tone as there were still a fair few inches of air between the phone and his ear.

'But he'th thouting, too, Mummy. HEWO, BA WITTEN!' Ben bellowed back.

Hayden gave in.

'Hello, Ben. Are you being good for Mummy?'

Silence.

'And what have you been doing?'

Muffled muttering from distant Hong Kong.

'HAVE YOU BEEN RIDING YOUR BIKE?' Hayden yelled.

'THETH!' shouted a suddenly animated voice. 'I FELL OFF. MUMMY TOLD OFF THE BIKE FOR BEING NAUGHTY. I GOT CHOCOLATE!'

'Oh, did Mummy give you chocolate when you fell off your bike?' asked Hayden.

Silence and then more mumbled muttering. Then Hayden heard something being tapped against the phone.

'NOOO. NOT THEN. I GOT CHOCOLATE IN MY HAND, HERE!'

Hayden smothered a laugh at the mental image of his grandson holding his chocolate to the phone. Then he heard Saffy trying to persuade Ben to say goodbye to Ba Ritten and give her back the phone.

'Here'th Mummy. BYE.'

'Hi, Dad, hang on… don't you want to blow a kiss all the way to Britain for Grandpa?' called Saffy.

Silence. Then a very distant shout.

'Bye, bye Ba Witten. Fank you for my bike.'

'He's blowing you very chocolaty kisses, Dad… Yes, and Ba Ritten is blowing kisses back to you, Ben… That's it. Good boy. Now go and find Daddy and ask him to wipe your mouth… and your hands… AL!' she called, 'He's got chocolate everywhere. Can you bring me a cloth for the phone? AL! Sorry about this, Dad, I'll be back in a mo.'

Hayden could hear raised voices but it was impossible to make out any words, then Saffy's voice came down the phone again.

'…chocolate, for Chrissake, he's only three…! Dad, sorry, are you still there? Sorry, it's chaos here as usual. Alistair's up early trying to get a report done for Monday and Ben's just got chocolate all over his laptop. I may have to cut this short...' She stopped talking – listening. 'No, we could be OK, it's all gone quiet – either that or there's been a suspicious death. Anyway, how are you?'

The remaining ten minutes of the conversation went largely uninterrupted. Saffy asked a lot of mostly appropriate questions about Madeleine and a few far less appropriate and unusually spiteful questions about her former stepmother.

'So what happened to the villa in Calabria? Don't tell me you let *her* have it?'

'Well, er, yes. But I never really liked the place anyway.'

'But she left *you*, Dad! Why should she get anything? And why did you ever agree to pay for those teeth? And as for those boobs – how did you manage in bed? They stuck out so far it must have been like sleeping in a tent – well, a marquee actually!'

'Now, now, Saf, they weren't that big – actually I was quite fond of them,' he said wistfully.

'So is Madeleine already sorted in that department or are you going in for a bulk deal?'

'She is perfectly lovely, Saffy. Now don't worry. We get on very well and she's good company. I was telling her about my involvement in Cornerstone this evening. Apparently she's very interested in children's literacy and really likes where we're going. I'm going to have a chat to a few of the board members at our next meeting – see if we can't use her skills somewhere.'

'Pretty *and* skilled – oh well, that's two advantages over Carla then! What's her thing?'

'Marketing, I think. Certainly sounds like she knows what she's talking about... just been made redundant. Could be good timing for us?'

'What, for Maylard's?'

'Oh, no. Cornerstone. She looks the part, too – nice smile, slim, very well spoken… yer, I think she could be good.'

'God, Dad, are you thinking of going out with her or giving her a job!'

Hayden laughed.

'Oh, you know. That's one of the things I really miss though. Not having anyone presentable to take to events. I had no idea I knew so many widows and divorcees – they've come out of the woodwork since Carla left!'

He heard Saffy laugh on the other end of the phone – it was her mother's laugh.

'Honestly, Saf. I go to all these events and within five minutes I can't move for women. I feel like I've had 'Single, *again*' tattooed on my forehead. It would be nice to be able to take some back-up to keep them off!'

'Well, it's good to hear you sounding so cheerful, Dad, so I guess I shouldn't be too worried. Just don't do anything too rushed, hey. …*WHAT?* She stopped, listened and then spoke again. 'Oh, sorry Dad, I knew the peace wouldn't last. Apparently Ben's dropped his chocolate down the loo. Better go before he fishes it out and finishes it! Look, just have some fun for a while – you deserve it!'

They exchanged hurried goodbyes and then she was gone.

Morris, lying sprawled across the carpet, flicked his amber eyes towards Hayden as if to say, 'Thank goodness for that. You were keeping me awake!' Then he crashed his head back down on the rug and shut his eyes tight as if to reinforce his message. Suddenly Landsmere Grange felt very quiet.

***

Monday 11th November, 11.05a.m.

The card read:

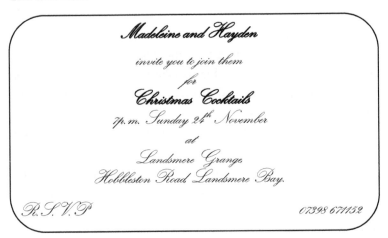

Madeleine and Hayden

invite you to join them

for

Christmas Cocktails

7p.m. Sunday 24th November

at

Landsmere Grange
Hobbleston Road, Landsmere Bay.

R.S.V.P   *07398 671152*

Nia reached for her diary, knowing full well that November 24th was blank – although, she noted, a tad early for 'Christmas Cocktails'.

She turned to Saturday 23rd and scrubbed through the words *'Out with Madeleine'* written neatly next to *'HAPPY BIRTHDAY TO ME!'* Then in the Sunday underneath she scrawled, *7p.m. Maddy – cocktails at Hayden's house,* before dialling the number on the card. It was Madeleine's mobile.

The answer phone kicked in after three rings.

'Hi, this is Madeleine Edwards. I'm in a meeting right now. Please leave a message and I'll get back to you as soon as I can.'

Nia gave a shrugging grin and spoke.

'Meeting, my backside! Hi, Maddy, Nia here. Thanks for the invite. Yes, I'd love to come. Thank Hayden, too. Hope you're well? See you soon. Bye.'

As she ended the call, her house phone rang.

'Nia, it's Ros. Um... did you get anything interesting in the post this morning?'

'If you mean the invitation to Hayden's, yes, and I've just accepted – via Maddy's answer phone. Not the greatest timing, have to admit, as I'll have to buy a cocktail dress and I'm skint.'

'Oh, no word back from Maylard's yet then?' said Ros, sounding genuinely concerned. 'I'm sure they'll use you. Did you give them both your numbers?'

'Yes,' answered Nia, averting her eyes from the pile of unopened bills lurking on the corner of her desk – one, she knew, was a final demand for her office phone.

'Isn't the twenty-fourth the day after your birthday? D'you think Madeleine's forgotten?'

'Not sure but it's the last year the number four will precede any number from one to nine on any of my birthday cards so I'm quite happy to play it down.'

'Oh, nonsense! More reason to celebrate!' argued Ros. 'Did you have anything planned? Do you want me to give her a call to remind her?'

'Gosh, no! Knowing Maddy she'll be far too busy making sure the napkins match the curtains to worry about changing her plans,' said Nia. 'No, going to a cocktail party at Hayden Elliot's, albeit the day after my birthday, will suit me fine. You never know, Maddy may have some grand plan? Haven't seen her for weeks. I'm sure she won't have forgotten.'

***

Sunday, 24th November 7.15p.m.

The appearance of four thin fingers around the edge of the front door coincided with the painful sound of wood scraping on quarry tiles, revealing, as the fingers did their work, a young girl clad in a plain black skirt and top, sporting a miniscule white apron and a vacant smile.

Nia and Ros waited to be invited in. Behind them, the sweep of rutted gravel that served as a courtyard for Landsmere Grange spilled into its long, equally pitted driveway – both were bumper to bumper with Jags, BMWs and Volvos. Arriving fashionably late, Nia had had no choice but to park her Mini right back out on the main road and the return journey on foot in the pitch dark had not been without incident; Ros had twisted her ankle falling down a pothole. It had also started to drizzle. By the time Nia finally pressed the doorbell both she and Ros were soggy and desperate for a glass of something cheering. Ivy (they had discovered the previous day during a very embarrassing lunch – with Ivy) had not been invited.

'Good even,' said the young lady, holding the door wide. 'Please to come in, I take your coats? Please yourself to a Buck Fizz.' She gave a vague wave in the direction of a side table groaning under the weight of cloudy orange bubbly and closed the door. She took Nia's coat. The bell rang again.

'Good even,' she said after a repeat performance of the struggle with the sticking door – opening *and* closing. 'Please to come in, I take your coats? Please yourself to a Buck Fizz.'

'Oh, my God,' whispered Ros. 'It's Poland's answer to the Stepford Wives!'

Madeleine's voice arrived just before she did.

'You're late!'

For a nanosecond Nia assumed she was joking but

Madeleine's expression as she bore down on them suggested not, and also rather spoilt the impact of her exceptionally short black cocktail dress – *pricey*, Nia observed (she also observed that the lace overlay across the shoulders just took it away from looking slutty). Ros did a neat, if somewhat painful, dodge and made a move for the Buck's Fizz.

'Fashionably, *mon amie*,' Nia soothed. 'We couldn't park anywhere near the house. Had to head back out on to the road. Do you think my car'll be alright there?'

'No idea,' said Madeleine, still vexed. 'There are a lot of people here who are meeting me for the first time and it just would have been nice to have had some familiar faces around!'

Ros handed Nia a long crystal glass and licked her fingers.

'Sorry, drinks delivery with a limp obviously isn't a good idea,' she said with an apologetic grin.

'Limp – oh God, what have you done?' demanded Madeleine, her expression now suggesting this was a disaster too far.

'Tripped down a pothole. The driveway's a bit dark,' understated Ros. She offered up a toast. 'Don't worry; I'll be fine after a few of these.'

A crash came from somewhere further into the house.

Only just loud enough for those very close to hear, Madeleine muttered, 'For fuck's sake, what now!' and stalked away, past an enormous blue and silver Christmas tree, towards the sound of fevered catering activities coming from, Nia guessed, the kitchen.

'And happy birthday, Nia,' said Nia, meeting Ros's uplifted glass with her own.

Hayden appeared from a noisy room to the left, looking anything but hassled. His face broke into an even wider beam when he spotted the errant pair.

'Nia, Ros! I'm so glad you could come. It was such a shame that so many of Maddy's other friends couldn't make it.' Nia threw Ros a questioning look – as far as she knew no one else had been invited and she knew that Paolo for one would have walked over molten *Mama Mia* DVDs to get to a cocktail party at Landsmere Grange!

Hayden held up his arm and beckoned Ros and Nia with his fingers.

'Shall I do some introductions, ladies? Maddy's around somewhere – crisis with the dim sum, I understand. I trust you have admired the tree?'

When Madeleine next appeared she was at least wearing a smile, even if it was a little forced.

'Right, I've finally managed to get the staff organised,' she said. 'The dum sim will be out any minute; although, honestly, I won't be using this lot again – half of them can't speak English!'

Ros was studying a row of photo frames set out along the marble mantelpiece – almost every one featured Madeleine at varying ages from early teens to almost present day.

'Gosh, Maddy. Are all these yours? Who's the chap with the child in that one, next to you?'

'Oh, that's my brother Martin and my nephew, Aaron. Taken a few years ago. Aaron's sixteen now.'

'And this one – is that your mother? You've got the same hair!' said Ros picking up the frame nearest to her. It was the only photograph that didn't feature Madeleine herself. Ros studied the sweep of hair of the woman in the black and white picture, posed 1950s film star style.

'Hmm, with any luck that's all I inherited!' breathed Madeleine.

'There aren't any of you and Hayden though, Maddy?' said Ros, carefully inspecting every picture. 'Unless I've made a mistake? Haven't got my glasses.' Madeleine regained her cross expression.

'Another sore point. We had some done in that new studio in town – cost a fortune. I ordered a big one to go over there.' She pointed to a wonderful seascape mounted above the mantelpiece that, Nia guessed, perfectly reflected the daylight view from the huge bay windows. Madeleine wrinkled her nose. 'But I wasn't happy with the print quality – the light wasn't right. Made my teeth look quite grey! Anyway, they're fiddling with it. It'll be an early Christmas present for Hayden – he doesn't know, so don't mention it. I told him we were just going to get a few shots done for a bit of fun.'

'Oh, so Hayden doesn't know it's going there?' said Ros. 'Do you think he'll mind?'

Madeleine glanced over to where Hayden and Jackson Tranter were in deep conversation – well, Hayden was – Jackson had one eye on the bottom of the waitress who had just staggered past him, wilting in the steam of the just-served dim sum.

'Ah, food, at last,' breathed Madeleine. The dim sum had been her idea when she and Hayden had first discussed the cocktail party. Hayden had voiced a preference for standard canapés, prepared by the caterers that he and Carla had used for years. But, after a mild sulk and one of the best blow jobs Hayden had enjoyed in years, Madeleine had got her way – although there had been moments during the past two hours when she had secretly wished she'd kept her mouth shut. 'Sorry, ladies, I'd better go and supervise...'

A second later Madeleine's voice carried out into the hall. 'Are those the prawns? Girls, make sure you tell people that those are filled with prawns! Is anyone going to bring in more drinks...? Buck's Fizz anyone? Dum sim?'

Nia studied the photographs again and took another sip of her drink.

'Do you think we should tell her?' said Ros.

Nia shook her head and took another sip of her Buck's Fizz.

'So, what's the betting there's a toothbrush with Maddy's name on it up in the en suite!'

Wednesday, 11th December, 11.50a.m.

Madeleine was brimming with excitement as she entered Horton's. She had just been to collect the framed photograph of her (teeth positively gleaming) and Hayden. It was now safely stowed behind the front seats of her car, ready for her to present to Hayden later that evening.

Nia's day, however, had not been going anywhere nearly as well: she had a splitting headache, the silence from Maylard's was deafening, and just before she'd left to meet Madeleine, she had discovered that her office phone had been cut off (the unpaid bill was lurking at the bottom of her in-tray – Nia's equivalent of putting her fingers in her ears, shutting her eyes tight and singing loudly). She had called BT from her mobile – trying not to cry – only to discover that the woman she finally did manage to speak to had clearly had the 'Care' bit removed from her 'Customer Care Representative' job title. What Nia really needed was the shoulder of a good friend, a large cup of Earl Grey and some chocolate – well, *lots* of chocolate, actually.

Madeleine positively shimmied across the stripped oak floor and plonked down into the leather armchair opposite Nia.

'I've got it!' she announced – triumph radiating from every pore.

Herpes? thought Nia; but, with her best interested look, she said, 'Got what?'

58

'The picture... for Hayden. Oh, Nia, it's fab. They finally managed to get my teeth right and my hair looks great – managed to persuade Alfonse to do it just before we went in.'

'Who's Alfonse?' asked Nia, still smarting at the BT woman's tone.

'My hairdresser!' said Madeleine. She didn't say 'Doh!' but Nia knew that expression. 'On the corner, opposite Number 68 – you know, that gorgeous little gallery. Have you been in? I've just bought a pair of candlesticks for the en suite in our room – Hayden loves them.'

'I thought it was Adam?' said Nia, ignoring the reference to the prohibitively expensive art gallery that had, only a few weeks ago, also been out of Madeleine's income bracket.

'God, no! I'm learning you get what you pay for with hairdressers. No, Alfonse is far better and much nearer to the Grange, too.'

Even Nia's disinterest was becoming disinterested. In desperation, she changed the subject back to the picture.

'So are you going to give Hayden the photograph on Christmas Day?'

'Gosh no! Where would I hide it?'

Nia's eyebrows shot skywards but Madeleine continued uninterrupted.

'No, keeping it a secret would be such a problem. I'm going to give it to him this evening after dinner. Actually it'll work out perfectly. We can get it hung ready for Sunday lunch – you are coming, aren't you?'

Nia had been dreading this question. Madeleine reached for her cappuccino.

'Look, I'm really sorry, Madeleine, but I can't. Mum's not too good again so I'm going to pop home to cheer her up.'

Madeleine sipped her coffee, her spine suddenly stiff.

'Oh! But you'll mess up my numbers. Are you sure you can't go to Wiltshire next week?'

'She's seventy-nine, Maddy; she's got acute angina and she's practically housebound – sorry, but I think my mum trumps Sunday lunch.'

Madeleine seemed to be concentrating very hard on reuniting her cup with its saucer.

'Oh..., well, yes. Of course. I'll ask Ros – I doubt she'll have plans for Sunday.'

'So why aren't you going to wait until Christmas Day to give Hayden the picture?' asked Nia, miffed but willing to change the subject.

'Well, as I said, it's going to be difficult keeping it a secret until then, now that I'm living there,' said Madeleine.

Nia gulped down a large mouthful of hot coffee.

'Oh… but what about your lovely little house?'

'On the market.'

'But, Maddy, don't you think this is all a bit quick? Don't you think… well, perhaps you could rent it out or something? You know… just in case.'

Madeleine gave a dismissive wave.

'No. Hayden did suggest something similar but we're going to be buying a flat in Spain after Christmas and I'm getting involved in some charity work now – at board level obviously, so I just can't see how I'd have the time to be a landlord.'

'But won't you lose money? The market's gone down terribly – I had a major shock when I had my flat valued last week,' said Nia, parking the "charity work" prompt for another time.

'There's still bits to do upstairs. Hayden's going to pay and I'll pay him back if I make anything on the sale.'

'And if you don't?'

Madeleine gave Nia an impish grin.

'Oh, I'm sure I can make it up to him in other ways!'

Sunday, 15th December, 12 noon

Ros glanced at her watch – twelve noon on the dot. She pressed the bell and cast a look back over her shoulder at the worryingly empty courtyard – had she got the right day? The last time she had been to Landsmere Grange, the courtyard and driveway had been backed up with expensive cars. Today, other than Madeleine's violently green Beetle haphazardly abandoned alongside a grey Saab and a very dirty Land Rover, it was deserted.

Behind her, the lock clicked and Hayden's smiling face appeared around the door: at his waist height, another very shaggy head nudged through the gap. Ros froze.

'Is that a dog?' she asked needlessly, fighting the extremely strong desire to scream. 'Does it bite?'

Hayden grinned, forced the door open and hooked his fingers under Morris's collar. 'It's alright, Ros. This is Morris. He's utterly harmless. We're just going for a quick wee before everyone arrives… him not me, that is! Don't worry. He'll sleep for the rest of the afternoon.'

'Oh, but he's so… big!' Ros's mouth was suddenly very dry.

Still hanging on to Morris's collar, Hayden pulled the door wide and stepped far enough back to create a reasonable gap between the entrance, the hound and Ros.

'No bigger than your average wolfie,' he grinned. 'Look, come in and make yourself comfortable. Maddy'll be down in a second. In the meantime I'll give Morris the opportunity to do what he has to, then I'll put him in the kitchen. Don't worry, he won't do anything.'

Unconvinced, Ros kept her back firmly pressed against the opposite doorjamb and slid across the threshold.

'Maddy!' Hayden called up the sweep of stairs leading from the middle of the expansive tiled hallway. Other than the two of them and the dog, this too was deserted. At the top, the stairs gave way right and left to a gallery of glossy white doors on three sides of the floor above. Madeleine's head popped out of one of the doors on the right wall.

'I'll be down in a mo. Can you show people into the drawing room, darling?'

Hayden held out his right arm, his left still resting on Morris's collar. Morris yawned.

'You heard the lady,' he said with a good-natured smile and waved towards a doorway off the hall. Then he dropped his voice and added, 'Although the last time I looked, it was the lounge!' His eyes twinkled with mischief. 'Anyway, help yourself to a G and T, sherry, whatever you fancy. I'll be back in a jiffy.'

Ros followed the direction of Hayden's guiding hand and found herself in a familiar room. Behind her, the front door scraped to a close. She was alone.

Ros wandered around the vast drawing room/lounge, sherry in hand. She spied the mantelpiece; it was now positively groaning under the weight of Madeleine's family photographs, as was the top of a gleaming baby grand piano that Ros didn't recall from her last visit. Above the fireplace, the seascape had gone – relegated, she noticed, to a dark corner at other end of the same room. In its place beamed Madeleine, with Hayden at her shoulder – it was only then that Ros noticed a sapphire gleaming on Madeleine's finger... her ring finger!

'Ros, I'm so sorry!' Ros jumped and spun around as if caught with the family silver jammed in her handbag. Amontillado spilled over her hand. Madeleine either didn't notice or chose to move on.

'Oh, has Hayden left you on your own? That blasted dog of his – I'm sure he cares more about that animal than me!'

'Oh, don't worry, Maddy. Gave me the chance to admire your photograph,' said Ros. She waved towards the portrait while surreptitiously trying to get a look at Madeleine's left hand.

'Yes, fab, isn't it?' Madeleine's face shone with self-satisfaction. 'Much better that that old thing he had there before. More sherry?' She reached for the decanter.

'Oh, no, thanks. I've got the car. I'll save myself for a glass of wine with lunch,' said Ros. Madeleine poured herself a large gin and tonic.

'Well, any news?' said Ros, getting desperate. 'Anything, er, new?'

'Not really,' answered Madeleine, carefully nudging the sleeves of a very new, very cashmere cardigan up her forearms. There… there it was, a flash of green! 'We've started to look for an apartment. Hayden likes Barcelona but I'd much rather Málaga. The flight's a bit longer but it's far nicer and of course, being much further south, so much warmer. We'll probably pop over after Christmas, you know, before the season starts again and the flights get busy.'

'And… any other plans?' prompted Ros as casually as she could. 'Any… special occasions?'

'Oh… Yes! I nearly forgot!' Ros put her drink on the baby grand ready to rush forward for the obligatory warm hug. Madeleine took a sip of her drink and then spoke. 'We're having the kitchen completely refitted and… guess what?' Ros held her breath. '…we're having a library!'

Defeated, Ros retrieved her drink and fought the temptation to ask Madeleine if she actually knew what a book was.

'Oh, how lovely!' she said instead.

'Yes. Of course at the party, I didn't really get the chance to show you around, did I? Come and have a look. How's the knee, by the way?'

'It was my ankle. I get the odd twinge but it's OK.'

As they talked, Madeleine led the way through the house. She showed Ros every room and, in every room, explained, in some detail, her redesign, redecoration and reorganisation plans. Ros wasn't entirely sure whether she was supposed to approve or put in an offer. By the time they returned to the drawing room, seven other people and Hayden were all quaffing something alcoholic.

Wednesday, 18th December, 8.05p.m.

'...and when Madeleine told me they were going to see "La Boame" I nearly choked,' said Ros, mirth forcing her eyebrows into her hairline. She propped her mobile under her chin and unpeeled an Elizabeth Shaw Mint Crisp.

'Oh, no!' said Nia. 'Didn't anyone correct her?'

'You must be joking,' said Ros, snapping the mint-flecked chocolate in two. 'I don't think those two bimbettes could spell *opera*, let alone La Bohème. I mentioned Puccini just to see what would happen and the red-head – you know the one called Kelli with an *i* – wrinkled her nose and told me that she didn't like fancy stuff on her pizza!'

Nia's laughter tinkled down the phone.

'Didn't Hayden say anything?' she asked. 'Or Jackson?'

Ros shook her head.

'Gosh no, Hayden's far too lovely and Jackson was too busy

staring down the cleavage of the *child* he'd brought along – Chloe, I think? Not that there was much to stare at! She didn't eat a mouthful the whole time and hardly said a word – honestly, I don't think she could have been more than about twenty-one!'

'I really didn't think Jackson was like that, you know,' said Nia, her voice loaded with disapproval. 'I mean, I know he's always been one for the younger woman – and with his money, I'm guessing that's a big attraction… but he's not bad-looking and he's actually quite good company…' She paused. Ros swallowed the chocolate she'd been savouring and picked up where Nia had left off.

'No, I didn't either. But he and that Roger; he's the one I reckon Madeleine had invited on my account, well, they were as bad as each other. I did wonder at one point if it was some kind of competition! The other chap, Paul, was OK but *his* wife had to be fifteen years younger than him. At least she had a sense of humour though; Madeleine asked her where she got her blouse from – it was really nice actually – and when she said Primark, Maddy nearly choked on her beef wellington.' It was Ros's turn to laugh again.

'Oh, I bet she only said that to see what Maddy would say,' said Nia.

'I have to admit, it was one of only a few laughs I had that lunchtime, that's for sure,' said Ros. 'I certainly don't think I'll be seeing Roger again; although I'll be dining out on the stories for weeks, obviously!'

Nia laughed this time.

'Oh, that reminds me,' added Ros. 'Did you know Maddy's wearing an engagement ring? Should I be buying a new hat?'

'Oh, gosh no!' said Nia, suddenly serious. 'It was her mother's. I really don't know why she's suddenly started wearing it though - she's had it for about fifteen years. Worth a fortune, apparently. Maddy got it after the divorce – her mother told her she couldn't bear to have it in the house after what her father did.'

'Why didn't her mother just sell it then?' asked Ros. 'She could have bought something really nice with the proceeds to spite Maddy's father! I would've, wouldn't you?'

'Mmm, by all accounts Maddy's mum wasn't the kind of lady that would be comfortable selling jewellery – would have sent out the wrong message, if you know what I mean,' said Nia. 'Maddy's had it in a jewellery box for ages. She showed it to me about five years ago. Maybe she's feeling nostalgic – you saw those photos at Hayden's.'

'Goodness me, you should see them now – they've bred! I was seriously worried that the mantelpiece may not be able to hold the weight!' said Ros. 'Talk about sending a message. And the plans she's got for the house... poor Hayden! Do you think he knows what he's letting himself in for? The newest member of the Trophy Wife Club, perhaps!'

'Now, now, Ros, that's a bit mean. I think they make a lovely couple,' said Nia. In the background, another phone started to ring. 'Oh, hang on... ooh, it's Maylard's – gotta go. Speak soon.' And the phone went dead.

Ros cast her eye around the bookcases that lined the living room of her little bungalow and pursed her lips.

'Damn, I forgot to tell her about the plan for the library!'

Sunday 9th February, 12.15p.m.

'Ladies and gentlemen, we will shortly be landing at Bristol Airport,' announced a disembodied voice. Almost to a man – or woman – the passengers of the ten-fifteen flight from Barcelona clicked their seatbelts and suddenly took an interest in the approaching ground. 'Please fasten your seatbelts and ensure that you remain seated until the plane is stationary. The local time is twelve-fifteen hundred hours and the temperature outside is a shade cooler than Barcelona, at nine degrees. Thank you for flying MBY. Have a pleasant day.'

Hayden's white fingers clutched his laptop case. He closed his eyes then opened them again and shook his head.

'You know, even after all these years and hundreds of flights, landing is still the bit I dread – it's the *maybe* factor that always worries me.'

Madeleine shifted in her seat. He reached across and squeezed her knee. 'You alright?'

'Gosh, yes, fine,' she replied stiffly. Actually she was still sulking because he had insisted they forgo a final shop the previous day in favour of a quiet afternoon spent mostly in, on or up against the huge, king-sized bed that seemed to fill the bedroom of the apartment, followed by an après shag lobster thermidor in the neighbouring yacht club, before heading back for more of the same – as far as Madeleine could see, after the last five days the shopping was the only good reason she would go back to Barcelona. 'Although my back's aching.'

'Can't think why that might be,' he whispered, giving her leg another gentle squeeze.

'Hm,' sniffed Madeleine. 'Well, if we do have that apartment, we'll be changing that bed.'

'I thought it was fine,' said Hayden, giving her leg yet another squeeze – a little further up this time.

A stewardess came past to check their seatbelts. Hayden moved his hand. Madeleine's belt lay limp at her side.

'Madam, please could you fasten your seatbelt. We'll be landing in a few minutes,' said the woman, and moved down the aisle with a polite smile.

Madeleine clicked the belt ends together without raising her eyes and muttered, 'It's ages yet. They always make you put them on too soon.'

'So, apart from the bed,' Hayden pressed on. 'Was there anything else you didn't like about the apartment?'

Madeleine pondered. The air hostess returned, glanced at Madeleine's lap and moved on.

'Well, apart from the fact that it was in Barcelona, no, it was fine,' said Madeleine.

While her reply was not unexpected, Hayden was still disappointed. She just hadn't seemed to share his enthusiasm for the spectacular Gaudi architecture that adorned the city; instead, she had developed a sudden and desperate need for a new pair of sunglasses... or a silk scarf... or a leather handbag. So while Hayden took in the breath-taking stonework of La Sagrada Familia, he had handed over his credit card and Madeleine had gone shopping. Later, cheered by a gin and tonic in a bar overlooking the harbour, Hayden had tried to share the experience by explaining that the basilica, started in 1882, was still under construction today, but Madeleine's dismissive, 'Well, they should have employed more people then, shouldn't they!' spoke volumes.

The sex, however, had been a real highlight and so Hayden agreed to move the apartment search to Málaga.

Tuesday 18th February, 3.15p.m.

Madeleine stood in the empty room surrounded by wall-to-wall barren, oak shelves – each one hand-jointed, sanded, fitted and varnished to her precise directions. She had spent days painstakingly researching the size of paperbacks and hardbacks; she had made amendment after amendment and had even had a run-in with the security guard at Waterstones (but once the misunderstanding about the tape measure and the spirit level had been sorted out, the staff there had actually been most accommodating.)

Behind her, the floorboard creaked and a warm, now familiar arm wound around her waist.

'Well, d'you like it?' she asked without turning around.

'Yes,' answered Hayden, gently kissing the back of her head. Her hair smelt of lemon and honey. With an unseen smile, he drew her closer. 'I also liked it as a music room but, well, with Saffy gone and no one to play the piano, I have to agree it was a bit wasted.'

'Oh, but the piano's much better where it is now,' said Madeleine, drawing away to face him. 'It'll be ideal when Emma and Nigel come to dinner next week – I was going to ask her to sing.'

Hayden's arm stiffened slightly.

'Maddy, they're coming to have a meal with friends! I've known Emma for years and I've never asked her to sing for her supper. If I start now she really will think our friendship is heading down a dark road!'

'But...' started Madeleine.

'Look, Maddy, Emma's coming to talk about Cornerstone. I'm really hoping that she'll agree to do some fund-raising for us this year. Maybe she might be up for doing something here in the summer as part of that?' Hayden said in an effort to divert Madeleine from one of her mini-strops (they were annoying but, as Hayden was relieved to discover, not nearly as bad as the clouds of talcum powder that Carla could conjure up when things weren't going her way); but, actually, the more he thought about the idea – a garden party perhaps? – the more he liked it.

Hayden surveyed the acres of bare wood that now lined the walls of his once spacious and uncluttered music room. A memory of Saffy sitting at the piano – pigtails as high as she could physically get them – practicing Gershwin's *It Ain't Necessarily So* sprang to life in his mind's eye. After a lot of finger-crashing and some surprisingly bad language for a twelve-year-old, she had eventually mastered the piece only the day before her Grade Five exam; she had played it perfectly, achieving the highest mark she had ever got, and never played the piano again. After that, it was Georgina who had persuaded Hayden that the piano should stay… just in case.

'So do you want a hand to put my books on these shelves, then?' he asked.

Madeleine stepped out of his gentle hold and shook her head.

'No, it's OK,' she said, not catching his eye. 'I, er, I want to make sure they go in the right place. I'll do it tomorrow… while you're away.'

'You sure?' frowned Hayden. 'There's about a dozen boxes up there, plus the ones in the study.'

'No, it's fine,' insisted Madeleine. 'I've got a plan. It's going to be a surprise.' A feline smile curled around her lips. 'I'll need something to keep me busy for the three whole days you'll be gone,' she purred.

She took one step back towards him. Hayden caught the middle button of her blouse and gently drew her one more step closer.

'You'll miss me, then?' he said, his voice soft in the empty room.

Her slate-grey eyes shone with mock innocence.

'How much?' asked Hayden in barely a whisper.

Madeleine stroked the top button of her blouse free of its buttonhole and ran her index finger down the parted silk. The innocence in her eyes evaporated. 'I'll show you, if you like.'

Thursday, 20th February 12.25p.m.

Madeleine stepped back to admire her handiwork. Her back ached and she had broken a nail, but she was pleased with the result of her efforts. Just over half of Hayden's books – the half she had decided to keep – were now lodged in their new home.

To placate Hayden, she had allowed him to pack the books away before the work on the library had even begun; with books all over the house, it had taken him hours. Now, however, with Hayden safely out of interfering distance, her initial sort through those same boxes had revealed a vast collection of texts featuring Mediterranean architecture – *lots* on Gaudi; he also had an indecent number of tomes on opera where something called 'bel canto' seemed to be a bit of a favourite. The rest of the collection was split largely across vintage cars, country walks in various parts of the UK (to Madeleine's horror!) and what could only be described as mountains of World War Two aircraft books. His fiction reading was exclusively crime thrillers – three boxes, two of which that she didn't even bother to open. There was also a box of children's books – obviously Saffy's – which again she dismissed immediately.

The initial sift had been less than sophisticated even for Madeleine; anything that looked well-thumbed was rejected and dropped back into the slot from where it had been lifted, as was anything that looked old. But there were still far too many books left that Madeleine simply did not want on her beautiful shelves, so the cull was broadened to include any volume that was an odd size, looked boring or (as quite a few seemed to be) looked like they had never been read. This strategy proved to be far more effective and by lunchtime Madeleine felt she was finally getting somewhere.

The phone rang.

'Maddy, hi, it's Ros. D'you fancy meeting up for tea this afternoon? I'm having a facial at one-thirty so I could see you at Horton's. Say three-ish?'

Madeleine scanned the boxes, like coffins, before her. Outside, Barry, Hayden's longstanding gardener, walked across the side lawn past the window, tree lopper in hand. Madeleine glanced at her watch – twelve-fifty – excellent.

'Sounds great, Ros,' she said. 'But can we make it three-thirty; I've got an errand to run in town first?'

Thursday, 20th February, 2.15p.m.

Barry slid the last of the boxes into the back of the Land Rover. He was sweating.

Madeleine had collared him on his way to make a cup of tea. It was mild for February and unseasonably dry, which had given him the chance to have a go at the overgrowth along the west garden. Before Hayden had gone off on his latest trip, he had mentioned something about a garden party later in the year and Barry knew that if some of those old shrubs weren't brought under control now, by the time the spring sun had done its work they would be another four feet wide. He had just demolished a rampant pyracantha and, nursing some pretty savage scratches, was heading down to the workshop at the edge of the walled garden for a plaster and a cup of tea, when Madeleine had called him from the front door.

All doe eyes and smiles, she had asked him to 'help' her put 'a couple' of boxes into Mr Elliot's Land Rover. But, he had quickly discovered, there were seven boxes – each one packed to the

72

gunwales – *and* 'help' didn't seem to involve the new lady of the house too much. To add insult to his injuries, heavy hints like 'I was about to have a cuppa with my lunch before I tackle that old buddleia,' had completely failed to conjure up the desired – or, in fact, *any* – refreshment. Barry was miffed – although not entirely surprised; after all, he had endured and survived the Mrs Elliot the Second years.

As Barry wedged the final box into the remaining space, the top popped open. He glanced at the row of book spines.

'Andy McNabb – haven't read one of his for ages,' he panted. 'And Lee Child… never enough time for reading.'

'Take the box, if you want,' said Madeleine.

Barry looked unsure.

'Really,' Madeleine insisted. 'They're going anyway.'

For a moment, Barry looked tempted but then shook his head and closed the rear door of the Land Rover with a slam.

'Nah, they'd only end up under my stairs.'

'Well, if you're sure?' said Madeleine. 'Right, well I'd better go change then I'm off into town.'

She peered at the driver's seat of the battered old Discovery.

'Better dress down, I think!' she said more to herself than to Barry, and headed back across the drive. Without a backward glance she called out, 'Thanks for that, Barry. Hope I didn't take up too much time – don't forget to add it to Hayden's bill.'

Friday, 21st February, 7.35p.m.

Madeleine glared at her watch – its mother of pearl, diamond-dotted face told her it was seven thirty-five p.m. Hayden had presented the watch to her as a Valentine's Day gift. Although a tad mainstream for Madeleine, it had rather eclipsed the Moët & Chandon she had bought him, so she had painted on her 'absolutely delighted and couldn't be happier' smile, ran a bath and let Hayden lick icy champagne out of her naturally ample cleavage.

At this moment, however, Madeleine was far from happy. Hayden had called her from the airport to suggest supper at The County Club. Not thrilled, Madeleine had only accepted because Hayden's housekeeper, Mrs Bosworth, had made chicken curry for supper, and having lived with the smell all afternoon, she really couldn't face it. So Brian had delivered her to the club well over an hour ago on his way to the airport. But now, with no sign of the merry travellers, Madeleine ordered another G and T and flicked through last month's edition of *Country Life*.

Hayden had first taken Madeleine to the club not long after that first night at the opera. From his enthusiastic description of the place, Madeleine had gathered that there were few places he would rather be; but, as she had quickly discovered, the County Club was every inch a *gentlemen's* club. Had she been even half as well read as her friend Ros, she probably would have likened it to a scene from P G Wodehouse – but she wasn't, and didn't.

The lounge – the only room, other than the *lower* dining room, in which ladies were welcome – had been deserted when she had arrived; at some stage two very elderly gentlemen had shuffled in and taken up residence on the far side of the room. She could hear their low voices interspersed with long pauses while they puffed on cucumber-thick cigars – apparently the smoking ban had side-stepped The County Club. Masculine murmurs in the Great Hall indicated the arrival of more members, but Hayden was not yet among them.

Bored now, Madeleine swirled her drink. The melting ice caught the light from one of the four chandeliers that dominated the ceiling. She tilted the glass as if daring its contents to spill while she watched the slice of lime drift through the cubes, unable to muster the energy to commit to any real bid for freedom.

'Is this seat taken?' said a gravely female voice beyond Madeleine's glass.

Madeleine jumped. Gin and tonic splashed over her trousers.

'Damn!' She sat tall to flick the icy moisture from the fabric.

'Sorry, didn't mean to make you jump.'

Taking the seat opposite, a leathery woman grinned an apology. 'Those are lovely trousers, by the way – Oska?' Her Marianne Faithful voice swamped the voices around them.

Madeleine's face lit up.

'Er… yes… yes,' she said.

'Thought so. Lovely, if you've got the figure!' said the woman. Madeleine noticed that the new arrival did not. Madeleine shifted slightly and drew her jacket over an annoying roll of flesh that had been gathering above her belt since she had started eating out with Hayden.

'Yes, I am lucky!'

'Just been writing about their spring collection,' said the woman, nodding to a passing waiter. 'If only I was three stone lighter!' She threw the waiter a fleeting glance. 'Get me a merlot, can you? A large one. Is my husband here yet?'

'Certainly, Mrs Avebury,' the waiter nodded. Then he shook his head. 'And no, Mr Avebury has not arrived yet. Will you want your usual table?'

'Please – but no damn flowers today – sneezed all night!' she said with a sniff.

The waiter bowed and retreated before raising his head.

'Sorry, did you say you were writing about Oska?' said Madeleine, hoping that Hayden and Jackson didn't choose that moment to arrive.

'Yes, darling – only for the *Western Express*, don't get too excited. Carolyn… Carolyn Avebury,' she said, holding out her hand.

'Madeleine Edwards,' said Madeleine, shaking the woman's offered fingers. 'So, you're a journalist?'

The woman laughed and drew a slim cigar from a silver case.

'Of sorts,' she said, flicking the lighter in her hand. 'Gosh, years ago I wrote for *The Times*. But then I met my wonderful husband and moved out here to the sticks. I only write now to keep up with what's going on. Oh God, I could tell you some stories!'

The waiter silently delivered a very large glass of ruby red merlot and an ashtray. Carolyn drew deeply on her cigar and eyed Madeleine.

'So you know your designer stuff, do you?' Smoke curled across the woman's creased face as she spoke.

Madeleine hesitated for a heartbeat. Fed up with being dragged around town or constantly handing over his credit card for internet shopping, Hayden had finally given her a gold card of her own for Christmas. Since Christmas, Madeleine really had got to know her designer stuff.

'Oh, yes,' she said. 'Well, you get what you pay for – so I *always* buy the best.'

With a glug of her wine, Carolyn asked, 'D'you shop locally?' Her expression was unreadable.

'Well, yes. When I can,' answered Madeleine. 'There are a few fab shops in town.' Then, to hedge her bets, she added, 'although if I'm looking for something extra special I have to admit to the odd internet purchase.'

Her companion peered over her wine glass for a few seconds and then spoke again.

'How would you like to do a little piece for us?'

Madeleine blinked.

'Well, I'm not sure… if you gave me the subject matter… I'd be happy to give it a go–'

Carolyn took a final puff of her cigar and, with one eye closed, gave a dismissive wave. 'No, no, dear. I'll write the bloody thing! You'd be wearing the clothes. I was thinking of something along the lines of 'A day in the life' – for the Women's section in the Saturday *Western Express*. You look the type.'

'Oh,' said Madeleine, flattered and not a little relieved. 'Well, yes. Sounds fab. When?'

Monday, 3rd March, 11.35a.m.

Nia scowled at the red bill on her desk and then scanned her emails again, willing the appearance of something that might offer even the tiniest financial promise. Maylard's was looking like a lame duck – on first name terms with Jackson's PA by now, she might be, but it seemed PA's weren't called gate-keepers for nothing.

Madeleine had promised to ask Hayden to do some gentle prodding but Nia hadn't heard from Madeleine for nearly three weeks… in fact, now that she thought about it, it was far longer than that.

Nia picked up her mobile phone – at least the bill for that was up to date. She scrolled down her calls log to see exactly when she and Madeleine had last communicated. Madeleine's number was not to be found, so she resorted to her contacts list, found Madeleine's number and pressed '*Call*'.

After half a dozen rings, Nia was framing a message that didn't sound too desperate when Madeleine answered.

'Madeleine Edwards.'

The cool tone threw Nia completely.

'Maddy, it's me. Nia,' she said, sounding desperate, despite her efforts.

'Oh, Nia! I'm just getting ready for a meeting. The *Western Express* is doing an article about me: 'A day in the life' fashion piece, you know, for this Saturday. I've insisted on a shopping trip, John Lewis, they're the best for labels. I've got to be there in two hours. Jack's doing my hair.'

'Jack?' asked Nia. From the jumble of information, 'Jack?' seemed the safest question.

'My hairdresser,' answered Madeleine, her tone adding 'Doh!'

'What happened to Alfonse?'

'Who? Oh, him. Idiot – no idea about colour. No, Jack is fab. Expensive, but really knows what he's doing. I'll introduce you.'

'Don't think I could afford to have my fringe cut at the moment,' said Nia.

'Oh, well, let me know when and we'll pop along. We could make a day of it. Their manicurist is excellent; I had an absolutely fab pedicure there before we went to Barcelona… that reminds me, must book again. We're off to Málaga on Sunday. Still apartment hunting. It's exhausting but at least we're going further south now, thank God. Oh, is that the time? Look Nia, it's lovely to talk but I've got to be at Jack's in fifteen–'

Determined to wedge in at least one question that wasn't about Madeleine, Nia said, 'Oh, OK. But just before you go, did you manage to have a word with Hayden about Jackson? I'm sorry to nag but I just can't get past his PA.'

'Oh, hasn't he called?' said Madeleine, just failing to sound casual. 'I spoke to Hayden before we went away. I'll mention it again. Look, sorry Nia, got to go. We'll catch up properly when I get back. We'll go for lunch at that new place down on the harbour.'

And with that the phone went dead.

Nia stared down at the red bill again and hit *Contacts* on her phone.

Saturday, 8th March, 5.05p.m

Bon Jovi's *Living on a Prayer* suddenly sang from Ros's handbag. She knew it was Nia before she dragged her finger across the screen to answer.

'Hi, Nia.'

'Ros, hi, it's Nia,' said Nia's voice.

Ros was standing in the food hall of Waitrose without a shred of inspiration; a yawning fridge packed with Meals for One stretched before her.

'Yes, I know. I'm in Waitrose trying to pick up something for supper. Not going out for a change so I thought I'd have a treat. What are dauphinoise potatoes? Do you think I'll like them? Oh, they've got cream in them... no...'

'Hmm, well their veggie meals are usually very good,' said Nia, an intermittent vegetarian.

'Oh, not sure if I fancy vegetables... They've got a Chinese thing here, do you know what that's like? It's got prawns in it. Do you think it's easy to cook? Ooh, no... there's something with salmon here, I'll have that. Sorry, Nia. How are you? Any more work coming in?'

Nia grinned. Ros might have the mind of an agitated butterfly, but at least she had the grace to show an interest.

'Nah! Still dire but I've finally got a meeting with Jackson Tranter. It's on Monday, so fingers crossed.'

'Oh, that sounds good. Have you spoken to Madeleine? Did she have a word with Hayden for you?'

'Not sure,' answered Nia generously. 'She's so busy at the moment… that's why I've called actually. I forgot to get a paper when I was out earlier. Have you seen the *Western Express* today?'

'Oh, good job you mentioned it, I nearly forgot, too. I'll go over now while we're talking,' said Ros, dropping a Beef Wellington Meal for One and a crème caramel into her basket. She headed towards the newspapers. 'What am I looking for? Anyone I know?'

'Not sure,' said Nia. 'But I spoke to Madeleine earlier in the week. She was in a bit of a rush but she mentioned something about doing a piece for the *Western Express*. Said it would be in the Saturday edition… see anything?'

'Hang on, I've got the paper in my hand. I'll just put my basket down and have a flick through… no… oh, that thing about the PM was ridiculous, wasn't it? Haven't they got anything better to… oh–'

Nia heard a crash and guessed Ros had dropped the phone.

'Ros… Ros, you OK…? Ro-os,' she sang down the silent phone.

'Nia, hi, yes, I'm here. Oh, has Madeleine seen this?'

Nia waited for Ros's standard second question. It didn't come.

'No, why?' said Nia, intrigued now by the missing question. She was already the wrong side of a large glass of red but was seriously toying with a quick trip to the Spar in search of a paper. 'Is it really good?'

Nia wasn't sure if the noise that came back down the phone was a laugh or a snort.

'Oh, Nia, you have got to see this. The headline is, 'A day in the life of a shopaholic' and the pictures are… well… who on earth gave her that hat! Oh, Nia, I'll be over in fifteen minutes – I'll bring wine.'

Thursday, 20th March, 11.40 a.m.

Madeleine swung her brand new Audi A3 cabriolet (Misano red, pearl effect) onto the double yellow lines outside Horton's and switched off the engine. The aftermath of the *Western Express* article still smarted (her brother had sent a text that read...)

Does my bum look big in this...? YEP! LOL☺.

...but it was amazing what a new car did to repair a dented ego.

When the article appeared in the paper, Hayden had been marvellous – he'd even picked over the photographs, pointed out his favourite and ordered a copy! It was currently taking pride of place on the baby grand but Madeleine had plans that would secure its disposal once a suitable time had elapsed (days, rather than weeks). To Madeleine's quiet relief, she and Hayden were between dinner engagements, thus significantly reducing the risk of having to discuss the article with anyone of influence.

The Audi had appeared on the drive last Saturday morning, decorated with a huge white bow and a bouquet that positively spilled across the back seats. Hayden had done his best to explain that the car was an early birthday present (her birthday being on 2nd April) rather than some sort of consolation gift in the wake of the article; however, Madeleine's squeals of noisy excitement suggested that she hadn't taken in that piece of information. Even so, by the following Wednesday morning, eleven days after the appearance of the article, Madeleine had already stowed two parking tickets in the glove compartment and appeared to have put the whole unfortunate episode of the article behind her.

She headed for the bar. Behind her, the Audi locked with a whisper; cats with cream had nothing on the smile Madeleine wore as she strode into Horton's.

Inside, Nia and Ros, already sipping cappuccinos, were deep

in conversation and didn't appear to have noticed Madeleine's Audi-wrapped arrival. It was only when Madeleine reached their table that Nia noticed her. She leapt to her feet, almost knocking Ros's cup from her hand; coffee splashed into the saucer sending tiny droplets splattering over the knee of Ros's cream chinos.

'Oh, Ros, are you alright? I'm so sorry. I didn't scald you, did I? Here, use this napkin. Oh dear, do you want me to get you another coffee? I was just going to get Maddy one.'

Seemingly oblivious of the drama, Madeleine sat opposite Ros, her smile now positively tickling her earlobes. Ros glanced at her... and choked on the remains of her coffee. Nia followed Ros's glance and lowered her bottom back onto her seat with a bump. Both women sat and stared although Nia did at least close her mouth.

'Tea, please,' said Madeleine, somehow managing to maintain her expansive, tooth-filled smile. 'Earl Grey, if they've got it. Travis.' She turned and beamed towards the bar, 'You have got Earl Grey, haven't you?'

Travis nodded, did a double take and disappeared into the kitchen.

Nia was first to find her voice while Ros continued to cough into her coffee-stained napkin.

'Gosh, Maddy, you, er, your teeth... um... gosh, they're white!'

Madeleine's smile was now almost obscuring her ears – her teeth were positively blinding.

'Oh, I'm so glad you've noticed. I've just had them done. It's a surprise for Hayden.'

'Yes, it will be,' spluttered Ros.

'But I couldn't see anything wrong with them before,' said Nia, frowning.

'Well, I've never been that happy with them and I was talking to Pietro last week. He's got the most fantastic teeth – brilliant white. *And* the most gorgeous smile–'

'Who's Pietro?' interrupted Ros, breathing normally at last. 'Is he your dentist?'

'Gosh, no,' said Madeleine. 'He's my hairdresser. Absolutely fab – specialises in colour.' As if to emphasis the point she slid her fingers through her newly uniform slightly-more-golden-than-soft-auburn hair.

'So did *he* do your teeth?' asked Ros. Her wide eyes were now in serious competition with her saucer. 'As well as your hair?'

Slight irritation dulled Madeleine's smile very briefly.

'No, Ros! He recommended a dentist over in Hartleymouth.'

Ros and Nia hooted with laughter. Madeleine completely missed the irony and flicked her hair with her fingers this time.

'We're going lighter.'

'What, your teeth or your hair?' said Ros, her eyes twinkling wickedly. 'Will your teeth go much lighter?'

With a weary look in Ros's direction, Madeleine pressed on. 'Pietro suggested I had my teeth whitened to enhance the overall effect. It was such a fab idea, I booked there and then – had them done yesterday. Hayden hasn't seen me yet. He's away again.'

'Yes, Singapore, isn't it?' said Nia with a nod. 'I spoke to Jackson this morning. They're back late tonight, I think – hope so, I've got a meeting with him tomorrow afternoon.' She grimaced.

'Ooh, so you got that project then?' asked Ros brightly. 'Did you negotiate a decent fee?'

Nia stuck her bottom lip out.

'Not really. They're quite keen, particularly on a re-brand. But from what I've seen so far, Jackson Tranter's allergic to spending money. We're meeting tomorrow to discuss a somewhat watered-down approach.' She made inverted comma signs with her fingers. 'But anything's better than nothing. Have to admit, the way things are now, I'd do it for half what I quoted.'

'Oh dear, is it really that bad? When's he likely to make a decision?' asked Ros, the stain on her chinos apparently forgotten. Nia's napkin now lay on the floor at her feet.

Travis appeared from the kitchen with a tray bearing a new cappuccino for Ros and a pot of Earl Grey and a cup for Madeleine.

'I'll get these,' said Ros and handed Travis a twenty pound note before Nia could reach for her bag.

'Thanks, Ros,' said Nia. 'I'll get the next ones.' She sipped her own coffee and then answered Ros's questions. 'Well, it's not too bad really, I guess. I'm sure there are people worst off than me but if I don't get some work in soon, things are going to get a bit tricky. I'm pretty sure Maylard's will go for something though – could mean a trip to Singapore too, if I do get it.'

'Really?' said Madeleine, mid-pour. 'When do you think that might be?'

'Oh, not for a few months,' answered Nia. 'If they go for the whole shebang, I'll certainly need to renew my passport though!'

'Weren't you supposed to be going away next week anyway?' asked Ros. 'With that architect chap? Peter, isn't it?'

'Weeell,' said Nia, guilt creeping across her face. 'We were. But he's suddenly decided he likes being married after all, bastard. So that's the end of another *belle amitié*. Bit gutted, actually. There's a gorgeous converted windmill just on the edge of the Norfolk Broads... Barton Mill. It's probably my favourite place in the world... well, in the UK certainly. Really quiet, so romantic. Four blissful days. It was going to be my belated birthday present as Peter couldn't get away in November.'

'So I'm guessing you won't be going now?' said Ros, adding, 'Had you booked? Will you lose any money?'

Nia wrinkled her nose.

'Well, I certainly don't fancy going on my own and it's not

really a take-a-friend kind of place.' As she spoke she made another inverted commas sign with just one hand this time. 'And yes, I had booked – less traceable, if you know what I mean, although in hindsight, stupid, too, I suspect I won't get it back from Mr Not-so-Wonderful-Afterall. So that's two hundred and fifty quid down the tubes, too – not the best timing, let's just say.'

'Oh dear, I wonder if…' said Ros, as she squinted unseeingly around the room as if she was searching for something in her mind. 'No, sorry, I'm– Oh, look, that traffic warden's booking that red car. Mind you, what a stupid place to park. Right on the double yellow lines!'

Madeleine shot forward and peered out of the window.

'Oh shit, I hope he hasn't started writing. That'll be the third in the last fortnight. I've started hiding them now.'

'Oh, so *that's* yours?' said Ros. 'What happened to your lovely Beetle?'

'Birthday present,' said Madeleine, grabbing up her bag. 'From Hayden. I'm selling the Beetle, if you know anyone who might be interested.'

And with that she dashed out. The warden was busy scribbling.

Tuesday 25th March, 3.35p.m.

Nia held her mobile phone to her ear and tapped the page of her open diary with a bundle of credit cards she was clutching in her other hand.

'So I thought we could all go out this weekend – say Saturday night, as it's your birthday next week? I checked with Ros and Ivy. Unfortunately, Paolo isn't around – he's in love again! Can't go too wild, of course, Maddy – although things are looking hopeful with Maylard's,' said Nia. She had spread her credit cards over the desk like playing cards while she talked. BT's refusal to reinstate her landline until her affairs were in order was forcing drastic action – all but one of her precious plastic lifelines simply had to go… but which one?

'Sorry, no can do, I'm afraid,' answered Madeleine. 'You know that mill you were talking about last week – well, I've booked it!'

Nia stopped mid-sort.

'Barton Mill? Where Peter and I were going this weekend? My special place?'

'Yes!' said Madeleine, her voice brimming with excitement. 'I Googled it and, well, obviously I knew it was free. It looks fab. And as they'd had your last minute cancellation I got it for next to nothing! I've had to get a whole new wardrobe obviously – some gorgeous silk pyjamas – not that I'll be wearing them for long, but you know!' She paused and then added. 'Any recommendations for good food – not pub grub?' Nia could tell Madeleine was wrinkling her nose.

Slightly taken aback, Nia's mind went into its default position of helpful and refusing to think the worst of anyone.

'Well, The Mint Leaf is nice. Peter and I went there for lunch last year,' she replied; after all, it wasn't Madeleine's fault that Peter's wife had taken a sudden and unforeseen interest in her marriage (there had been an out of character introduction of whipped cream that certainly Peter, let alone Nia, had not anticipated – Nia wasn't a fan of cream, whipped or not). Nia thought for a moment and then added, 'Ooh, if you want *really* expensive, there's The Wren's Egg in Chittleworth – tiny village off the A146 outside Hales – chateaubriand to die for.' As she spoke, she smiled at a long-held memory.

'Ooh, that sounds fab. I love champagne. Haven't heard of that one though… Wonder if they've got a website? I'll have a look. Thanks for that, Nia.'

'Well, have a lovely birthday,' called Nia: Madeleine's tone told her she was being dismissed.

'Er… yer…, I will. We'll catch up when I'm back. I'll take lots of photos.'

'Lovely,' said Nia. 'We could go out for breakfast.'

But the phone was silent.

Nia looked down at her credit cards, now in a neat row.

'Eeny, meeny, chateaubriand, mo,' she said, flicking a card across her desk on each word (and two for 'chateaubriand). But on 'mo' there were still three cards stubbornly staring up at her. 'Oh, sod it,' she said and jammed all three back into her purse – the ones on the floor would be retrieved later.

Thursday 27ᵗʰ March, 10.35p.m.

Hayden's eyes skimmed quickly over the words of the email for a third time. He'd had no inkling that Saffy's marriage was anything but blissfully happy. So to read that Alistair had not only left her for another woman, but had given her a black eye in the process, was news he was having a great deal of difficulty absorbing.

> Hi Dad
> I'm really sorry to break this to you in an email but I was too upset to phone last night and by tonight Ben and I will be on our way to the airport. We're coming home, Dad.
> I hope this will be good news for you but I'd better give you

the gory details before we get to Heathrow - 1) so that you understand why we have had to leave so suddenly, and 2) so that you have a bit of time to calm down before we get to Landsmere – it is OK for us to come, isn't it? It's just for a while. I just need some time to think and to plan what's best for Ben and me.

I'm crying again, so ignore any typpos…

Al and I have been rowing a lot recently and last week Ben's nusrery school teacher called me in to tell me that Ben had suddenly become aggressive towards other children and had started using some really baf language – he said fuck, Dad, when his pencil snapped! And he called the Principle, Emily Brinkner, a pathetic bitch! Of course I knew straight away where it had come frm so I tried to talk to Al. Well once we'd started, it all just came out.

He's been seeing someone called Charlize for nearly a year. She works in his office but apart from being the office bike I've no idea what she's paid for – well… anyway he says he loves her. I though tit was just because he was wrking such long hours – working!? God, what a compete fool I've beeen. I got upset and we argued (*again*). I tod him I wasgoing home and that I wwas takin Ben – he went mad, Dad. Absolutely crazy. I won't repeat what he called me but Ben got really upset. I picked him up to give him a cuddle but Al tried to get him away from me and we all fell over and I got hit in the face. When he saw the cut over my eye he cried – Al not Ben. At the hospital the nurse tried to make me report him. But I couldn't – but I don't want to stay. I don't feel safe. He losst his temper so quickly. Sorry, can't seee the wordz now.

We'' be lanfing in Londom Satutday evening – can you pick ud up?   Sorrry x

Hayden looked out of the window across his favourite view. Tears flowed unchecked down his cheeks. How could he have let this happen? Why hadn't he picked up on this before?

He toyed with getting on a plane to Hong Kong to beat the living crap out of that boy – to think he'd trusted Alistair with the two most precious things in his entire life!

Hayden scrutinised the email yet again. Saffy hadn't given him the arrival time for the flight but there seemed little point in replying so he Googled Heathrow Airport. Within a few minutes, he'd narrowed the arrival time down to three possibilities – 16.55hrs, 19.40hrs or 21.05hrs, after all, she had said evening. It was too late now to call Grace, his PA at Maylard's and lifeline to the real world, but he resolved to get her to do some proper detective work in the morning to find out exactly what flight Saffy and Ben would be on. If anyone could find out it would be Grace.

Instead, he picked up his mobile and searched for Mrs Bosworth's number – cakes were definitely in order, together with two beds freshly made up. As the phone rang, he wondered if he should ask her to do two beds in the guest room, or make up Saffy's old room for Ben.

Brief but efficient as ever, Mrs B had quickly decided that both rooms would be made up (thus justifying the retention of a charity bag stuffed full of Saffy's old teddies that Hayden had discovered on the doorstep at Landsmere on Monday morning, after he had left early for a meeting only to return having forgotten the briefing papers); Mrs B also assured Hayden that a beef casserole and a Victoria sponge would be delivered on Saturday afternoon, while he was at Heathrow with flowers and chocolate at the ready.

It was only then that Hayden remembered… 'Bollocks, Madeleine's mill!'

Wednesday, 3rd April 9.15 a.m.

'Well I'm struggling to see why they can't move into my house,' said Madeleine in a strangled whisper. 'I mean, it's not as if people are queuing up to buy it. They've been here four days now *and* they ruined my birthday!'

Hayden sighed. His eyes flicked to the kitchen door, slightly ajar; although having checked only half an hour previously, he was fairly sure that Saffy and Ben were still fast asleep upstairs, having not quite caught up with the time difference.

'Oh, come on, darling. This is Saffy's house too! And anyway, I'm not sure she should be on her own just yet. You've seen that cut over her eye, haven't you? And Ben's so excited to be here. Bet it's all a bit of an adventure for him.'

'Yes, he certainly is highly strung!' hissed Madeleine. 'It's a shame the word *please* doesn't seem to be in his limited vocabulary!'

'He's been through a lot, bless him,' said Hayden.

'Well, you might be able to weather broken reading glasses and chocolate up the banister,' said Madeleine, working herself up to abject horror. 'But jamming a slipper down the toilet! The en suite has been blocked all weekend! I've had to use the main bathroom! And that V & A suite hasn't been in two weeks – have you any idea how much it cost?!'

'Oh, yes,' said Hayden, with the slightest hint of annoyance in his voice. 'And it was my slipper… and with five other bathrooms to choose from, it's hardly a hardship!'

But Madeleine wasn't finished.

'And as for that dog! He's all over him with that "MowithMowithMowith" constantly. God, it's annoying!'

Hayden opened his mouth to retaliate but instead closed his eyes, took a deep breath and then spoke. 'Look, my darling, they've been through a lot.' His voice was suddenly soothing. 'If Ben wants to make a fuss of Morris, surely that's up to his mother. I don't mind and neither should you. Just give them some time. I promise, I'll make it up to you.'

In actual fact, a weekend in Paris had already been promised as a consolation gift for missing their break at Barton Mill. Confirmation of the flights had been sitting on Hayden's desk since Monday, along with four rather old and crumpled parking fines that had appeared the same day, all bearing the registration number of Madeleine's Beetle (the ones for the Audi, registration ME 1001 were still stashed in its glove box). But as Madeleine had already hinted at how grateful she might be while they were away, Hayden had done the paperwork, written the cheque and was determined to stay silent.

Thursday 4th April 7.30p.m.

Saffy inched back towards the bedroom door, not daring to take a breath. After a tantrum that would have rated an '11' on any amplifier, Ben had finally given in and peace once again wrapped around Landsmere Grange, the tired but beautiful, grey stone pile that had been Saffy's home for the first twenty-four years of her life.

The door creaked as she made her escape but Ben didn't stir – the jet lag that had turned his little world upside down had finally taken its toll. It had not escaped Saffy's notice that her father's new lady was less than impressed by their sudden arrival and Ben's challenging behaviour over the past four days had definitely not oiled any wheels. Saffy made her escape from the quiet bedroom, leaving behind the regular, steady breathing of a sleeping child. She pulled the door almost shut and after a final pause to listen, headed for a large glass of merlot, praying that they might at last be back to a more normal routine.

Across the landing, through the open door of his study, Saffy spied the top of her father's head over the back of the chair. She smiled. His hair might have got a few shades greyer but was still hanging in there. And that old chair was as battered and bruised as the last time she had set eyes on it four years ago. She remembered the smell of its ancient leather when, as a child, she would twirl it around as fast as she could, before stopping with a foot-slapping jolt to watch the view of Landsmere Bay swim in front of her dizzy eyes – once she had actually vomited into the wastepaper bin; later on, she would sit on a high stool next to her father while he struggled with her physics homework. Eventually he had given in and hired a tutor. Every Wednesday after school she would try to think up any excuse not to sit with poor Roger Bosworth, Mrs B's son, who was trying to scrape his way through college by offering maths and physics tuition to disinterested sixteen-year-olds like Saffy, whose heart was in English and Art, not Ohm's Law. But, to Master Bosworth's credit (and her father's refusal to bow to any amount of emotional blackmail she had tried to throw at him) Saffy had come out of school with a grade 'C' Physics 'O' level to add to the other eight she achieved at far higher grades. Secretly, she had thanked her father many times since.

Saffy pushed the study door wide.

'Ben gone off?' asked her father without looking around.

'Thank God,' answered Saffy. She rested her hands on his shoulders and kissed his cheek. 'I'm going to have a glass of wine. You want one?'

Hayden closed the sheaf of papers he had been trying to read for the last half hour and nodded gratefully. 'Mmm, that doesn't sound like a bad idea at all. How long do you think we've got?'

He nodded his head towards the guest room.

'I'm hoping hours,' said Saffy with a weary grin. 'I'm so sorry he's been such a nightmare, Dad. I promise he's not usually quite this bad!'

Hayden studied his daughter over the top of his spare pair of reading glasses. She was so like her mother: hazel eyes, gold streaks in her chestnut hair, even her voice had the same soft tone. His gaze drifted to the deep cut over Saffy's eye. It wasn't quite as swollen now but the bruise was red-black and going green around the edges. The rage he had felt when he first saw her at the airport had subsided to a smouldering angry pain but he gave her a kind smile and hoped it didn't show.

'Oh, believe me, you were ten times worse when you were tired!' he said. 'I'll never forget when we took you to Panama. D'you remember? We stayed with your mother's sister. God, you were so young. I think you finally got used to the time difference the day before we left – she didn't ask us again.'

'Oh dear, I don't remember that at all. Sorry, Dad.'

'Oh, it was nothing that time didn't heal,' said Hayden with a mischievous grin. 'Come on, let's have that wine.'

Saffy turned towards the door.

'Where's Madeleine? I'll give her a shout.'

'You're OK. She's headed into town to meet Ros and Nia,' said Hayden. 'Brian's taken her in. I got the feeling she's planning on being late.'

'I don't think she's ever going to forgive me for ruining her birthday,' said Saffy as they padded downstairs and headed for the kitchen. Hayden waved a hand casually.

'She'll be fine. I'm taking her to Paris in a fortnight. Good food, wine and shops. Believe me, she'll forgive you! Red or white?'

'Red for me,' said Saffy. She retrieved two elegant goblets from the dishwasher – cold and dry now, where Mrs Bosworth had filled the machine long before she had departed at four. Hayden let the merlot glug noisily into Saffy's glass. She smiled gratefully. 'I love that sound.'

'Me, too,' said Hayden, filling his own glass half full.

Saffy tipped the glass to her lips and allowed the grapey aroma to fill her nose before she took a sip. She could feel the wine slip down her throat and felt that first hit of alcohol warm her insides.

'I found one of my old books up there, in my old desk. *Dougal's Scottish Holiday*. Just been reading it to Ben, although I think I got more out of it than he did. Those books really were quite funny - I'd forgotten,' she said taking another sip.

'Dougal?' said Hayden.

'You know, those Magic Roundabout books we got at that book festival. We met the author, remember? Eric Thompson. You bought me all five books – *The Adventures of Dougal, Brian, Dylan*... I'm sure there was *The Adventures of Ermintrude*, too? And the Scottish Holiday one – that was my favourite. Can't see the others in my room though? Any idea where they'd be?'

Hayden frowned. 'In the new library, I suspect. Didn't you have quite a lot of signed books? Have you been in the library?'

Saffy gulped on her wine.

'Lord no! Every time Ben makes a beeline for the door Madeleine positively throws herself in front of it. I get the feeling the books in there aren't for reading!'

Hayden laughed affectionately.

'Yes, she is a bit protective. Mind, she did work hard on it. She's just proud. I think it looks lovely, I have to admit – quite professional. I'll ask her in the morning, about your books. That reminds me, I wonder what she did with my World War Two books. I had a quick look for one of them on Sunday but couldn't spot them. She's got her own system, I'm sure she'll find them in no time.'

Thursday 4th April 9.15p.m.

Madeleine glowered into her pinot grigio.

'And that child! Absolutely no discipline – almost flooded the master bathroom. After all my hard work. He filled Hayden's slipper with my Clarins day lotion and shoved the whole lot down the toilet!'

'Oh, that's terrible! Was that the extra-firming one?' asked Ros, looking appalled. 'Do you think it works?'

Madeleine ignored both questions.

'Thank God we're off to Paris soon,' she said, brushing her hand down her thigh. 'I've laid heavy hints that Saffy and Ben should move into my house but Hayden's not keen. He's going to Sweden Monday so I'll do some gentle persuasion while he's away. God, I hope they're gone soon or I might be forced to lace that child's Smarties with strychnine.'

'Maddy, that's a terrible thing to say!' said Nia, disapproval brimming over her glasses. 'He's not that bad. He was really sweet on Tuesday when I called over with your birthday card. He was telling me about Morris – an 'Iwith wolf hound' apparently – bless.'

'Bugger bless!' said Madeleine, looking cross. 'It's bad enough that I have to put up with that manky old animal but adding a marauding three-year-old really is too much. God, I'm just praying that they're gone by June!'

Ros suddenly looked interested and put her phone down mid-text.

'Ooh, June? What's happening? It isn't going to clash with the Wimbledon Finals, is it? Can't be bothered with the rest of it but I do like the final weekend – great excuse to eat the odd strawberry and drink a lot of bubbly!'

Madeleine looked at her nails.

'Not sure... nothing's definite yet of course... just a little garden party for Cornerstone. I thought we should do something in the garden to raise money for the charity. Suggested it to Hayden. He loved the idea. Emma Jenkins is coming.'

'Oh, I think she's wonderful!' breathed Ros. 'Will she be singing? You saw her in La Traviata, didn't you?'

Madeleine gave Ros a gleaming beam.

'Oh yes. She does like playing here – you know, her old home town. More personal than the Albert Hall, she said.'

Ros took a moment to find her tongue.

'What? You know her? But you haven't mentioned this before.'

'Oh yes,' replied Madeleine with a dismissive wave. She took another gulp of her wine before giving away any more detail. 'Yes, she's been up to the house quite a few times. I suppose I haven't known her that long, but it seems like ages. We've got loads in common. Anyway, she's agreed to do one song – although she hasn't decided what yet. I did suggest *I've a Maria* but she said she'd rather choose something a bit more upbeat – we're going to have a chat about it next week. Oh, that reminds me, I must phone the printer.'

'Printer?' said Nia. 'Wouldn't caterers be more relevant?'

'Invites. I'm taking the opportunity to do some re-branding for the charity – it's about time. Hayden thinks it's a great idea – we're going to use the garden party to launch the new face of Cornerstone.'

'Oh,' said Nia, looking mildly hurt. 'Anything I can help with?'

'No, it's OK,' replied Madeleine, draining her glass. 'I've got it covered. There just isn't any slack in the budget for anyone else.'

'But I thought you'd retired?' said Ros. Nia gulped back almost half a glass of pinot noir.

'I was toying with it,' replied Madeleine. 'But the trouble with being retired is that you get to spend time with people who have a lot of time on their hands… and they're just so boring.'

'Oh!' said Ros. This time it was her turn to look hurt.

'Another drink anyone?' Nia cut in. 'So, is Saffy going to move into your house then, Maddy?' She waved her hand towards the nearest waitress. 'Two large pinot grigios and another large red for me, please?'

'Pinot noir or the house red?' asked the girl with a smile.

'Oh, pinot noir, please.' Nia threw a guilty look towards Ros and Madeleine. 'Yes, I know… but it is Maddy's birthday, and I've got my credit card!'

Tuesday, 8th April 9.05p.m.

Hayden sat on the edge of the crisply made bed in his pleasant, personality-less hotel room and listened to the unanswered phone ringing in his ear. He was cross that he'd had to come away so soon after Saffy and Ben had arrived at Landsmere but Jackson had been called to Singapore rather suddenly – trouble with an errant contractor and a packet of herbal tea, apparently.

Hayden's stomach rumbled. He was just about to abandon his attempt to check in at home when a breathless voice answered.

'Hi… I mean, Landsmere Grange, hello.'

'Saffy? Hi, it's Dad. Madeleine not around?'

'Um, I thought she was… but apparently not. I'd just dozed off with Ben… bollocks, he's awake again. Oh, well… I'LL BE UP IN A MINUTE, DARLING. BA RITTEN'S ON THE PHONE… NO, STAY THERE, I'LL BE THERE NOW… Sorry Dad. You OK?'

Hayden smiled down the phone – if only she knew what a

nightmare she'd been at Ben's age.

'Yer, I'm fine. The flight was a bit delayed but I'm here now. Two meetings tomorrow and one on Thursday morning before my flight home. How're you getting on?'

'Oh, we're fine. Went to see one of the local schools today. The head was nice but the school was a bit shabby.'

'Which one was that? Not Rockmoore, I hope?' Hayden asked. He had already planned to pay for Ben's schooling but hadn't had chance to broach the subject with Saffy.

'No. The local primary. Gosh, Dad, I don't think Al's going to be able to pay for anything private. Rockmoore would cost a fortune!'

'So what did you think? Did you have a chat to Madeleine? Did she go with you?'

Saffy sounded genuinely appalled when she answered.

'God, no. She's made it pretty clear already that Ben is not her Number 1 child. I think she'd have him packed off to boarding school on the other side of the country, if it was up to her!'

'Oh, I'm sure that's not the case, Saf. She's just not used to children.'

'I noticed - mine, nor yours!' said Saffy with a laugh. 'She mentioned us moving into her house again today. If you're not careful she'll have us packed off before you come home!'

'Oh, she doesn't mean it. Take no notice. You can stay as long as you want – Landsmere's your home, too. I'll have a chat with her – she's not there now, is she?'

'It would appear not. She was in your study, on the computer. I mentioned those books, by the way. Not sure where she is now... well, her car's gone,' said Saffy, obviously looking out of the hall window onto the drive. 'Guess she went out. Can I give her a message? What time is it there, by the way?'

Hayden was a little disappointed but shrugged.

'Just after seven. No, don't worry. I'll catch her in the morning. She's throwing herself into the re-branding thing – you know. Did I mention it? Cornerstone is to have a facelift. I asked her if she knew anyone who could do it and she jumped at it. I guess she's either gone to a late meeting or to see the girls. Anyway, don't worry, I'll catch her at some stage. Go and give Ben a kiss from me. See you Thursday, love.'

Tuesday, 8th April 9.10p.m.

Madeleine reversed the Audi neatly into the last remaining parking bay outside Horton's, talking as she steered, it was so much easier now she was hands-free.

'Oh, please, Ros. You're always claiming to be a bit of an expert on books,' she pulled the handbrake and turned the key. 'And after all, you aren't working so I rather hoped you might be able to help me out. Nia can't do it – got some new client or something.'

The voice that came back through the car speaker did not sound overly impressed.

'Well, good news about Nia, but contrary to popular opinion my diary is actually quite full. And anyway, I'm not terribly sure what you want me to do. If you gave them the books, really you should be the one to try to get them back – or buy them back. How many were signed? Do you know how much they're worth?'

'No idea,' answered Madeleine, touching up her lipstick in the rear view mirror. 'Apparently there were a couple by some guy called Thomas – Ian, I think… *Magic Roundabout* books – honestly, you'd think she would have grown out of those by now! There were some others too but I've got no idea who they were written by. I'm sure they'll remember me though, in the shop – I did take in seven boxes!'

'My goodness, Madeleine! They weren't all Saffy's, were they? Has Hayden said anything?'

'Gosh no, he's away so much I don't think he's spent more than ten minutes in the library since it's been finished! I'm sure most of them were his – Lee Child, Ian Rankin, stuff like that – read them all, so I couldn't see any point in keeping them – some war stuff too, I think. Planes. Exceptionally dull – they just didn't work in my bookscape.'

'Please don't tell me any of those were signed, Maddy – they're probably really rare – collector's items!'

Madeleine opened the glove box and squinted over from the driver's seat.

'So could you have a go, Ros? If you can get them all back that would be fab. Tell them I've had a breakdown or something and didn't know what I was doing. I've got to go now – I'm flat out with the re-brand. Meeting John Cavendish now about the logo.'

'Gosh, that's a late meeting! Isn't your friend Josh doing it? Have you seen him lately?' asked Ros.

'Who – oh, Josh?' said Madeleine retrieving a bottle of Christian Dior from a twist of crumpled parking tickets. She squirted a dribble behind both ears. 'Oh, no. Red Hot're far too small-town for Cornerstone. No, I've brought in Cavendish Major from over the bridge. I really need a company who knows what it's doing – you know, has a bit of profile.'

'And could Nia help out at all? Isn't that what she does? I think Maylard's are using her now but I know money's still an issue,' said Ros.

Madeleine threw the Dior back into the glove box and slammed it shut.

'Not sure yet,' she said, opening the car door before cutting Ros off. 'Look, I've got to go, Ros. Let me know how you get on with the books – tomorrow would be ideal. Thanks, bye.'

'Well, tomorrow's not–' The phone line went dead. Madeleine jumped out of the car and threw her arms wide to greet the man now standing on the opposite pavement.

'John, hi! What excellent timing!'

Thursday 10th April 12.30p.m.

The phone in Ros's neat little house was tastefully placed on a stylish little occasional table beside a tall Dartington Crystal vase out of which currently spilled a dozen bright red tulips. As is the wont of tulips, their long green stems had given up any attempt to support the cheerful heads almost as soon as they had been placed in their new home, giving the vase a somewhat Medusan appearance that Ros rather liked.

On this occasion, however, the phone being quite so far from the end of the settee on which she was currently languishing was a distinct disadvantage. She ignored the first four rings; if it was anyone she knew doubtless they would try her mobile, which was beside her on the settee (being easy to reach when one had put one's back out hauling boxes of books between charity shops and cars). But by the eighth ring she did start to wonder if perhaps she should struggle up to answer it. By the eleventh ring she was inching her way painfully along the sofa, convinced it must be something urgent concerning her father (the home in which he had lived for the last two years only ever called if there was a real problem which, thankfully given his condition, was infrequent).

Just as Ros reached for the phone it went silent.

'Fuck!' she said, rather more loudly than perhaps was necessary and turned to make her way back along the sofa. A hot knife of pain shot down her back and through her thigh. 'Fucking, fuck!' she repeated – between gasps.

From the other end of the settee, her mobile sprang into life and *The Ride of the Valkyries* filled the room.

'Hi, Madeleine,' she said, having stretched for the phone from where she was now rooted by pain.

'Ros, hi! How did you get on? Just tried your home number. You did go yesterday, didn't you? Only Hayden's due home this evening and that blasted girl asked about Dougal again today – honestly, I think she's becoming obsessed!' Madeleine sounded decidedly ruffled.

'I couldn't go yesterday, sorry. I did try to tell you, but anyway I went this morning–'

'Did you get them? I do need them back today before Hayden gets home.' There was a very slight hint of what Ros thought she recognised as concern in Madeleine's voice. 'I Googled some of those war books – they're worth a fortune!'

'Mmm, I thought so. They're in mint condition, Madeleine,' said Ros, thinking, *Well, if you've got salt, seems a shame to not to rub it in.*

'Oh, so you have got them then? Oh, thank goodness. Can you bring them over? I've got another meeting with John Cavendish at three so ideally I need them in the next hour.'

Ros carefully lowered her bottom on to the leather foot stool behind her knees.

'Sorry, Maddy. I don't think I'm going anywhere for a few days. I put my back out lifting one of the boxes into my car.'

'Oh no, that's terrible! How am I going to get them over here before my meeting?'

Ros pressed on.

'I think I've slipped a disc but I couldn't get an appointment with my doctor until tomorrow afternoon so I certainly won't be going anywhere until then; although I'm not sure if I'll even be able to get in the car to go around to the surgery.'

Madeleine was silent for a few seconds.

'Madeleine, are you still there?' asked Ros.

'Oh, yer, sorry. Just trying to think... Probably the best thing to do is for Brian to drive me to my meeting, then he can call around to your house to pick up the books.' Ros could hear Madeleine picking up steam as her mind worked its way around her problem. 'Yes, he can put them in the garage and then come back for me. Whatever you do, don't tell him you got them back from the charity shop... say you were keeping them safe, or something. He should be back here by five and Hayden won't be home until at least eight... I'll just give Saffy her books in the box... can always say I'd put them into storage or something... yes, right... you'll be there anyway so Brian will call in about forty-five minutes. I'm sure he won't be doing anything. Are the books in your house?'

'Hardly! I only just managed to drive myself home. Luckily a very nice chap came into the shop. He put the last two boxes in the car for me. It was all I could do not to cry,' said Ros. Another hot knife brought back the memory – her lip wobbled.

'Oh dear,' said Madeline finally. 'Well, I'm sure Brian can get them in the car without your help, so don't worry.'

'I won't,' said Ros. 'By the way, I had to buy them back, Maddy. Two hundred and fifty pounds.'

'What!' Madeleine shrieked. 'But they're mine! How... why did you pay?'

'Well, technically they weren't yours, Maddy,' said Ros. 'You did give them to the shop. It just seemed the easiest way to get them. The woman in there today was utterly disinterested –

someone had just brought in a huge suitcase of designer wear. I got the distinct impression she just wanted to get rid of me so I made her an offer. Luckily they'd only unpacked two of the boxes – I think you would have had a problem if they'd all been out on display.'

'Yes, but–' Madeleine started, but Ros had her argument planned.

'There were at least two hundred books there, Maddy. And it was The Red Cross – a charity. You didn't honestly think they would have just let you take them back without at least insisting on a donation, did you?'

'Well, no… I suppose not. God, I should've just given them a cheque in the first place instead of going to all that trouble taking them in!'

Ros opened her mouth but closed it again, incredulity washing over her like a giant wave. Madeleine was, as usual, irony-free.

'Right, well at least we've got them,' Madeleine continued. 'So, Brian will be over after he's dropped me off – damn, look at the time! I've got to go, meeting John in half an hour.'

'OK,' said Ros, pain interrupting her briefly. 'Tell him the door'll be on the latch. He can let himself in and I'll give him the key. Could you ask him to bring a pint of milk – I've run out?'

'Oh, OK. Will you have change? Hayden only gave me twenties. You'll need to pay Brian back when he arrives.'

'Or you could take it out of the two-fifty you owe me,' prompted Ros.

'Oh…, oh, yes,' laughed Madeleine. 'Of course. I'll give you a cheque for that, don't worry. Right, I've got to go, see you soon. Bye.'

***

Friday 17ᵗʰ April, 9.45a.m.

Hayden watched Saffy pouring her second coffee while she absently offered her son a square of toast. Equally disinterested, as he was driving a little red bus around his breakfast plate, Ben took it and jammed the whole piece into his mouth adding another Marmitey smear to his now liberally-coated chin. Beside Hayden, Madeleine winced.

'I thought Marmite was bad for children,' she said, picking at a sliver of honeydew melon with a fork. Saffy looked up. The bruise around her eye was almost gone now, but it was obvious that the scar would be a permanent reminder of the reason she and her son were now living at Landsmere Grange.

'Gosh, no,' she said, handing Ben the final square. 'Well, probably by the pot, I would imagine. There's a fair amount of salt in it; but as he ends up wearing most of it I don't think it'll do him too much harm.' Cup in hand, she wandered over to her son, pulling a tissue from her jeans pocket. 'Have you had enough, darling? Here, wipe your hands and face, please.'

Ben chucked the tissue on the floor and threw an unreadable glance at Madeleine.

'Oh, Ben! That was naughty!' said Saffy sharply. 'The Easter bunny won't leave you any eggs if you carry on like that!'

Hayden bent to retrieve the tissue.

'It's OK, Saf. I've got it. Here we go, Ben. Look at Ba Ritten. Mouth closed. Well done. There – shiny as an apple!' Hayden scrumpled the Marmite-covered tissue into one hand, pushed it into his closed fist with his finger and then opened his empty hand. Ben looked at Hayden's fist, then at his grandfather's face waiting for an answer to his unasked question, to which Hayden replied, 'Gone!'

Madeleine looked skywards.

'You'd think he would have worked that one out by now,' she said. 'You've done that trick every day.'

'Well, I've been away for three days,' said Hayden with a good-natured grin. Then he turned back to Ben. 'And it amuses you, doesn't it, little man?'

Ben grabbed Hayden's fingers and turned his grandfather's hand over. Madeleine opened the fridge and scrutinised the bottom shelf. It was packed with nail varnish bottles. After some moments she found what she seemed to be looking for and perched one cheek of her slightly smaller (but not getting small enough, quickly enough) bottom on a stool at the breakfast bar.

'It'th gone! Can I have it back, now?' Ben asked Hayden.

With an exaggerated frown, Hayden patted his trouser pockets.

'Hmm, I don't know about that – I think the Easter Bunny's taken it.'

'But it'th my tithue,' objected Ben. 'Tell him to give it back.'

'Well, there's a special magic word that just might work,' said Hayden.

'What?' demanded Ben, now captivated by curiosity.

'Please!' whispered Hayden and tapped the side of his nose.

'What?' said Ben. Saffy laughed.

'Ba Ritten meant that the magic word is please, I think, Ben,' she said. 'Dad, I've got no idea why my darling son has suddenly become allergic to the word please, but I think you're going to have to work harder than that.'

'Can I have an Eathsterwegg now?' said Ben with a frown.

'How about, you ask the Easter Bunny for your tissue first. If you remember to say please as well, we'll see about an egg?' suggested Hayden.

Ben clamped his mouth shut and resumed his game with the bus.

With Ben not giving an inch, Saffy turned to Madeleine.

'Thanks for the books, by the way. Ben absolutely loves the *Magic Roundabout* ones.'

Madeleine swept the brush of her rose pink Dior along her nail.

'Oh, that's fine. I'd forgotten I put them in the garage to send out to you weeks ago,' she said without looking up.

'You found them then?' said Hayden, temporarily abandoning his battle of wills with his grandson.

'Gosh, yes. Just needed a hand to get at them. I asked Brian yesterday. Those war books of yours, too, I put them there to keep them safe. You know some of them are very rare, don't you? There's a load of Lee Child and Ian Rankins, too. Do you still want them? If not, I'll give them to charity.'

Hayden wrinkled his nose and thought for a moment.

'Well, the World War Two books, yes, of course. But I guess the others… can't we squeeze them into the library? I noticed some empty shelves when I was in there the other day.'

Madeleine continued her rose-pink sweeps.

'I rather thought we might leave room for when we go to Book Plus. We're bound to come back with some signed first editions. Why don't we see how much room we've got after that?'

'Book Plus Literature Festival? Oh, lovely!' exclaimed Saffy. 'Oh, Dad, that's where we went when I was little; you, me and Mum. That's where we met Eric Thompson!'

'Oh!' said Madeleine, mid-sweep. 'But we've already booked The Mount. I doubt they'll have any availability now.'

'Well, if you and Ben would like to come, I'm sure we can sort something,' said Hayden. 'I'll give Tom Wilkins, the manager, a call. He'll get you in, I'm sure.'

***

Wednesday 16th April 3.05p.m.

Nia glanced down at her phone. It had just sent out an indignant trill reminding her that she had an unanswered text. She raised an eyebrow. Madeleine took a cautious sip of her skinny latte and grimaced.

'It's not as if I'm not doing my bit, you know, Nia,' Madeleine said putting the mug down in a way that suggested it was unlikely to be picked up again – well, not by her anyway. 'I helped with the bloody Easter egg hunt; I ignored the chocolate finger marks on my Prada bag – it's old anyway. *And* I've been to every sodding school in the county, smiled at paint-coated children and shaken hands with so many heads that I'm at serious risk of getting capello tunnel syndrome – not that any of them were good enough for her! Hayden has mentioned going private – I'm sure that husband of hers could afford it… along with somewhere for his ex-wife and son to live! Honestly, I can't wait 'til I'm on that plane on Friday. Although the way things are going, that girl and her devil child will be sitting across the fucking aisle!' She snatched up the remaining shortbread biscuit from the plate between them and snapped it in two. Nia could practically hear the grinding of Madeline's now *ultra* pearly-whites.

The clip of lightly tapping heels behind them made both Nia and Madeleine turn. Ros, looking positively euphoric, was advancing at speed.

'Helloo,' she said, from a distance of some ten feet, and without pausing for a return greeting, or indeed breath, she announced, 'Did everyone have a good Easter? I've got some fabulous news… well, you know I missed out on tickets for Centre Court at Wimbledon for the Men's Final? Well, I've just managed to pick up the last two tickets to hear Jo Hartley speak at Book Plus!' She skidded to a halt at the table. 'You are going this year, aren't you, Nia? If you're not too busy with your new client, would you like to come with me?'

'Hi, Ros. Yes. Very excited but early days,' said Nia with a shrug. 'How's your back?' Nia got to her feet to give Ros an air kiss. 'Gosh, Jo Hartley – fantastic! Yes, I'd love that. I heard her at Cheltenham about three years ago. She was wonderful.'

'Jo Hartley?' said Madeleine.

'Yes, she's got a new book out next month – *The Dior Inheritance*,' said Ros, sitting down very carefully. 'What she doesn't know about Christian Dior really isn't worth knowing. I can't wait to get it. Obviously I'll wait until Book Plus to get a signed copy to go with the rest of my collection.' She turned back to Nia. 'My back's much better, thanks. Just took loads of ibuprofen and read for three days – it was bliss.'

Nia's phone trilled again.

'Oh, honestly, if he thinks I'm just going to come running because his wife has discovered she doesn't like cream he's even more naive than I gave him credit for!'

Ros's face took a fleeting break from its joyous state.

'Not Peter again? How many times now?'

'Thirteen since yesterday,' said Nia, casting her eyes skywards.

'Goodness, Nia, that's practically stalking! Have you told him to go away? You're not going to give him another chance are you?'

Nia paused before she answered.

'Not sure yet. Anyway, Maddy was telling me about her Book Plus trip. *Tout n'est pas bien*, from what she was saying.' She threw Madeleine a sympathy-packed look. Madeleine took her cue.

'Yes, it seems we can't even go to a book festival without the perfect daughter and her delightful son muscling in!'

'Oh, well, that's not too bad,' said Ros, looking genuinely relieved. 'Book Plus's wonderful for children. They have a whole programme of events. Trust me, you won't see them.' Travis appeared at the table, his eyebrows raised to prompt a response – preferably one in the form of an order. Ros's eyes twinkled with mischief. 'Um, yes. Anyone fancy a glass of wine? Well, I am celebrating!'

'I'll have a spritzer – lots of ice,' said Madeleine, leaping on Ros's suggestion before Ros had closed her lips.

Nia requested a merlot. Travis removed her empty cup and Madeline's abandoned latte but then Nia changed her mind and ordered another coffee. 'I'll have one later,' she said in answer to Ros's questioning glance. 'Meeting the new client – I'm pretty sure you know him, Maddy.'

But Madeleine obviously wasn't listening.

'Yes, well, children's events are all very well but they're also staying in The Mount with us. *And* Hayden's asked Saffy to join us when we go to see Sting.'

'Oh, wonderful! I'd heard he was going to be there,' said Nia. 'As you know Maddy, I've always been a huge fan of Sting.'

'Sting?' enquired Ros, with a lost look.

'Yes, he was in The Police,' answered Nia.

'Oh,' exclaimed Ros brightly. 'My friend Margaret was in the police. Special Branch, before she retired. Where was he based? I wonder if they worked together?'

'The band,' said Madeleine. Ros frowned.

'Band, what band? Have the police got a band?' she said and shook her head decisively. 'I don't think Margaret plays any musical instruments.'

'No, Ros, I think we need to backtrack a bit here,' interrupted Nia. 'Sting was in a pop band called The Police, in the eighties. Surely you've heard of them?'

Ros peered at Nia over her glasses as an aging aunt might peer at a child.

'And did they have anything to do with Charlie Parker or Thelonius Monk… Dizzy Gillespie, perhaps?' (Ros had discovered modern jazz in her early twenties and had steadfastly refused to ever move on).

Nia gave up. Madeleine had already lost interest.

'Yes, he's friends with Emma; she was in school with his wife. We're meeting them all for drinks after Sting's done his interview,' said Madeleine. 'There's talk of a meal at the hotel if Hayden can get a table. But, well, with one extra now, that's an even more remote chance!'

'What day is his event?' asked Nia.

'The first Friday evening,' replied Madeleine. 'One of the biggest apparently, not that you can get a ticket now for love nor money.'

'Ooh, that's the same day as Jo Hartley!' Ros said, turning to Nia. 'Her talk is at five-thirty.' She turned back to Madeleine. 'We could meet up after. Maybe you could get Sting to pose with Nia for a photo?' But her encouraging nod towards Madeleine went unnoticed – the drinks had arrived. Ros's expression suggested a change of direction in her thoughts. 'I wonder if Jo Hartley would be interested in doing a fund raising event? One of the McMillan Trust nurses who look after Dad has asked for ideas for this year. I always try to help out. They've been so brilliant with him.'

'How is he, by the way?' asked Nia.

'Oh, you know. Not great but stoically battling on,' Ros answered with a cheerfulness her eyes didn't share. 'What about your mother? Any better since Christmas?'

'Not too bad at the moment.' Nia crossed her fingers. 'We had that scare over New Year but she seems to have rallied since then. We actually got her out for half an hour on Mother's Day. Well, it was my sister, in fairness – only round the park but she really enjoyed it.'

'Wonderful. Wish I could get Dad out.' Desperate sadness

clouded Ros's face. Nia shifted the subject.

'So what fundraising have you got in mind, you know, if Jo Hartley did say yes?'

'Oh, I don't know? Someone suggested a fashion show,' answered Ros, clearly thinking as she was talking. 'I think it's quite a nice idea. And we have got some lovely fashion shops locally. Could be fun - sometime in the summer, possibly?'

'Well, as long as it's not the twenty-first of June,' Madeleine cut in. 'We're having a garden party for Cornerstone and I don't want you hijacking my guests; although lots have already accepted.'

'Oh, have the invitations gone out then?' asked Nia. 'Mine hasn't arrived yet. Mind you, the post has been abysmal lately – they managed to lose a draft presentation pack that Red Hot sent me last week and a cheque for six hundred pounds! Honestly!'

Madeleine shifted in her seat. 'Don't worry, I haven't sent you one. I decided to concentrate on the moneyed end of my social circle for this one. I'll need you two to help.'

It was fairly obvious that Nia was lost for words; Ros, on the other hand, dug around in her handbag and produced her diary.

'What date did you say? The twenty-first? Oh, good, well clear of the Wimbledon finals, so you're OK. Shall I put it in my diary? What would you like us to do?'

Through an expansive smile, Madeleine's teeth positively sparkled.

'Oh, fab! As I'll be with Emma for most of the afternoon, I'll need bodies to meet and greet, take coats and show people into the west garden.'

'Bodies!' Nia squeaked.

'Yes, so if you could both do that,' she said, talking as she got to her feet. 'Oh, must just nip to the loo.'

Madeleine headed for the Ladies, leaving Ros scribbling and Nia aghast. Nia turned on Ros.

'Well, if she thinks I'm playing *staff*!' she said. 'I mean, what happened to the Poles? They were good enough for the Christmas cocktails!'

Ros could see that while *Good Nia* might agree, *Cross Nia* was definitely giving her a run for her money.

'Yes, Nia,' she offered. 'But just think. We can meet Emma Jenkins… and if we go to help we won't need to make a donation. *And* as Emma's now Madeleine's new best friend, maybe Sting will be there, too!'

Thursday 17ᵗʰ April, 11a.m.

Hayden clipped his seatbelt into place and glanced at his daughter. Already buckled up, she was staring out of the Saab's passenger side window, the knuckle of her index finger resting on her teeth.

'Well, what did you think?' he asked.

Saffy didn't look around.

'Don't get me wrong, Dad, it's wonderful. Mr Francis certainly talks the talk and Ben would absolutely love that pool… but it's thirteen thousand a year. I didn't catch what happens when they go up to the senior school; my mind had gone into blind panic by then as I imagined what Alistair would say if I even suggested it. He's never been big on the public school idea as it is!'

'Never mind Alistair for a moment,' said Hayden gently. 'What did you think? How does it compare to the other schools you've seen? After all, you and Maddy must've been to them all by now.'

'Yer,' grinned Saffy. 'In fairness to Madeleine, I really didn't think she'd help, but actually she's been great, driving me around.

There was just no point in learning to drive in Hong Kong but I'd better get my act together if we're going to be staying over here! Won't be able to rely on lifts from you or Madeleine, once we're out of your hair.'

Hayden's face told Saffy exactly what he was thinking. Saffy sighed.

'Ben and I can't lodge with you forever, Dad. Don't get me wrong, it's absolutely lovely and Ben's having a whale of a time. But... well, you and Madeleine, in the grip of love's young...,' she paused and then said, 'OK, not so young – dream.' Hayden laughed, but Saffy's face was serious again. 'We're in the way, Dad.'

'Look, Saffy, I don't want you to ever think you are outstaying your welcome. Landsmere will always be your home. Anyway it's far too big for just Maddy and me.' He paused and grinned. 'And it's not as if we're likely to be adding to the family stock, is it? As you said, *not so young.*'

Saffy returned her gaze to the expansive, bowls-perfect lawns that rolled either side of the driveway leading to Rockmoore Hall School for Boys.

'I'm not sure Madeleine would agree,' she said. 'Well, about us staying anyway. Can't see her with kids somehow!'

'She just likes her own space,' said Hayden.

'I noticed.' Saffy paused, opened her mouth to add something but closed it again.

'Look,' said Hayden, 'Maddy and I are off to Paris tomorrow and in another couple of weeks we'll be going to Málaga. So we're hardly going to be under one another's feet. And who'll look after Morris? He certainly can't go into kennels now, not with his hips.' He turned the key and the Saab purred into life. 'But let's just get back to why we're here for a minute. You liked the school?'

'Yes, Dad. It's wonderful. That Head of Year, Ms O'Reilly

was lovely. The facilities are fantastic; the exam results are way up there with the best and it's practically next door to Landsmere – what's not to like, but as I said, Al–'

'Alistair won't have to trouble himself about his son's education unless he wants to,' Hayden interrupted, indicating left out of the school drive. 'I'm going to pay.'

'What? Dad, look, this is very generous, but really... Al and I'll sort something out.' The car sped along the leafy lane back towards town. 'The primary school at Little Landscombe was fine. A bit of a trek from Landsmere but Madeleine liked it – it was the first one we went to see.'

Hayden stopped the car at a red light.

'Look, Saffy. I want to do this. Ben's my only grandchild and I didn't think I would ever get to spend any real time with him. I want you and Ben to stay at Landsmere, and I want to pay for Ben to have the best chance he can have.'

Saturday, 19th April, 9.15a.m.

Hayden lay on the bed, a linen sheet covering his modesty. He gazed vaguely over the front cover of *Le Figaro*; it seemed that the somewhat tarnished outgoing President was not going quietly, or indeed graciously. The photograph under the leading headline showed him with some young thing, half-dressed and half his age, escaping into a limousine with the President's hand firmly planted on the girl's nymph-like and barely clad backside.

Madeleine was standing at the door to the balcony draped only in a white bath towel. She was on the phone. Beyond the open door, the Avenue des Champs Élysées stretched away below her, traffic roaring and hooting its way through what looked to Hayden from the bed like a glorious Parisian morning.

'Hi, John... Maddy... Madeleine Edwards, yes. Hi.' She paused to listen.

'Oh, sorry, I forgot about the hour difference. You're teeing off now, are you? Oh, OK. Just wanted to touch base about the banners. I'm still not happy about that shade of red.'

She turned to Hayden, rolled her eyes and mouthed, 'Golf!'

Hayden, not a fan of golf, was a firm believer that it really was a good walk spoiled. Madeleine had not played a game since they had met and her golf clubs were now swathed in cobwebs in a dark corner of Josh's garage, where she had left them after their last game (not wanting them in the hall of her own tiny house, which was now sitting empty and annoyingly buyer-free).

'No, I'm just not happy to sign it off until that red's right – it needs to be deeper. It's too pinky at the moment. I think I'd better have another look at the Pantone charts. Can we meet next week?'

She flicked the nail of her index finger across the corner of a Louis XIV occasional table that occupied a small corner in the expansive suite. Hayden watched. The table, he knew by the price of the room, was highly likely to be an original. Madeleine's other arm, hooked to hold her phone, also held the towel in place while she looked out over the city – the River Seine, pegged to the city by a plethora of bridges, just visible in the distance. As Madeleine talked, Hayden watched one end of the towel escape and drift to the floor, exposing her peach-like bottom to the room. Hayden smiled; France's former President would definitely have appreciated this positively splendid, hand-filling view.

Pleased that he had decided to hang the 'Do not disturb' sign on the door the evening before, Hayden dropped the newspaper across his warming form and waited for Madeleine to finish her call – by the sound of it, it wouldn't be too long and he would once again be able to have that glorious bottom all to himself.

Tuesday, 22nd April, 10.45a.m.

Madeleine was deeply unhappy that their flight home had been booked for twelve noon. In the far too few hours (in her opinion) spent shopping between the many hours they had spent in the bed of their capacious suite, she had found a wonderful little shop just off the Louvre Tuileries and had promised herself another visit there before they came home. To her irritation, however, Hayden had had *other* plans for that morning and their resulting late departure from the hotel (after a somewhat hurried brunch in the hotel bar as they had missed breakfast) had meant that her final session of retail therapy was not to be. She had also discovered that keeping her legs in the air for quite so long, and spread quite so wide, made her hip ache – this discovery did nothing for her mood.

At the airport, Hayden pressed a bundle of Euros into the taxi driver's hand before grabbing up the handles of the newly purchased case, now stuffed full of Madeleine's purchases, and the weekend bag they had come with. Hayden had been very generous with his credit card and Paris had been very willing to help him use it. Madeleine turned slowly and winced.

'You OK?' Hayden asked, looking her up and down with a concerned frown.

'Er, yer. My hip's aching a bit, that's all. Must have been all the walking.' Hayden hooked his arm around Madeleine's waist and drew her closer.

'Well, next time we won't do quite so much then.' He kissed her cheek softly. 'I'm sure once we're home, we can find other ways to while away the time.'

Madeleine had hoped to speak to Hayden about their lodgers at Landsmere but thus far hadn't found the right moment; at Hayden's words, however, she spotted the door of opportunity throwing itself open before her.

'Well,' she said and with a naughty glint in her eye. 'If we ever have Landsmere to ourselves again, maybe we won't have to travel all the way to Paris.' Slowing, she drew him back, letting her lips brush his ear, and whispered, 'You could fuck me in every room in the house – there are plenty we haven't tried yet.'

Tuesday, 6th May, 10.45a.m.

Madeleine nestled into the king-sized tub chair in the reception of Cavendish Major and glanced down at the diamond watch Hayden had given her the year before. Rather small for her taste, and as a result seldom worn, the watch showed ten forty-five a.m. She was fashionably late.

Ultra glossy annual reports were splayed in a gaudy fan across a bright red, equally glossy table in front of her. She leant forward to retrieve one. The black leather seat creaked expensively. To her left, a gigantic cube boasted phrases that included, 'The light at the end of the tunnel will not come on by itself', and 'Those who try may succeed; those who strive, win!'

The bold san serif phrases were carefully placed on each side of the cube across a solid block of colour: lime green on navy; aubergine on bright yellow. In fact, the whole room was a smorgasbord of colours that smacked the onlooker in the face on arrival. Madeleine loved it.

A wasp-waisted receptionist answered a bleeping phone, spoke in hushed tones and then got to her feet.

'If you'd like to follow me to the lift, Mr Cavendish is ready for you now,' she said and, with an efficient smile, led the way to the lift where she showed Madeleine in with a wave of her waif-like hand. One Madeleine was safely on board, she pressed the button marked '3' and sprang backwards to exit the lift just before the doors closed. At the third floor the lift doors opened.

John Cavendish smiled the smile of a man who knew how to smile. Madeleine oozed charm back at him. Stepping forward, she bypassed his offered hand and kissed the air in the region of his left cheek.

'John, hi,' she breathed.

'Madeleine,' purred John. 'Coffee? Let's use the meeting room. It's just through there… no, on the right.'

Slightly disappointed, Madeleine veered right, away from a huge office that overlooked the newly developed harbour. Below, restaurants battled for the steady drip of tourists while all around executives sat in their ergonomically perfect waterside offices ignoring the defiant scream of gulls shitting across the car park, bumper-to-bumper full of guano-coated company Alfa Romeos. Madeleine's pulse picked up the pace.

'So, was that coffee or tea?' said John.

'Oh, coffee would be fab. Thanks. Black.' John picked up a coffee pot and raised his eyebrows.

'Perfect.' It was Madeleine's turn to purr.

Within moments two gloss-black cups steaming with hot coffee were delivered to the vast board table where Madeleine was already scrutinising a colour chart, holding it against a mock-up of the new Cornerstone logo – version thirteen.

'You can see what I mean, can't you?' she began before the cups hit the oak laminate. 'Needs to be about two shades darker then I think we'll be there. See.' She held up another colour card. 'This is more like it.'

John tapped two fingers on the table, breathed in sharply through his nose and nodded.

'Yep, that looks great. So, we'll make that change and go ahead, yes? The pens shouldn't be a problem but leave it much longer and we'll be cutting it fine for the chinaware you wanted. Did you have a think about the wraps for the buckets, far cheaper than those boxes you showed me?'

Madeleine shook her head.

'Well, I'd like to see the final proofs obviously, and really I'd prefer the boxes but...' She paused studying the logo again. 'The spacing between the letters looks better now, doesn't it? I couldn't sleep once I'd realized it was wrong!'

'Oh, yes, definitely looks better... so, the wraps?' John prompted.

Madeleine pursed her lips, tucked in her chin and threw a doe-eyed gaze in John's direction.

'Those collection boxes are way more expensive, Maddy,' said John, reading her expression correctly. 'And with the date on them they'll have a very short shelf-life. To be honest, my advice would be to go for the buckets; they're easier to carry around and won't collapse if it rains or if they get sat on. Bespoke design collecting boxes, especially in the shape of a real hardback book – that's a hell of a lot of cutting and folding. It'll really push up the price!'

It was Madeleine's turn to tap her finger. She dropped her gaze to her beautifully manicured nail. The *Rose Exubérant* she had applied only that morning was chipped – not what you'd expect from Chanel, she thought with a silent tut.

Parking her disappointment with Chanel for a moment, she said out loud, 'No John. Buckets just won't give the right impression. This is a garden party. There'll be a lot of very influential people. I simply must have those boxes.'

John picked up his pen and flicked it across his fingers.

'Have you discussed this with Ha–'

Madeleine had anticipated this line of objection. She was aware of some business link between Hayden and Cavendish Major but had lost interest in the detail as Hayden had explained it.

'Hayden's fine,' she interrupted. 'We talked about it in Paris at the weekend. He wants the garden party to be as much of a success as I do and I'm just not prepared to risk letting him down by scrimping, especially at this late stage!' Madeleine paused and took a sip of coffee – if she was going to get her way here she knew she had to concede something. 'Look. John, I've got an idea. Let's take the date off the boxes. Keep the rest of the wording, obviously. That way we can use them next year.'

'So the garden party's going to be an annual event?' said John.

'Of course!' replied Madeleine. 'Landsmere Grange is perfect. Once we've got the business model, why not?' She beamed the glorious smile of one who didn't pay her own dental bills and her voice softened. 'No, Cornerstone has been looking for someone to do this sort of thing on an ongoing basis for a while, so now I've proved I can do the job I'm just waiting for the green light. I can really start planning properly then. I've already got some fab ideas.'

John twiddled with his pen again. He didn't look entirely convinced.

'Well, if you've got plans to make the spend stretch… and if you've talked to Hayden I'm guessing the board are OK with it.'

Madeleine glanced at the diamond face on her wrist.

'Oh, is that the time! Sorry, John, I've got another meeting at noon!' She jumped up, swung her bag under her arm and bent forward in anticipation of a parting kiss on the cheek. John obliged as she carried on talking. 'The logo looks fab, John. Really pleased.

Hayden will be, too.'

'Right, good. Thanks, Maddy. I'll get the proofs over to you by Friday... actually you can have the logo this afternoon – it's the other stuff that'll take the time.'

Victorious, Madeleine strode back towards the lift.

'You're a love, John. Give me a call when it's ready. I'll get Brian to pick it up for me.' The lift door opened obediently. 'Oh, we didn't discuss quantities.'

'A hundred mugs; pens,' he paused and wrinkled his nose. 'A thousand? Not worth going for less. I'll get the price for the boxes and we'll decide from there.'

The lift doors closed.

'Wonderful!' Madeleine called out and pressed the button marked 'G'. Looking at her watch, she saw that the time was eleven fifty-five a.m. Her hair appointment was booked for noon. She was going to be late – fashionably, of course.

Thursday 8th May, 5.05p.m.

Ros added the name *Hannah Butrills* to a long list neatly arranged into two columns in her pale lilac notebook; the columns had now spilled over onto a third page. She was pleased with progress. Hannah, Ros had just discovered, was the new fashion columnist for the Western Express. Apparently Carolyn Avebury had finally retired – a shame, thought Ros, she had grown to like Mrs Avebury.

Looking down at the name she had just written, she tapped her lip with her pen and then added another 't', then crossed the added letter out and put an asterisk against the name. This, according to the little key she had devised long ago (when she had first started listing), denoted that she would need to find out the correct spelling before making contact with Hannah. She was scanning this, her most recent list, tapping her lip as she read, when the peace that was Horton's on a rainy Thursday afternoon was shattered. Nia and Ivy arrived.

'Bejesus, Ros, have you seen that car of Madeleine's?' said Ivy, more loudly than her proximity required. 'She's out there now making a pig's ear of parking it!'

'It's a birthday present from Hayden,' said Ros, almost with a note of apology. 'Didn't you know he bought her a car? So Madeleine's joining us, is she?'

'Yes,' said Nia, making hand signals towards Travis for a bottle of merlot and two glasses. 'You won't have red, will you, Ros?'

'Gosh no. White, for me – ABC,' replied Ros, tapping her half full glass with her pen. 'You know, anything but Chardonnay.' She wrinkled her nose and gave a toothy chuckle.

Nia signalled two fingers towards Travis. Madeleine walked in, and Nia held up a third finger.

Ivy plonked down next to Ros.

'Not another list, Ros! No idea why you bother, it's always the same names! What're you going to get us to do this time? God, I hope it's not another one of those surprise cabaret performances you were trying to rope us into for Margie's wedding!'

Ros looked over her glasses at Ivy, her face passive, her pen poised.

'I don't know what you mean, Ivy. That was a perfectly good idea. If people had only applied themselves I'm sure it would have been excellent.'

'Hilarious, more like – at our expense!' said Ivy. 'So what're you up to, then?'

'Well,' said Ros, clicking her pen and closing her book. 'As you know, I try to do some fundraising for the McMillan Trust when I can.'

'So, another sponsored read, then,' interrupted Ivy. 'I just hope you pick some better books this year! I fell asleep twice!'

Ros pursed her lips.

'No,' she said very deliberately. 'We're going to try something different this year – to try to get a few more people involved. A fashion show, actually.'

'Well, I hope you're not going to involve that bloody Carolyn Avebury woman!' Madeleine cut in. She plonked down in the seat next to Nia. 'Not a clue about fashion!'

'Mmm,' said Ros, with a frown. 'That article she did with you certainly was a surprise. Generally I always thought she was quite good. I've used some of her recommendations myself – she was always excellent on colour.' Ros tugged proudly on the lapel of the jade jacket she was wearing.

Madelaine gave a derisory snort.

'Well, I'm sorry, Ros. I certainly wasn't impressed. She tried to put me in navy! No, after the second outfit I simply had to take over!'

'So, the piece in the paper... Carolyn Avebury didn't choose *any* of those clothes... or hats?' said Ros, evidently picking her words with care. 'She didn't actually give you any advice on what to wear?'

'She tried but God, No!' said Maddy. 'Didn't know what the hell she was doing! Me... in navy, for chrissake!'

'Well, with your hair and teeth, I'd have thought navy would look great – very classic,' said Ivy without catching anyone's eye. She took a sip of the wine Travis had just delivered. Back suddenly straight, Madeleine opened her mouth but her phone rang. The change was spectacular.

'Oh, fab! That'll be John with the proofs – better take it,' she said digging deep into her bag. Her smile positively sparkled as she said, 'John, hi, yes… hang on, I'll go outside, too noisy in here… Now? Oh fab, you're a darling…'

Nia and Ros exchanged glances. Ivy took another swig. Madeleine disappeared out into the street.

'I knew Carolyn Avebury would never have chosen that hat,' said Ros.

Tuesday 13th May, 10.45a.m.

Hayden hit 'Confirm Payment' and sat back from his computer with a smile. He and Saffy had visited Rockmoore School again that morning and after another somewhat animated discussion in the car on the way home, he had finally persuaded her to let him pay for Ben to start there in the autumn – he had also reiterated his hope that she and Ben would regard Landsmere as their permanent home. Winning Madeleine around, however, he knew, might be a bit more of a challenge. So in an effort to maintain the peace, he had booked two first class seats to Málaga, flying out the day after their return from Book Plus (another sore point for Madeleine). He had also arranged four viewings – including a delightful villa out to the east that he really was hoping Madeleine would fall for.

It would be nice to get away again. Madeleine definitely seemed happier when they were away. He smiled at the memory of a particularly enjoyable breakfast in Paris (or 'sexfast' as Madeleine had christened it); as he had discovered with champagne, honey would certainly never be quite the same again.

Morris wandered into the study and nudged Hayden's elbow. Jolted back from that glorious king-sized Parisian bed, Hayden sought out the clock in the corner of his computer screen. It read 18.07

'Hello, old man. Is it walk o'clock already?' said Hayden, scratching the hound's ear. Morris gave a low moan of appreciation and pressed his ear into Hayden's hand for more. Since Madeleine had thrown herself into the re-branding of Cornerstone, Hayden had seen a lot less of her. He was pleased in a way. After all, she had started to allude to early retirement (the thought of his own retirement filled Hayden with dread), but he was happy working and was worried that she might get bored. Cornerstone had provided the perfect distraction and if the garden party went well he was seriously considering asking her to get a bit more involved – on a voluntary basis, of course – but that was a thought for another day.

From downstairs he heard the front door scrape open.

'Dad, you upstairs?' Saffy called.

'Ba Ritten, where'th Mowwith? Hath he had hith walk yet?' shouted Ben, before Hayden could answer.

Hayden laughed and got to his feet.

'Just coming down. I'm just about to take Morris out actually. Is it too late for my favourite grandson to join me, Mummy?'

'What's the time? Six-fifteen. Where you going? If you're not going to be too long he can go with you. We've just been swimming so he won't need a bath and with the amount of corned beef pie he packed away earlier, I don't think he's going to need any supper either!' said Saffy as Hayden, followed by Morris, headed down the sweep of stairs.

'Ah, Mrs Bosworth's famous corned beef pie. Haven't had that for ages, any left?'

'Yes. But I thought you'd want to eat with Madeleine later?' said Saffy, glancing out of the still open front door as if looking for Madeleine's Audi.

'Another meeting apparently, then I think she's meeting Nia. So if there's a piece of Mrs B's corned beef pie going I'm perfectly happy to have that – might even leave a bit for Maddy.'

'Ooh, don't think corned beef pie is quite in her league, Dad,' Saffy said with a mock frown. 'Anyway I'm sure I heard her mention a diet. She's got some new dress that she wants to wear for Book Plus – you know, meeting Sting.' Saffy rolled her eyes. 'She does know that Sting's married, doesn't she?'

Hayden pulled on his wellies.

'She just wants to look her best, Saf. Don't be mean.' He glanced out of the window at the gathering clouds. 'I think Ben might need a coat.'

Friday 16th May, 11.45a.m.

Madeleine threw a fleeting glance over the proofs spread across the expansive desk in John Cavendish's expansive office. After their last meeting she had insisted that they now knew each other well enough for her to be allowed into this inner sanctum. She had been there for nearly an hour, mainly talking about sailing (Madeleine refused to let her ignorance of the subject stifle the conversation) and golf (apparently he had played at Turnberry three times, once having to move aside to let Sean Connery play through – Madeleine could hardly breathe, she was so impressed). The time had flown.

'Tell you what, John darling,' said Madeleine, peering into her empty coffee cup. 'We'll have another coffee and just go through that leaflet again, then let's go for lunch. I think we're pretty much there and there's a fab new tapas bar in the next block. How do you fancy giving it a go?'

John glanced at his watch and shook his head.

'Sorry, Maddy. I've got a one-thirty. New account. Not sure it'd be a good idea to breathe wine and garlic over our newest client. Maybe next time?'

'Ooh, anything I can help with? Now that we've worked together on Cornerstone, you can see what I'm capable of,' said Madeleine brightly.

Again, John shook his head.

'Thanks, Maddy, but Nia Griffin's working with us on that one. Do you know her? It's her first project with us and I have to say I'm impressed so far. Sadly her client hasn't got your budget but Nia's very practical – some very neat low-cost ideas. I really like her approach actually.'

Madeleine pushed the handle of her cup with her pristine *Dragon Red* nail; the cup turned slowly in the saucer.

'Oh, Nia's doing some work for you now, is she? Yes, Nia and I go back a long way. Used to work together,' she said with a wry smile. 'So what's she doing for you?'

'Well, it's a new business actually – they make shoes out of old tyres… well, the soles anyway. Treddies – great name; Nia came up with it. They approached Deart Marketing but you know start-ups, no budget. So their Marketing Director, Beth Franklyn – you probably know her, too? Well, she recommended Nia. She's top notch at the PR, too, you know, the profile stuff, very hands on. We're doing some packaging designs for them. It's a great product; I think they're really gonna go places.'

'Sounds fab, good luck with that one; I'm sure Nia'll be OK.' She reached to the corner of the desk and drew over the annual report that only half an hour ago she had dismissed as fine and ready to go to print. 'You know, John, I'd just like to go through this again.' She flicked over a couple of pages and gave a light laugh. 'Talking about Nia reminded me. We were working on a new brochure a few years back, well Nia was. Anyway, no idea how but a director's name got missed out. Really embarrassing and I had to do some quick talking to smooth things over.' She tapped her nail on the cover of the report, then with a decisive breath picked it up and slid it into her open briefcase. 'Yes, think I'd better have a quick look at this again over the weekend. I'll let you know if there are any amendments first thing Monday. Is that OK?' She gave him a scrunchy-nosed smile. 'Good job you mentioned Nia!'

Monday 19th May, 9.35a.m.

Hayden's voice echoed up from the hall. He was holding Madeleine's phone. It was showing three missed calls.

'Maddy, it's John Cavendish. Are you available for a quick word?'

Madeleine had just applied an avocado and yogurt face pack and had absolutely no intention of letting Saffy, or worse still, Ben, see her owl-eyed white face.

'No, it's OK,' she called from the en suite. Her briefcase lay unopened on the floor by the window where she had left it on Friday afternoon. 'Tell him the AP is fab. No amends needed. Tell him everything can go to print... Oh, Hayden darling, ask him to arrange delivery here. Tell him to let me know when he's got the date and time?'

**

Wednesday 21ˢᵗ May, 1.45p.m.

'No, it's OK, I won't come in, Ros, thanks,' said Nia, on the doorstep of Ros's little house. The border between Ros's house and her elderly, flower-obsessed neighbour was exploding with Sweet Williams just coming into bloom. A grateful bee buzzed loudly around the newly opened heads. 'Just wanted to drop off the money for the Jo Hartley tickets before I forget. Thank you so much for getting them. I don't know where the time's gone over the past few weeks.'

'Thanks, Nia. Wish everyone paid their debts as quickly!' said Ros, and pursed her lips. She still hadn't had the two hundred and fifty pounds back from Madeleine for the books she had bought back for her. It had gone on for so long now she was embarrassed to ask for it. 'So this new client is keeping you busy then? Are you enjoying the work?'

'Gosh yes! It's great to be busy again. John Cavendish is an absolute sweetie. Ironically, Jack Tranter rang me last week, too. They've finally agreed a budget for their re-brand – it's ten times what Treddies have got! I've brought Cavendish Major on board with that one, too, which has gone down very well.' Nia paused and frowned. 'Although for some reason John's started double-checking my work. Bit odd but they're good payers, so hey-ho!'

Ros watched Nia as she talked. The lines around Nia's eyes weren't quite as deep as the last time they had met, and there was a good colour in her more recently pale cheeks. Ros smiled.

'Well, as long as they're paying!' she said, and then crossed her arms – ready for a bit of a gossip. 'So, do you think Madeleine will introduce us to Sting next week? What are you going to wear?'

'I can't see why she won't; she knows how much I love Sting. God, when we worked together I had a Police calendar for Christmas one year and kept it on my wall ages after the year passed.' Nia laughed as she talked. 'I used to play *Zenyattà Mondatta* every time we went to a meeting together – that was always my favourite album – until she begged me to change the CD – she hates The Police – well, she did then, anyway!'

Ros guffawed.

'Oh, that's marvellous. And now she's meeting one of them. I wonder if she'll mug up beforehand. You know Maddy, she'll do just enough to come across as some sort of Police aficionado! But I bet she gets the name of that album wrong...! Hey,' she said, suddenly looking very mischievous. 'Have you got a CD I can borrow? I'll do some research on the internet, we can ask Sting some really detailed questions to catch Maddy out!'

She guffawed again.

'That's a bit mean, Ros,' said Nia, grinning. 'He is their guest after all; but I've got *Zen* in the car as it happens, if you want to have a listen. At least then, when we do meet him, you won't feel totally lost.'

Ros was not to be deterred.

'Oh, that would be lovely. I'll Google Sting this afternoon and do some reading. Oh, what fun, I'm quite looking forward to this now!'

Friday 30th May 1.30p.m.

It was rare for Hayden to get irritated, let alone angry – very rare. Anger, he believed, was a wasted emotion. He had learned long ago that leaping about ranting rarely changed the course of events – especially if events were going badly already; a twinkly-eyed grin generally proved more effective even in a crisis and served to really piss off your opponent if things turned nasty. Madeleine had recognised this in Hayden very early on – her only dilemma was whether to file it under *Threats* or *Opportunities*.

Today, however, at this moment, Hayden was a tad annoyed.

Brian had picked him up that morning at seven for an early meeting the other side of Bristol – a journey of about forty-five nicely air-conditioned minutes with John Humphries providing just the right balance of news and comment to allow Hayden to arrive at his meeting relaxed, informed and unchallenged. Hayden was expecting a similar journey home, albeit the *Today* programme would have given way by then to something equally topical; unless it was a phone-in, in which case he could always ask Brian to hit the off switch.

Just as a huge plate of warm croissants had arrived (after all, being the non-executive director of a struggling coolant systems manufacturer had to have *some* high points) Hayden's phone had buzzed in his trouser pocket. Helping himself to a serviette-wrapped croissant, Hayden had retrieved his phone. There was a text from Brian; he had been called back to Landsmere – apparently it was 'urgent' but nothing for Hayden to worry about, so he didn't. (An answer phone message left a little later by a very apologetic Brian explained that Madeleine had just discovered that all of the garden party merchandise had been delivered to Losemere House on the other side of town and a Mrs Everly was not at all happy to discover a mountain of cardboard boxes on her doorstep when she opened the front door to retrieve her milk).

More amused than concerned (at that stage), Hayden had put his phone back into his pocket, helped himself to a second croissant (Madeleine's spartan diet had started to encroach into his own meals, although for the moment he was choosing not to notice) and tuned back in to the meeting that was continuing around him. The MD, sweating profusely, was limping through a very long-winded tale about economic influences in an effort to explain the company's current lacklustre performance. Hayden listened, trying to pick the truth from the words while he skimmed through the trading figures laid out in the quarterly report. On the third column he spotted a howling error that unfortunately reduced sales still further; however, in the light of MD's current nervous state, Hayden decided to stay quiet. Instead he listened patiently, enjoyed his croissant, made notes, had another coffee, and, when eventually asked, laid out a step-by-step plan for remedial action. The downside was that his recommendations would result in the loss of two jobs; the upside was that these could be soaked up by one long-term sickness that was coming to its own sad but natural conclusion, and a retirement.

At eleven fifty-five a.m. Hayden walked to the railway station as a man who in a matter of hours would be taking his lovely lady away to the Book Plus Festival for what he sincerely hoped would be a small amount of listening to people talking about books and a lot of sex. He liked having sex with Madeleine. She always threw herself into it with enthusiasm and surprising agility for someone of her age – and some of her ideas would have made even Carla's hair curl, which he liked even more. By the time Hayden got to the platform he had to buy a newspaper simply to maintain his modesty.

Unfortunately, an hour and a half later, as the taxi rolled away down the gravel drive, weaving from side to side to avoid the potholes that the unsuspecting driver had endured on the way in, the cooling of Hayden's ardour was sudden and rapid.

A dozen boxes were piled on the drive just in front of the currently open, ancient garage door; Brian, knees buckling under the weight of a vast carton, nodded a weary head to acknowledge Hayden who returned the greeting by raising his briefcase before heading into the hallway of his home. Inside, the hall was littered with more cartons stacked in perilously high piles.

'Hayden, darling, is that you?' Madeleine's voice came from the library. 'I'm in here. You've got to come and see. This stuff is fab!'

A stack of letters lay unopened on the barely negotiable hall table and it was with some difficulty that Hayden managed to retrieve them. There was no sign of the slender silver letter knife that normally lived on the post table so, flicking through the envelopes, he picked his way through the maze of cardboard cases towards the disembodied voice.

Madeleine's phone trilled.

'John, hi!'

Hayden continued to flick through the brown envelopes. Madeleine spoke again.

'Yes. Once we'd persuaded her that they really were for me and that I really did live at Landsmere Grange, she was fine – off her head, mind! Couldn't believe Hayden's parents were dead and that Hayden was no longer Head Boy at Rockmoore School – he kept that one quiet!' She paused again and then laughed. Hayden, now standing in the doorway, spotted Cavendish Major's logo on a bulging envelope in his hand. He slid his finger along the top edge to open it. Madeleine caught Hayden's eye, shot a look skywards and then said, 'Yes, he's just arrived, I'll tell him... anyway, I'm going through this stuff. It's fab.' She paused again before answering. Hayden scanned the sheaf of papers he had just drawn from the envelope. 'Yer, sure,' said Madeleine nodding. 'Came this morning. I've left it out for him. Yer, I'll give him a prod.' She nodded again towards Hayden, waved her fingers at the papers in his hand and then gave a thumbs-up. 'Now, you are going to come, aren't you?' she added and paused. Then she smiled. 'Oh, fab. And don't forget, that invitation is for you plus one...' She let the sentence hang. An answer to the unsaid question obviously came back. She giggled. 'Oh, you big meany. Come on, you can tell me.' She laughed again. 'Oh well, I'll find out soon enough. Look, I'll go through the rest of the things and give you a call in a bit. Take care.'

She pressed a button on her mobile, held it to her ear as if checking the caller had gone and then, still grinning, pushed the phone back into her jeans pocket.

'John Cavendish, checking everything's here. God, it's going to take an age to sort but what I've seen so far is fab. The colours are spot on – took a bit of a battle but I knew it would be worth it… That the invoice? God, they're on the ball, aren't they! Bit of a cheek really.'

As she spoke she dived into another box.

'Ah, the crockery! Just look at these!' Her voice filled with triumph as she drew out a jet black cup and saucer. Even from where Hayden was standing he could see that both items of china bore the Cornerstone logo. Madeleine's face fell.

'Well, a bit of enthusiasm would be appreciated. I've worked bloody hard to get this sorted… Hayden, darling, are you alright? You've gone a funny colour. Mrs B left one of her lunchtime specials in the oven – no idea what it is.'

She stepped over the box she had just opened, knelt next to another and slid Hayden's letter knife down the brown tape that secured the lid.

'Oh fab, the pens… oh no. Oh, bloody hell, look at that colour! No… these'll have to go back.'

Hayden's voice was hollow when he next spoke.

'Will they give a refund?'

Madeleine gave a brief snort.

'No, silly. They'll have to be re-done. I'll phone John. That red just isn't right. And the top half of the barrel should be black, too! We discussed this. I'll call him now.'

She dragged her phone out of her pocket.

'Maddy, have you any idea how much this lot cost?' asked Hayden.

Madeleine found John's number and pressed 'Call'.

'Of course! Sorry, darling, but if I don't call John now I'll miss him. Just remembered he's playing golf this afternoon.' She waited briefly and then said, 'Oh, hi Tonia, John still there?'

'Put the phone down, Maddy,' said Hayden quietly. Madeleine waved her hand in a request for quiet and carried on talking.

'Oh, damn! I've missed him, have I? No worries, I'll give his mobile a call... yes, it is urgent... no, no, it's OK, I've got it. Thanks... No, no message. We're off to Book Plus later so I really need to speak to him now. Thanks, Tonia darling. Bye.'

She studied the phone again, finger poised.

'Madeleine, put the fucking phone down and speak to me, damn it!'

Madeleine dropped the phone. It bounced off the edge of the pen box and clipped the black branded cup – there was a ping and the cup's handle tinkled into the saucer.

Hayden's breathing had suddenly become laboured.

'Have you any idea how much this lot cost?' he repeated, waving the paper as if trying to shake the numbers off the page.

'Yes,' said Madeleine defensively. 'Well, John did mention that we were a tad over budget, but...'

'And when did John mention this "tad over budget" issue?' demanded Hayden, his voice now so dangerous even Morris had wandered in to check he wasn't needed.

Madeleine shuffled.

'Oh, I can't remember. He didn't say it was much though – couple of thousand.'

'And did you carry on ordering – after he's mentioned this *couple of thousand*?' asked Hayden.

Madeleine got to her feet. Morris lay down.

'Now, hang on, Hayden. You asked me to sort the re-branding, which, if you'd care to look at this stuff, is bloody good;

you didn't tell me that the budget was set in stone. God, how much do you think a re-brand costs if you want it done properly?'

'Not, fifteen thousand, two hundred and eighteen pounds and...' he paused to check the now crumpled paper, 'thirty-two pence... plus VAT!'

Madeleine's eyebrows momentarily rose then her face broke into a beam.

'Oh, thank God for that! I thought it was going to be heaps more!'

'Fucking hell, Maddy, the budget was ten – including VAT! How the fuck am I going to explain this to the board? Is there any more on the way? Can it be stopped?' Hayden's mind was racing as he talked. How could Madeleine have got it so wrong? (Although, furious as he was, he had to admit the new logo was a great improvement on the original.)

Madeleine's lip started to quiver. Her mobile rang. She looked at the illuminated face chirruping from the floor. 'It's John,' she whispered, an unchecked tear now trickling down her cheek. Hayden was lost. He had never made a woman cry – ever.

'I'll get it,' he said gently, bending to pick up the phone. 'John? No, Maddy's busy. It's Hayden. How're you? Yer, I'm great. Look, I'm glad I've caught you...'

As he talked he turned and walked from the room, Morris got up and padded after his master.

Friday 30th May 2.15p.m

Following a long conversation with John Cavendish, Hayden did not return to the library. Instead he made for the kitchen and was silently delighted to find one of Mrs B's utterly splendid shepherd's pies with *extra* gravy – one of a large number of dishes in the housekeeper's repertoire that Madeleine had banned on account of the amount of butter Mrs B insisted on putting into… well, almost everything. He spooned a very generous portion onto a plate, ate it all and then helped himself to the remaining third; after which, whistling the chorus of a nameless tune that someone on the train had generously shared with him all the way from Temple Meads, he had packed his dinner suit into his car along with a long dress cover that Madeleine had left strategically hanging on the bedroom door frame, and their bags; then he sent Saffy a text telling her to be ready by four and took Morris for a long walk, leaving Madeleine to do whatever it was she did before they went on a trip.

Friday 30th May 8.15p.m

Hayden and Madeleine were now ensconced in the bar of The Mount Hotel. The journey there had been punctuated by two vomit stops for Ben and a bladder stop for Madeleine (or to be more accurate, a lipstick and perfume check, just in case they bumped into Sting on their arrival).

Madeleine sipped a gin and tonic while Hayden swirled a double Glenfiddich around a heavy-bottomed crystal glass. Madeleine broke the silence.

'It was definitely a sensible move for Saffy to take Ben for an early tea and then off to bed. Judging by the number of tickets you booked for him he's got a big day tomorrow. Must have cost a fortune – I hope he appreciates it!'

Hayden took a slow, savouring sip of his whisky before he spoke.

'Oh, I'm sure he will.' The malty liquor hit his empty stomach, warming him to his boots. 'Did you enjoy the talk? Sting's depth of knowledge was quite remarkable, wasn't it?'

'Oh yes, fab!' said Madeleine. 'Shame about the photo though. We must remember to get one at dinner now. It'll be better actually, more intimate.'

'Oh, I nearly forgot,' said Hayden, tipping his glass towards her. 'Did you see Nia and Ros in the audience? At the back. They waved as we walked in. Nia certainly looked pleased to be there. Mouthed "see you later". Did you see her?'

'No,' said Madeleine, swigging back the remaining half of her G and T. 'Are we having another?'

She waved at a passing waiter.

'Two more?' she smiled, gesturing at both glasses. Her blood-red nails caught the soft glow of the table lamp beside them.

'Gin and tonic and… Glenfiddich for sir?' asked the waiter with a nod. 'Water with that, sir? Spring, wasn't it?'

'Oh, yes, spring, please. Just a splash, mind.' Hayden handed the waiter his empty glass and glanced at Madeleine's dangerously low neckline. 'That's a nice dress. You should wear black more often.'

He did like it, too. Tight-fitting all the way to the floor; it certainly showed off Madeleine's slimmer but, he was pleased to observe, still very satisfyingly curvy frame. In fact, her almost obsessive mission to lose weight had not had the slightest impact on her cleavage, he noted,… and if she leant forwards… he wondered if he might catch a glimpse of her nipples, as big as cherries and just as–

'What time do you think they'll come down?' said Madeleine, interrupting Hayden's exceptionally pleasant musing. 'I'm starving.'

'Well, that guy from *The Guardian* seemed very keen to get a few words,' answered Hayden, inwardly dwelling on her nipples. 'And he was third in the queue. You know what press conferences can be like, I'm sure. They'll be down in a while.'

Madeleine shifted in her seat.

'Look, I just need to pop to the loo.' She got to her feet and ran her hands down her hips because, well, she could (and looking at Hayden's eyes, she knew *he* wanted to). Then she headed for the Ladies.

Friday 30th May 8.55p.m.

Behind her, the cloakroom door brushed to a close. Ahead, the mirrored wall at the end of the long room confirmed how wonderful Madeleine knew she looked.

Her dress was based on a gorgeous Amy Childs number that she'd found in a tiny little boutique in town; but much to Madeleine's irritation she had not been able to get anywhere near the original. Refusing, however, to let a sizing discrepancy stand in her way she had promptly commissioned a seamstress (recommended by the local though recently discovered executive dry-cleaning service) to rustle up something with echoes of Childs but for a woman with breasts and hips. Madeleine's design featured the sweetheart bustier neckline of the original but, unlike the Amy Childs creation, continued *past* her knicker-line keeping the black chiffon pulled tight around her body right to the floor. This design tweak had the advantage of *not* showing off Madeleine's legs – she had better attributes (especially since discovering a varicose vein, which she planned to have done privately at her earliest convenience); the disadvantage of the design variation was that the wearer could only take very tiny steps (the seamstress, identifying this as a problem early on, had tried to introduce a slit up the back to the knee; however, Madeleine's design was fixed in her mind and changes were not an option).

The zipper was the ace – extra long, it held the soft chiffon folds around her body like a grasp, fastening from just below her bottom up to the centre of her back. Meticulous practice meant that Madeleine could now reach and locate the tiny fastener with two fingers and, with one seductive sweep, undo the zipper. Later tonight, when the dress fell, she would stand before Hayden completely naked with the exception of her glossy black five-inch heels (six being just an inch too far, she had discovered in the shoe shop – although, thankfully, she had been fully clothed at the time). Standing to admire her reflection, Madeleine knew that in this dress Hayden would forgive her for anything.

The door behind her opened with a bang and after a moment a girl reeled in. She stopped and stared at Madeleine's side-on reflection in the mirror above the nearest basin.

'Oh, that dress is lush,' she said. Her eyes made a valiant effort to maintain a uniform direction but failed. 'Is it Top Shop? I'm not bein' funny but I loves Top Shop stuff, it's lush. My boyfriend got me one a bit like your one for last New Year's – gor, fancied me something wicked in it, mind. Fucked me in the park... on the swings – couldn't wait to ger home, dirty bugger! The dress got ripped but I din mind.'

She shrugged and hit the bar of the tap. Water trickled into the china bowl unchecked.

'You stayin' yer?' she asked, swaying slightly.

'Yes,' said Madeleine simply, hoping that the girl might give up her conversational efforts.

'Me, too,' said the girl. 'It's me twenty-first. From Abertillery.

I'm not bein' funny but it's lovely yer, in' it.' She hiccupped. 'Sorry, I've had a bit too much to drink. Tequila – it's lush.'

'Oh, well, er, many happy returns,' said Madeleine. 'Anyway…'

She backed into the nearest cubicle and locked the door. The sound of running water continued from the cloakroom.

As undoing the dress was now a practiced art, within a second Madeleine stood butt-naked, clutching the fabric in her arms to avoid weeing on the chiffon. Job done, she stood up, wrapped the bodice broadly over her torso with one arm ('arrangement' was better negotiated when the dress was once again secured) and reached for the zipper…

It was only at that moment that it dawned on Madeleine that she had only ever practiced undoing the dress. Her dressmaker had always been on hand for assembly.

On the other side of the cubicle door, the water stopped running.

In a flash Madeleine, still clutching the dress around her, was out of the cubicle, a beaming smile at the ready.

'Oh, I wonder if you could just give me a hand to do this up?' she asked, placing herself between the swaying girl and the exit.

'No problem,' said the girl with a vacuous smile. 'My boyfriend was only ever interested in the zipper goin' down. I'm not being funny but my mam had to help me ger it on! Mine was short though, see, so I din need to undo it when I needed a pee… or anything else.' She giggled.

'Well, if you could just…' said Madeleine turning around. 'Thanks.'

She cupped the bodice tighter under her boobs and felt the girl's cool fingers touch her skin as she fought with the fabric.

'Ooha! No pants, you slapper! Fucking hell, go girl!' said the girl rather louder than Madeleine felt was strictly necessary.

'Er, yer,' Madeleine whispered, hoping the girl might follow suit. 'Can you just…' She wriggled to emphasise the urgency.

'Well, I would say keep your knickers on, but seein' as you're not wearing any,' shrieked the girl. Madeleine felt the girl's hand grab the zipper. 'Sorry, was that you bum? Don't want you thinkin' I'm gay or nothin'!'

As the girl got more enthusiastic her Welshness got louder.

'No, no, it's fine but please, could you just do it up,' hissed Madeleine.

'OK,' said the girl brightly and Madeleine felt the warm fabric once again envelop her like a cocoon – just before it fell away again.

'Oops,' said a suddenly quiet voice. The girl reappeared at Madeleine's side. She was staring cross-eyed at the now detached zipper clutched in her chubby, pale fingers.

Madeleine's throat suddenly constricted. The girl gave a coy smile.

'I think I pulled too 'ard,' she said quietly. 'Sorry.'

'Will it go back on?' asked Madeleine, knowing the answer.

'Oh, no!' shrieked the girl. 'Another bit flew over there somewhere.' Madeleine didn't look.

'D'you want me to go get your 'usband or anythin'?' the girl offered.

Still clutching the bodice Madeleine said, 'Er, um, yes… er, I think that might be a good idea. Tell him to bring his jacket.'

Brightening at this plan, the girl listened obediently while Madeleine gave her a meticulous description of where Hayden was sitting and what he was wearing. She even remembered the colour of his hair – although grey would have been a fairly safe bet even if she hadn't.

'If you can't find him, ask the waiter to take you to the man drinking the Glenfiddich and spring water,' whispered Madeleine as the girl exited through the cloakroom door.

Silence reigned. Madeleine stood alone, clutching the bodice around her chest, her gaze now avoiding the mirror she had only minutes before admired. A sudden horrific thought that Sting and his wife may have now arrived did nothing to help the situation. Would she just have time to whip upstairs and change? There was a pair of velvet trousers and a Jacques Vert top in her case, yes, that would have to do – God, that stupid girl!

A gentle knock on the door preceded the sound of a disembodied whisper. 'Maddy, Madeleine. Are you in there?'

'Hayden, is that you?' Madeleine hissed back. 'Of course I'm bloody well in here!'

The door opened a crack and then swished wide.

'My God, Maddy, you look magnificent!'

Behind Hayden the door closed once again and it was only then that Madeleine spotted a sister mirror at the opposite end of the cloakroom. Between the two ends of the room the reflection of Madeleine's naked bottom bounced back and for, exposed to infinity… and beyond.

'Just give me your jacket,' she hissed. 'Has Sting arrived yet?'

'No,' said Hayden, struggling to concentrate. 'I, er, I've just had a message. They, uh, had to cancel… Trudie's pu– God, I–'

'Oh, great! I go to all this trouble and they let us down. What about Sting, couldn't he come on his own?'

'Fuck Sting!' said Hayden. 'He can go to hell! Madeleine Edwards, get up to our room now.'

With his jacket wrapped haphazardly around Madeleine's shoulders, Hayden escorted her to the lift. He noted on the way that the makeshift cloak wasn't quite long enough to cover that wonderful bottom and toyed with mentioning it… but well, there wasn't anything he could do about it, so he didn't.

The lift doors finally closed. Hayden slipped his arm under the hem of the jacket and caressed Madeleine's warm back with the flat of his hand before letting the tip of his finger drift down between her buttocks.

'So does this mean I'm forgiven for the overspend?' said Madeleine softly.

'What overspend?' whispered Hayden.

Thursday 12th June, 11.30a.m.

Madeleine scraped her *Blush Pink* nails up and down her ankle and made another note in her diary. With the garden party now less than two weeks away the pressure was starting to mount; the weather didn't look good, she'd had to change the caterers at the last minute after a row over blinis that got completely out of hand and, while she and Hayden had been in Málaga, Madeleine had been bitten by something that buzzed. Five days after the attack, what had started as a tiny lump was now the size of her thumbnail and was driving her mad.

On the far side of the wine bar, Nia emerged from the Ladies looking relieved. She stopped at the counter.

'Coffee, Maddy? Latte?'

Lounging in one of the brand new, cool leather sofas (one of many little changes Travis, now the proud new owner of Horton's, had recently made) Madeleine nodded before returning to her diary. The notes pages at the back were filling nicely; lists of guests sat next to lists of potential donors (and estimated donation amounts) that were interspersed with to-do lists and seemingly endless lists of suppliers.

'I bumped into Paolo last week,' said Nia, moving the umbrella and raincoat she had hastily dumped on her arrival before heading for the loo. 'He's just got a place in the chorus for Tosca – very pleased! Oh, and he's met someone!'

'Really,' said Madeleine, frowning and crossing through a supplier's name with her newly purchased Mont Blanc pen. 'Well, I would say fab, but you know Paolo; more rides than the harbour bike hire service but none of them stay around more than ten minutes.'

Nia laughed.

'That's a bit mean, even for you!' she said. 'No, honestly, this time, I think it might just last a bit longer… *and* he assures me, they haven't done the *deed* yet!' She scribed inverted commas in the air with her fingers to stress the word.

'He's lying,' sniffed Madeleine. 'I know Paolo. A sucker for a nice arse! D'you know where I can get peonies?'

'Peonies?' echoed Nia.

'Yes.' Madeleine tapped her leg with her pen before using it to scratch her ankle. 'I want the old fashioned, pompom style, you know. Pinky-white with huge heads. They'll look fab against the new black and red logo – especially the crockery.'

'Y'know, I still can't believe that you got that lot past Hayden,' said Nia, her expression now a mix of envy and admiration. 'A little bird hinted at your budget-busting order. God, Maddy, just how much did you spend? And more to the point, how did you get Hayden to agree?'

Madeleine made another note.

'Oh, he was fine. Once I'd laid out my marketing strategy he could see the cost versus benefits. Do you think I'd get them locally or should I order them? I found a company in Hereford but they'd have to ship in the colour I want from New Zealand.'

Nia laughed out loud.

'Maddy, are you mad? I really don't think shipping peonies from New Zealand is a good idea for a charity event! OK, you've just about managed to justify the costs so far but believe me, if you go laying on a lavish do people will start to wonder where their donations are really going.'

'Yes, but–' Madeleine started, giving her ankle an aggressive scratch.

'Look, Maddy, I know you want to do a good job and impress your man but quite honestly, *I'd* certainly be a bit wary of asking people for money and I can bet Ros would positively refuse. No, if you want our help I think it's time to stop spending and start talking tactics so we can make the most of the day.'

The coffees arrived. Madeleine threw her pen and diary onto the table and sat back into the sofa, arms folded and legs firmly crossed. Nia spotted her ankle.

'My God, Maddy. What happened there?'

Madeleine rubbed the bright red wheal just above her ankle bone.

'Oh, something got me when we were away. It'll be fine.'

'So, did you find anything you liked?'

'Nah,' answered Madeleine, wrinkling her nose. 'One was too small; one had no pool, for God's sake! Can't image what Hayden was thinking! The one that Hayden liked was OK but it was miles from the beach. The last one we were due to see on Monday before we left had been sold that morning – shame, I liked the look of it, too.'

'Oh, *quel dommage*. So what are you going to do?'

A clatter from the doorway interrupted Madeleine's answer.

'Nia, Nia! Oh, have you seen *The Guardian*? Look, look.' Ros advanced at speed. Water dripping everywhere, she wrestled with a folding umbrella that in her rush she had obviously forgotten to close before entering the building. In the hand unencumbered by said umbrella Ros was clutching a damp newspaper.

It was only when the brolly was finally under control that Ros slid both coffees to one side, laid the newspaper on the table and flicked through the pages to the centre spread.

It took Madeleine and Nia a few seconds but Nia suddenly said, 'Oh, it's me! And Sting!'

'What! Where?' demanded Madeleine.

Ros pointed to a tiny photograph among a montage of six others featuring Sting through the years since The Police up to the present day. Madeleine followed Ros's pointing finger; it was true. There was Nia, standing right next to Sting. She was beaming right into the camera; Sting was looking the other way.

Nia roared with laughter.

'Oh, that is brilliant! I wondered if that photographer had got me in the frame!'

'Yes,' Ros agreed. 'And if you look closely, here use this.' She produced a magnifying glass from her handbag. 'I'm there too – look, that's my shoulder!'

'What? So you spoke to Sting?' Madeleine bristled. Nia was definitely there in the photograph with the former lead singer of one of the most famous and influential bands to come out of the eighties; although Madeleine was yet to be convinced about Ros's claimed presence.

'Gosh no!' laughed Nia. 'Unlike you actually dining with Mr Sumner – AKA Sting.' Madeleine said nothing. Nia continued. 'I just bought one of his books, see, in my hands, there – he'd just signed it and suddenly there were cameras everywhere. I couldn't see how to get out so I just looked into one of the lenses and smiled. That's his wife, there, too. Apparently she'd just agreed some new book deal. It was all supposed to have been a secret until after Book Plus but as usual somebody blabbed. She was furious actually but you can't tell from the picture, can you? And look at that one, when Sting had hair! God, some of these pictures make me feel really old!'

Madeleine studied the photograph of Nia and Sting.

'God, Nia, was that dress a wise choice?' she asked, magnifying glass in hand.

'Oh,' said Ros brightly. 'That reminds me – I bought a new outfit for the garden party.'

'Yes,' said Nia, looking slightly envious. 'Work might be picking up but not fast enough. I could have spent a fortune. Mind you, Ros, that suit is lovely.'

Madeleine raked her ankle with renewed vigour.

'Well, I'm sorry, Ros, but you'll just have to save it for some other time. I've already ordered T-shirts for you both. Black trousers'll be fine; you have both got those, I trust?'

'Oh, but I–' Ros started, but Madeleine held up her hand.

'I'm sorry, Ros, but I've put a hundred and ten percent into this new brand design for Cornerstone. We need to look the part. I'm going to be asking my guests for money and I intend to make sure they give more than a grubby little tenner!'

'So what are we going to be doing?' asked Ros, somewhat crestfallen. 'Are you sure I can't wear my new suit?'

'Absolutely!' said Madeleine. She grabbed up her diary and flicked through her many lists. 'Right, let's see… ah, yes. Nia, you'll be directing the guests through to the garden on arrival. I've ordered pre-mixed Buck's Fizz – no one'll notice as long as you keep the bottles in the kitchen – you'll be offering people a glass as they come through… aaannnd…' She ran her pen down a list of about ten names. Ros was the final entry. 'Ah… Ros… you'll be taking any coats and if it does rain – please God, no – I've ordered some branded golf umbrellas for you to give out. Nia.' She glanced at Nia's umbrella propped against the seat. 'Oh good, you've got a brolly you can bring.'

'And will I need to count them back in?' asked Ros, peering over her still rain-dotted glasses.

Madeleine laughed.

'Gosh no! But a little joke about them being freebies subject to the size of the donation might not go amiss. Oh, that reminds me, I haven't forgotten about that money Hayden owes you for those books.' Her eyes flicked to the clock above the bar, its huge mock-antique face clearly visible to the aging eye from even this distance. 'Oh, bollocks, is that the time? Look, I've got to go. I'm learning Spanish – Sebastian – very handsome; private of course. He's marvellous. I had my first lesson Tuesday. Well, thought I'd better make the effort as we're going to be spending quite a lot of time in Spain once we've found the right place.'

As she talked she gathered up her diary, pen and handbag.

'Right, if you have any questions give me a buzz or text… actually text, I'll be too busy to take calls unless they're important. Over the next week or so I'll be answering all my texts in the evening. Probably best if you both come over to Landsmere next week. I'll text. Oh, nearly forgot. I'll need you there at seven-thirty a.m. on the day. Gotta go, *buenos aries*, as they say!'

Madeleine bundled out. Ros, steam almost coming from her ears, opened her mouth. But Nia grinned.

'It's one day, Ros. And we did say we'd help.' Then her eyes flashed mischievously to the clock. 'Do'y think it's too early for a glass?'

Sunday 15th June 8.35p.m.

Saffy settled onto the ancient wooden bench. She could feel the slats on her back still warm from the evening sun. Far out at sea a boat, fishing, she presumed, bobbed through the waves heading back towards the little harbour far below where she sat. She loved this time of year at Landsmere – and especially this time of day, when the heat had gone out of the sun but everything around still carried its legacy of warmth long into the evening.

Above her, through an open window of what had now become Ben's bedroom, she could hear her son's voice; he was talking to his teddy. She smiled. It was something he had only recently started to do and from some of the conversations she had overheard, Ben and his teddy, Madagascar, were definitely the very best of friends. At the moment Ben was recounting one of the stories he had heard at Book Plus; the one about the rabbit who liked toffee but didn't like carrots. She had heard him tell the tale over and over, changing crucial elements each time – he had even subjected "Aunty Madadalain" to a particularly detailed and somewhat lengthy version which she had at least had the good grace to sit through, even if she had been surreptitiously texting the whole time.

As Saffy sat enjoying the sound of her son's animated, albeit one-sided, conversation drift across the dahlias, Hayden appeared through the French windows from the lounge, a glass of something white in each hand.

'Thought you might like to join me?' he said, handing her one of the misted goblets.

'Mmm, yes. Thanks, Dad.' She looked past her father. 'No Madeleine?'

'No,' answered Hayden. 'Well, she's around, but still up to her arms in black and red. I've left her in the study, working through her lists. We're on to the moving of the piano now. I'm sure I've got the Steinway guy's number somewhere but for the life of me I can't put my hands on it. Maddy wants to sort it out tomorrow morning. My only worry is rain… But I'm sure she's got that on one of her lists, too.'

Saffy sipped the delicious, ice cold offering. 'Pinot grigio?'

'Is there any other white?' Hayden asked over his glasses. He took a sip of his own drink and sat silent for a moment. Then he grinned. 'So the rabbit's made friends with a tiger called Mrs Boswoof, unless my hearing is deceiving me.'

'So it would seem,' said Saffy with a light laugh. 'Mind, when he was telling Madeleine the story yesterday, it was a water buffalo called Mabby and all of her sparkly teeth fell out because she ate too much toffee. Fortunately for Ben, Madeleine wasn't really listening.'

'A water buffalo!' said Hayden quietly. 'Where did he get that from?'

Above them, the tiger was explaining to the rabbit that he should eat carrots, not toffee, so that his teeth would always be nice and sharp.

'Oh, you know, one of those animal programmes he likes,' answered Saffy. 'The Longleat one, most likely, it's his favourite.' She paused and then added, 'Mind you, he was watching a wildlife programme in the week about cheetahs. There was a water buffalo in that, although, it didn't end well for the poor thing.'

'Oh dear,' said Hayden. 'Maybe we shouldn't try to read too much into that one then.'

They were both quiet again for quite a while before Saffy realised that Ben was no longer talking.

'Thank goodness,' she said, taking another glug of wine. 'He was exhausted. It's funny how they don't give up, isn't it? God, I'm asleep before my head hits the pillow these days!'

Hayden gave a smiling shrug.

'Little minds, I guess. It's all just too interesting and they don't want to miss a moment. He was very good in the pool today. Can't get him to kick his legs though, not even with a float; his doggy paddle is actually quite efficient though.'

'Yes. Thanks for taking him, Dad,' said Saffy. A shadow of sadness crossed her face. 'That was Al's project. To teach Ben to swim properly.'

Hayden stayed quiet as if expecting her to say more but she didn't.

'Have you heard from him... since you told him about Rockmoore?' he asked eventually.

'An email. He's not happy. I think it's finally sinking in that we're not going back.' She gave a sad sigh.

Hayden put his arm around her shoulders and drew her closer.

'Well, I suppose sending Ben to school over here is a bit of a marker in the sand... So you are going to stay then?'

Saffy nodded.

'If you'll have us. I'm still not convinced Madeleine's as keen as you, Dad. But, yes, I'd like that. And I'm pretty sure Ben's stories would take a turn for the murderous if I told him anything else.'

'Doesn't he miss his Dad?' Hayden asked.

Saffy took a deep, shaky breath before she answered.

'Oh, I think he does but he doesn't say much. He certainly wants to know his Daddy's OK. But he seems quite happy to be told that Daddy's still working in Hong Kong. To be honest, Dad, after the fight... Well, I think Ben was frightened and... well, yesterday I told him that Al might come and visit him later in the year and...' Saffy swallowed hard. Hayden felt his polo shirt suddenly wet and realised his daughter was crying. She continued, her voice thick. 'Well, Ben got really upset and asked me if Al was going to hit me again if he came to stay.'

It was Hayden's turn to swallow back his tears. Every time he looked at Saffy's beautiful face he had to force himself not to look at the scar above her right eye; now, hearing that his grandson was frightened of his father was almost too much for Hayden to bear.

For a long time they sat without saying anything, watching the sun drift towards the horizon.

Wednesday, 18th June 4.05p.m.

'…coming Friday,' said Madeleine. She rubbed her ankle and glared accusingly at the rain now pounding on the kitchen window. 'God, I'm praying that forecast is right.'

At the breakfast bar Ros stirred a spoonful of sugar into her tea and slid the sugar bowl towards Nia.

'So what will you do if it is raining?' Ros asked Madeleine. 'Where will Emma sing then?'

Madeleine dismissed this shaft of doubt with a shake of her head.

'Ros, that just isn't the attitude!' She reached for a chocolate finger and then put it back on the plate. 'It is *not* going to rain; they *are* coming to put the marquee up tomorrow, the Steinway *will* be moved in there as late on Friday as we dare leave it *and* the two hundred people I have invited will come, they will eat the bloody canapés that I feel I've made myself they've been such a nightmare, and Cornerstone's new brand image *will* be an absolutely fabulous success.'

'*And*,' said Nia pointedly, 'we'll raise lots of lovely money for said charity that will go a long way to helping improve the currently woeful literacy standards in this country – well, the county anyway. By the way, Maddy, did you have any luck with the Children's Laureate for Literature?'

Madeleine gave a derisory snort.

'No! Another engagement – apparently.'

'Oh, that's such a shame. She could have done a reading,' lamented Ros. 'How about *The Sea, The Sea* by Iris Murdoch? So fitting with that view, don't you think?'

Madeleine perked up.

'Oh! I'll invite her. I'll Google her later and give her publisher a call.'

'Well that would certainly draw a crowd,' said Nia.

'Oh, why?' Madeleine asked, looking from Nia to Ros while Nia's irony sped over her head.

'She's dead,' said Nia. 'Has been for some time. And things weren't that great before she went.'

'Well as it's a children's literacy charity,' said Ros pointedly. 'Don't you think it would be nice to have a child, or even *some* children, doing a couple of readings?'

'Yes,' said Nia. 'Kids are always great as money raisers, too.'

Madeleine's face said it all but just in case they hadn't got the message she added, 'I am not going to all this trouble to have jelly and blancmange smeared over the furniture!'

Saturday, 22nd June 3.10p.m

Nia sipped at a glass of Buck's Fizz. It was slightly warm but she didn't care. She had just spent the last hour standing in twenty-five degrees of unrelenting sunshine (without the offer of even a smear of sun-screen) directing traffic, apologising for the potholes and smiling as if her life depended on it. Hayden's kitchen, by contrast, was an oasis of cool.

In fairness, Nia had to commend Madeleine on the quality of the guest list – the suspected weight of the wallets now sipping sweet, warm Buck's Fizz on the west lawn was something to behold; although Nia was in no doubt that the arrival of the more decorated guests would have had more to do with Hayden and, of course, Emma Jenkins (there were whispers of a gong in the next Honours List). Emma had also been very sporting about the extra, *extra* large team T-shirts, insisting on donning one despite Madeleine's protestations (although, by contrast, Madeleine had been most insistent that Nia and Ros wore theirs).

Now, standing in the kitchen, Nia wafted her own expansive T-shirt in an attempt to cool her clammy midriff, and topped up her glass.

Ros, also looking frazzled, wandered in.

'Oh, wonderful – cool!' She waved a weary hand towards the half-empty bottle on the breakfast bar. 'Glass, me.'

'Not much call for brollies then,' Nia grinned, and filled the nearest glass to almost to the brim.

'Honestly, I swear, if one more person calls me Mary *Fucking* Poppins…' she took a grateful swig but wrinkled her nose. 'Ewe, that's a bit sweet.'

'It's better cold. I put a load of bottles in the freezer after I'd tasted it and I've sent Brian out for more ice. Thankfully so far no one's said anything,' confessed Nia. 'Did you notice Madeleine's Beetle is still out there? What a waste!'

'Wasn't she selling it? Gosh, that was ages ago,' said Ros. She brightened. 'Why don't you buy it? Ivy told me about your unfortunate breakdown at Waitrose last week.'

'Yes,' said Nia darkly. 'The alternator this time; it's just one thing after another now. I suppose I have had it for nearly ten years but at least it's paid for… I certainly couldn't even consider a car loan at the moment. The bank would laugh. How're the caterers doing out there?' she asked, changing the subject with a nod in the direction of the garden.

'Well, I can see that the marquee was a good idea based on the weather we've had recently, but those poor people must be melting in there today,' said Ros. 'And Madeleine won't let them open the back – apparently she told them she doesn't want people to be distracted by the view when she gives her talk. Have you seen her, by the way?'

As if on cue Madeleine swept in, wiping beads of sweat from her forehead with the back of her hand.

'What happened to *your* T-shirt?' asked Nia. Madeleine's jeans and the extra, extra-large had been replaced by a dress; lace with a flared handkerchief hem now fell in elegant drapes to her ankles.

'Just changed! Can't seem to get cool… and anyway, now everyone's here I've got to look the part.' She performed a slightly unsteady twirl. 'Ralph Lauren, Battenberg lace.'

'You OK?' asked Nia with a sudden look of concern.

'God, yes. Fab!' insisted Madeleine, her eyes overly bright. The beads of sweat had returned.

'Well, it certainly seems to be going well so far,' said Ros brightly. 'Have you had a look at the gift aid list? Some of the sums are amazing and Emma hasn't even sung yet! Have you seen her with that bucket? And she's still wearing that God-awful T-shirt!'

Madeleine didn't answer. She was leaning on the breakfast bar nursing her ankle.

'That thing still bothering you?' asked Nia.

'Oh, what's that?' asked Ros. 'Gosh, you are looking a bit pale Madeleine. Are you alright?'

'No… I mean yes, I'm fine. It's just this bite thing. I'll be fine. Plastered it in antihistamine just now.' She lifted one of the lace folds to reveal a very swollen and exceptionally red ankle.

'Shit, Maddy!' Nia's face filled with genuinely shock. 'That looks far worse than it did last week!'

'Have you seen anyone about it?' added Ros. 'What about Hayden? Has he seen it?'

Madeleine dropped the lace irritably.

'No, when have I had time? Honestly, for God's sake, stop fussing. If it's still bad Monday, I'll do something about it but right now I've got a garden party to host.'

And with that, she marched back out into the heat.

Saturday, 22nd June 3.30p.m.

The final notes of Emma's aria rang out over the garden, soothing the sea to a mill pond (the caterers had finally defied instructions and opened the back end of the marquee. A delicious breeze now flowed through the canvas corridor and the view behind was indeed breath-taking). Making ready to applaud, Ros set her plate on the grass at her feet while goose-bumps tingled down her neck; she might never forgive Madeleine for the raven-black, tent-like T-shirt but Ros was forced to admit that the girl did know how to put on a good do – and the signs so far were that this was going to be a corker.

As the applause peeled away, Madeleine, looking coy and extremely pale, took centre stage. Standing a little way off in the shade of an ancient willow, Ros could see Hayden standing with Jackson Tranter. Both were beaming.

Madeleine waited for quiet; white-knuckled hands clasped at her waist. Then she spoke.

'Well, I think I can say, on behalf of everyone here, Emma, that that was truly fabulous and such a fitting start to what I hope... er... what I hope will... um...' Ros, being nearest spotted a bead of sweat trickle down Madeleine's temple. 'I... we... welcome...' Madeleine's voice faded. The baby grand broke her fall as her knees buckled and very gracefully, Ros noted, Madeleine slid to the floor.

Sunday, 23rd June. 10.15a.m.

The sound of disembodied voices drifted into Madeleine's consciousness but she didn't open her eyes. It wasn't that she couldn't, she just didn't really want to. She was aware of sheets pinning her down, too... and a bustle that suggested she was not in that familiar bed at Landsmere in which she had spent many hours working to secure her future as Lady of the House.

Brisk footsteps approached.

'Hello, Hayden,' whispered Ros's voice. 'How is she today? Has she opened her eyes yet?'

'Not yet. But she's much better,' answered Hayden's voice, equally hushed. 'They took the drip out about an hour ago and her blood pressure has stabilized. God, she gave me such a fright. Why on earth didn't she mention that bite?'

'No idea,' said Ros. 'Do you think she was hoping it would get better on its own? Have they said how long she'll be in?'

'Well, I'm hoping I can take her home today, later on, the nurse said. Going to be on penicillin for a week or so, but at least the leg's safe.'

Madeleine's heart jumped. She scrunched her toes – definitely two legs.

'Oh, she's stirring,' said Ros. 'Has she woken up at all today? Do you think she'll remember what happened?'

'Don't know,' answered Hayden. 'She hasn't really moved at all until just then. She really was very distressed. They had to sedate her in the end. Poor thing. Gave her enough sedatives to knock out a water buffalo!'

'Have you seen Nia this morning?' said Ros, either missing or choosing not to pick up on the water buffalo reference. 'Has she phoned?'

'No. God, I hope she's OK. She was brilliant, wasn't she?' Hayden really did sound impressed. 'The way she took charge.'

'Yes,' agreed Ros. 'Even after Madeline gave her that black eye. I've never seen anyone delirious like that before.'

'Neither have I,' said Hayden, his voice grave. 'I think it was the shock of that ice. Not that I think Nia did the wrong thing, of course. In fact the nurse said Nia did exactly the right thing; Maddy's temperature was over a hundred and four when they got her in here!'

'My God!' exclaimed Ros. 'All caused by a tiny insect bite!'

Another set of footsteps tapped closer.

'Nia, hello! We were just talking about you,' said Hayden, obviously getting to his feet. Madeleine could sense kisses on cheeks. 'How's that eye?'

'Gosh, Nia, does that hurt?' asked Ros, her voice positively impressed. 'Have you got plenty of steak?'

'Here, have my seat,' said Hayden. 'Never enough chairs in NHS hospitals.'

The legs of a heavy seat scrapped across lino.

'Thanks, Hayden,' whispered Nia. 'I'm fine, looks worse than it is. How's the patient? A bit calmer now at least.'

'Sedated – heavily,' repeated Hayden.

'Well, I'm not really surprised,' said Nia, still in a hushed voice. 'She was wound up enough without being poisoned by that infected bite. *Travailler trop dur, je pense.*'

'Yes, I think so,' said Hayden, suddenly sounding upset. 'But she was so happy, you know, being busy. I just left her to it; could kick myself now. I should have at least noticed her ankle.' (Eyes still closed, Madeleine knew Hayden had had little hope of noticing the bite – he only ever got close up and personal with her legs when they were clamped around his waist... for a fleeting moment as she pictured the scene, she wondered if now was the time to get her varicose veins sorted out).

'Well, the good news,' said Nia, suddenly considerably more up-beat, 'is that the garden party raised twenty-eight thousand and fifty-seven pounds!'

'Gosh!' said Ros.

'Yes, and there's still a lot more in change and notes from the buckets. Emma was such a star, she kept that T-shirt on 'til the bitter end and went around again with her bucket once the ambulance had gone, but sorry, Hayden,' said Nia, suddenly sounding apologetic. 'I just didn't have time to count it this morning. My brother called. Mum's not well again.'

'Oh, I'm so sorry to hear that, Nia,' said Hayden. 'I didn't know she was poorly. Madeleine hasn't said anything. But that really is a fantastic sum. Thank you.'

'Well, I think Madeleine really should get the credit,' said Nia.

'Yes, she certainly did very well to get it all organised,' agreed Hayden. 'But you reading the Iris Murdoch piece was a triumph. I must get the book for Maddy, for the library. Such a great distraction when the ambulance arrived. And those statistics – I think they shocked a lot of people. Don't think Maddy had them in her speech... unless she changed it last night? Honestly, Nia, you stepping into the brink like that made a significant impact on the amount of donations. Not to mention your efforts, Ros, and of course Emma's. When Madeleine does wake up I'm sure she'll be absolutely delighted!'

'It's fine, Hayden. I like to have a back-up plan, you know, just in case,' said Nia. 'And we all really enjoyed it, didn't we, Ros? In fact we're meeting Emma for a drink later.'

In the bed, Madeleine decided it was time to wake up. She opened her eyes, sat up… and vomited over Nia's feet.

Thursday, 26th June 7a.m.

Madeleine lay on her back and stared up at the ceiling, glad to be back at Landsmere Grange. The bedroom was already filled with bright warmth and a light breeze wafted in through the open balcony door, billowing the draped curtains in its path. It was one of Hayden's little summer-morning rituals: get up at six-thirty a.m, go down to let Morris out for a wee, then return to the bedroom. During the week, he would open the balcony door on his way to the shower; on the weekend, he would open it on his way back to bed.

From between the crisp cotton sheets, Madeleine could hear Hayden's soft humming interspersed with the sound of cascading water from the shower.

She had been discharged from the hospital late Sunday afternoon under the strict instructions that she was to rest and definitely not to have a bath until the penicillin had started to kick in. They hadn't mentioned anything about sex though, and finally, the previous night, surveying her lower legs bouncing above Hayden's naked shoulders, Madeleine had noticed that her ankles were at last far closer to matching in girth than they had been for some days. Pleased, and not a little relieved, she resolved to immerse herself in the jacuzzi in the morning, as soon as Hayden was out of the way. A soft thud indicated that Hayden had turned off the water in the shower.

'I'm going to take Ben swimming again after the meeting,' he called from the bathroom. 'You don't mind, do you, darling?'

While Madeleine was extremely piqued that Saffy and Ben appeared to have taken up permanent residence at Landsmere, she had been so busy with the re-brand that any chance to quiz Hayden about when they might be departing had been missed; and, of course, since Sunday, with her blasted ankle–

'Oh, I forgot to say,' Hayden continued from the en suite. 'Nia rang yesterday while you were having your nap. Wants to know if you're up for a glass of wine this evening. I got the impression Ros and Ivy'll be there, too.'

Madeleine was still smarting from the humiliation of passing out in front of the great and the good of Western Vale; let alone Nia then taking over and coaxing almost thirty thousand pounds out of said great and good (Madeleine remained in denial about blacking anyone's eye).

'Oh, that's a shame, I've still got two days left on my tablets,' she said, her eyes following a cobweb that extended from the end of the curtain rail to the corner of the most recent portrait of her, this time, clad in the evening gown she had worn, or rather almost worn, at The Mount. Brushing aside the couture catastrophe, she made a mental note to speak to Mrs B about dusting *above* eye level.

'It's OK,' said Hayden cheerfully and appeared from the bathroom wearing the silk robe Madeleine had chosen for him in Paris. 'I checked those tablets. You're fine, just don't go too wild.'

'Oh, right, I'll call her later.' She rolled over onto her side, allowing the sheet to slide away exposing her breasts. 'So has Saffy made any mention of when she and Ben might move out?'

Hayden glanced at her nipples; Madeleine could see he was enjoying the view.

'Well, I… no, not yet.' He turned away and headed into the walk-in wardrobe. 'It's just that they've been through a lot… and Ben is settling in so well. Have to admit, I like having them around.'

Hayden reappeared holding up a pair of linen trousers and a short-sleeved shirt. Madeleine draped her forearm across her forehead.

'Oh, I know. And it's fab having them here.' She gave him a beguiling smile. 'It's just that I thought, well, you know.' She drew the sheet back with her other arm. Naked other than the bandage around her ankle, she crooked her finger and purred, 'If Saffy is anything like me, when she does find a wonderful man, she'll want to make the most of him without the risk of interruption.'

Hayden draped the clothes over the back of a chair and stood at the end of the bed. Letting the silk robe slip to the floor, he put one knee on the edge of the mattress and gently rolled Madeleine onto her stomach. She giggled softly and lifted her bottom.

'You know, you're going to make me late,' said Hayden.

'I don't care,' whispered Madeleine.

Thursday, 26th June 6.30p.m.

Ros raised her glass.

'Well, congratulations, Nia, on your new client; although, I'd love to be a fly on the wall when Hayden tells Maddy!'

'I thought she'd retired,' said Ivy, knocking back an orange juice. 'I was going to ask if she wanted to join the gym to keep me company. God, this new healthy lifestyle is so damn boring!'

'I think she wants to retire,' said Nia, her expression

positively sympathetic – an odd look when you're sporting a *very* black eye. 'And she certainly could, if she and Hayden stay together. Trouble is, I think she gets bored.'

'So why didn't Hayden just get Cornerstone to appoint her then?' asked Ros. 'Didn't they like the new logo?'

'Gosh, no, it's nothing like that,' Nia insisted. 'No, they're delighted. No, apparently Hayden doesn't want Maddy to overdo it. I think he got a bit of a shock on Saturday – after all, she really was quite ill. And reading between the lines I don't think the board were comfortable with such a close,' she held up her fingers to make her trade mark inverted commas, '*informal* link between the two of them.'

'What do you mean by that?' asked Ros, looking appalled. 'Isn't that a bit old fashioned?'

'No, no, nothing like that either,' said Nia hastily. 'But Cornerstone's a very small charity, Ros. Can you imagine if the Chairman and the Director of Marketing and PR fell out because of a failed romantic attachment? A tad awkward, *je crois.*'

'Well, knowing Maddy, she'd have to get run over by a steamroller to allow that to happen!' said Ivy. 'No, that girl knows when she's on to a good thing.'

Nia continued.

'I think the main reason is that the board wanted to employ a sub-contractor under a formal contract. Much cleaner and cheaper for the charity. I've got a great track record and I can deliver through my own limited company. Keeps it all nice and neat. I think it just would've been too messy if they'd given it to Maddy.' She took off her jacket and sat back into the sofa. 'Hayden's going to talk to her this afternoon. She'll be fine.'

'Where is she, by the way?' asked Ivy, looking around as if expecting Madeleine to appear.

'At home, well, Landsmere,' corrected Nia. 'D'you know, she

still hasn't sold her place?'

'Or her car,' added Ros darkly. Madeleine still hadn't repaid her the two hundred and fifty pounds and it was starting to gall.

'She called to apologise,' said Nia. 'Said she thinks she's coming out in some sort of reaction to the tablets. Didn't go into detail but mentioned itching.'

'Oh, do you think the bite's flared up again?' asked Ros. 'Is her ankle still as swollen as it was?'

Ivy laughed out loud.

'Nah,' she guffawed. 'I know what it is. She's on penicillin, isn't she? Bet she's got thrush!'

'Oh, God, I hadn't thought of that,' said Nia. 'Poor thing.'

'Nonsense!' laughed Ros. 'Serves her right for making us wear those bloody T-shirts *and* for punching you in the face!'

Friday, 27th June, 8.50a.m.

'Right, Dad, are you sure you don't want to come with us?' asked Saffy, brushing Weetabix out of Ben's fringe.

'No, I'm fine. I've gotta go get cleaned up,' said Hayden, abandoning his mud-splattered wellies on the mat before hanging Morris's lead on the hook behind the door. He looked down at his grandson. 'And you, young man, are going to be far too busy making new friends to worry about Ba Ritten while you try out your new school, aren't you?'

'Yeth!' said Ben, nodding enthusiastically. 'And Mummy thed they've got lotth of toyz. I'm going to play wiv them all!'

'And you're going to meet Mrs O'Reilly, too, aren't you?' said Hayden, also nodding.

'Yeth,' said Ben. Then he turned to his mother. 'Who'th Mithus O'Reilly, I've forgotten again?'

'She's going to be your teacher when you go to Rockmoore School in September, Ben. She's very nice, isn't she, Ba Ritten?'

'Oh yes,' agreed Hayden and bent his knees so that he could look his grandson in the eye. 'And if *I* liked her, I'm quite sure you will, too.' Then, straightening up, he ruffled the little boy's hair affectionately. 'And as long as you're a good boy, I'm absolutely sure she'll like you.'

Madeleine appeared at the kitchen door.

'The estate agent's just called. Fab news – they've got a viewing booked for this afternoon. Obviously I don't need to be there. Can you ask Mrs B to pop over and whip round with the vacuum? She could wipe a duster over everything too, while she's there. I've got Spanish at eleven.'

'Oh,' said Hayden, looking surprised. 'Well, that's not really Mrs Bosworth's job, darling. She might have other plans for today – Friday's can be quite hectic for her. You know, with cooking for the weekend.'

'Oh, she can fit it in; it's such a tiny house. Anyway, she won't say no to the extra money. So, will you ask her, darling?' She gave him one of her promise-filled smiles and made to move back but stopped. 'Gosh, Saffy, you look quite smart! Not off viewing anywhere yourself, are you?'

Saffy hesitated for a nanosecond then said cheerfully, 'Ben and I are off to visit Ben's new school, aren't we, Ben? They've got an open day today for the little ones, you know, so it's not such a shock in September.'

'Oh, fab! I've heard lots of good things about Little Landscombe Primary,' Madeleine lied. 'I'm sure he'll be fine.'

'Oh! He's not–' Saffy began. But Hayden cut in.

'Oh, Saf, look, Brian's just arrived. Don't keep him waiting;

he's got to come back for me at ten.'

The Jaguar purred into view. Saffy threw Hayden a knowing look.

'Oh, OK. Come on then, Ben. Mustn't keep Miss O'Reilly waiting either. Give Ba Ritten a kiss.'

Ben rushed at his grandfather and hugged his knees. Hayden bent to kiss the boy's cheek.

'And Aunty Madeleine. Come on, quick, quick,' said Saffy, heading for the kitchen door that led out into the courtyard.

'Oh, don't mind me, Ben darling' said Madeleine, backing away from the advancing child. 'Just put my make-up on. Don't want anything smudged.'

Saffy put her hand on her father's shoulder and stretched up to kiss him.

'Good luck,' she whispered and pecked him lightly on the cheek. Then she grabbed Ben's hand. 'Oh, and don't forget I've got a driving lesson at four. You don't mind looking after Ben for an hour, d'you, Dad?'

Hayden shook his head.

'I'm looking forward to it,' he smiled.

And with that Saffy and Ben were gone.

Madeleine slid up onto a seat at the breakfast bar. Hayden reached for the half-full coffee pot.

'Latte?'

'Did she say O'Reilly?' said Madeleine, with a frown that suggested she was trying to remember something not really cared about. 'Don't remember any Irish names. They all seemed to be called Thomas… or Jones. Must be new. Oh, well, you know what these state schools are like; can't keep teachers for five minutes on the salaries they pay!' She took a sip of her coffee and added a splash more milk. 'Well? How did the Cornerstone meeting go yesterday? You were back late; did you go to the club? Sorry I wasn't awake when you got in; those tablets just knock me out.'

Hayden took a deep breath.

'Maddy, darling, I've got a couple of things to tell you.'

Friday, 27th June, 10.15a.m.

'You fucking pillock!' said Jackson, shaking his head. Speeding past an Eddie Stobart lorry, Brian manoeuvred the Jag off the slip road straight into the outside lane of the motorway.

'Thanks, Jack, I knew I'd be able to rely on your heartfelt support,' said Hayden, gazing up at the Stobart logo.

'Well, for fuck's sake, Hayden!' Jackson rubbed his hand down his leathery face. 'OK, so you told Madeleine that you're paying for your grandson to go to private school, your daughter's not moving out and *she* didn't get the marketing job at Cornerstone. A shit-load of bad news for one breakfast, I'll admit, and yep, I'd be pissed off with you, too. But you didn't have to ask her to fucking marry you! Jeez!'

Hayden shifted uncomfortably. He hadn't really planned to propose to Madeleine this morning... or at all, if he was honest. And she hadn't actually said yes. But she really had been very cross.

The news of Ben's new school had set the mood, which got a whole lot darker as Hayden had gone on to explain that Saffy and Ben would not be moving out of Landsmere any time soon. By the time Hayden got to the bit about Nia becoming Director of Marketing and PR for Cornerstone, he could practically hear ice crystallizing across the kitchen windows (he had failed to tell her about it the previous morning, deciding that after some of the best sex he'd had even with Madeleine, the Cornerstone appointment might not have been the most appropriate post-coital topic of conversation).

The worst bit had been Madeleine's silence.

With the calm of an assassin about to strike, she had sat at the breakfast bar flicking through a copy of *Harper's Bazaar* that had lain abandoned on the worktop for days. Hayden had sipped his coffee, trying not to feel intimidated but failing.

Then, like a cobra, she had struck.

'Ah!' With an unreadable smile, she had laid the magazine flat. 'I've just ordered something very similar.'

Her smile remained fixed as she tapped the page with a perfectly manicured *Midnight Blue* nail.

Staring out at Hayden, in high gloss, was a cleavage almost adorned in a black lace basque: some high-flying fashionista was experimenting with burlesque, according to the few words of the headline that Hayden managed to take in. He became aware that Madeleine was talking again.

'Although, y'know, I think I'll cancel it… not sure if a peephole style is really me anyway. Is your computer on?'

Sliding off the stool she sauntered towards the door. Hayden stared down at what there was of the black lace; the image of Madeleine's delightful breasts there for his pleasure among that whalebone (or whatever it was now – at that moment Hayden really didn't care) almost stopped his breath.

She was all, but not quite, out of the kitchen before he found his tongue.

'Er, no! Um, don't… don't cancel it.' He cleared his throat. It was suddenly quite hot in the kitchen. 'You'll look wonderful in it… good enough to… er, good enough to marry.'

Madeleine stopped but didn't turn back.

'Was that a proposal, Hayden Elliot?'

Hayden was still admiring the image in his mind of Madeleine in a peephole basque and not a lot else.

'Um, yer... I mean, yes. Yes, it was!'

'Hmm, I'll think about it,' said Madeleine, and she walked out of the room.

Friday, 27th June 5.25p.m.

'Married? Oh, Madeleine, how exciting! Congratulations,' said Nia, her eyes shining with genuine delight.

'Well, as I said, I haven't actually said yes... yet,' corrected Madeleine.

'Well you'll be a fucking idiot if you don't,' offered Ivy.

'Is it too early for champagne?' asked Nia.

Ivy's jaw set in defiance. 'God, no! Bollocks to my new regime. I'm having a glass and that's that!'

Right outside the bar, Madeleine's Audi was in its usual position – parked across the double yellow lines. A traffic warden was writing out a ticket – her second that week.

'Yes, I suppose there would be advantages,' she said with a vague glance out of the window. 'At least I'd have a bit more security... *and* I'd have a formal say in what goes on at Landsmere, at last.'

'Hmm, am I guessing that Saffy hasn't mentioned moving out then?' Nia asked her. Travis appeared. She ordered a bottle of Moët & Chandon and four glasses. 'Not sure where Ros is. I can't wait to see her face when you tell her that Hayden's just proposed.'

'Oh, I don't want to tell anyone just yet,' said Madeleine.

'After all, as I said, I haven't said yes… and I might yet say no.'

'And what exactly might sway you to decline one of the richest, most eligible men in the Western Vale, pray tell?' asked Ivy, her eyebrows almost reaching her hairline.

'Well, I think we might be having words about Saffy and Ben, for a start,' said Madeleine. 'I mean, Amrose Street still hasn't sold. They could move in there. It's certainly closer to the wonderful Rockmoore School for a start. And Saffy's going for her test next week so once she's driving she can start looking for a job. She's getting money from Alastair obviously but she can't live off her ex-husband and her father forever. Has she no self-respect?'

Ivy's eyebrows rose even higher. Travis approached the table with a laden tray.

'Ooh, champagne!' said Ros from the bar entrance. 'And what are we celebrating?'

'Nia's new job,' said Madeleine, quick as a flash. 'I felt very bad that I wasn't here the other night when she heard about Cornerstone. Thought we could celebrate now.' She raised her glass and handed another to Ros as she sat down. 'To Nia, and may your experiences with Cornerstone be good ones.'

Ivy and Ros echoed the toast. The faintly awkward silence that followed as they all sipped at their glasses was broken by Ros.

'So, Nia, when does the work start? How many days a week will it be?'

'Well, to start it's actually only five days a month,' said Nia with a grimace.

Madeleine looked aghast.

'Five days! The re-brand alone was practically a full-time job! Honestly, Nia, do you think they know what they're doing?'

'Actually it was my suggestion. Their budget isn't that great, you see,' said Nia carefully. She studied her glass, looking suddenly awkward. 'You know, after your… the new brand work, well, they haven't really got a lot of spare money. I've agreed to give them a bit of extra time pro bono if they need it, for now, in the hope that come the new financial year things moneywise might be easier. There's still bits and pieces coming in from other places, although Maylard's have gone very quiet for some reason.'

'Oh, that's such a shame! You must be really disappointed,' said Madeleine, looking anything but.

'So no new car just yet?' said Ros with a sympathetic pout.

'No, *malheureusement*,' said Nia. 'My old banger'll just have to keep going for a few months yet.'

'Now don't forget,' said Madeleine, giving Nia an odd, scrunchy nosed smile. 'My old Beetle is still sat outside at Landsmere. I could always hire it to you or do some kind of monthly payment thing if yours gives up the ghost.'

Saturday, 5th July 10.05a.m.

Ros peered into her fridge. Capacious it certainly was, if somewhat lacking in nutritional content. This was fine as far as Ros was concerned – more room for champagne! In one hand she held her phone to her ear. Nia had just mentioned Madeleine's wedding and then lied about when she'd found out to cover for Madeleine's omission the previous evening.

'Gosh, that was quick! But no date yet, I take it? D'you think Madeleine'll make him wait until he agrees that Saffy and Ben will move out?' she said, silently counting bottles of Moet & Chandon. 'Has she had any interest in her house yet?'

'No,' answered Nia. 'Those people put in a ridiculous offer – twenty thousand less than the asking. The cheek of some people!'

'Well, the market's so depressed now. Perhaps she should accept just to get rid of it. I would, wouldn't you?' As she talked, Ros took a punnet of strawberries from the top shelf of the fridge, threw an approving eye over the shining fruit and replaced it on a lower shelf. 'Oh, I've only got four bottles of champagne. D'you think I should get some more? Ivy's coming and I'm never quite sure which part of the wagon she's on.'

'Hmm, I know what you mean… Who's playing, by the way?'

'No idea of names but one of the women is a very young Australian girl apparently – it was on the news last night. Tomorrow, it's two Spanish chaps. Is Madeleine coming? Do you think she'd be prepared to add to the ambience by commentating in Spanish?' said Ros with an impish grin. She popped a strawberry into her mouth and pulled off the stalk before closing her lips.

'Sadly not,' said Nia, adopting a hint of melodrama as she continued. 'She's going to have a look at wedding dresses and then Hayden's meeting her to buy the ring!' She paused as if reflecting and added, 'She really is lucky, y'know. Hayden's such a sweetie. Hey, let's go out for some something to eat before the match?'

Ros swallowed her strawberry in a gulp.

'That would be lovely but… well, are you sure? Have Cornerstone paid you?'

Nia laughed.

'Well, yes actually. But thank you for your concern, Ros, it is appreciated. As it happens, Cavendish Major have also come up with three lovely jobs for me to do before Christmas, and John's paid up-front for one. So I'm sure I can run to a bite out – it's been ages anyway and I'm fed up of scrimping all the damn time.'

'Well in that case, let's try that new coffee shop on the high street,' suggested Ros. 'Martha's, isn't it? Will you let Ivy know? We could have brunch; I've heard they do an Eggs Benedict to die for. As you'll be going past M&S on the way, can you pick up another two bottles of bubbly? Nothing fancy. After a few Moets we won't notice the difference anyway! Although I insist on giving you the cash for those. Shall we say eleven-fifteen?'

Saturday, 5th July 5.10p.m.

The doorbell rang just as the umpire called, 'Game, set and match.' The exceptionally young Australian girl had just beaten the US Number One seed in three very convincing straight sets and it was fairly obvious that Ms Numero Uno was not happy.

Ros reached for her glass and tottered to the porch.

Through the obscured windows of the Georgian-style front door she could see the outline of a figure in a large hat. Ros pulled the door open.

From under a very wide-brimmed sun hat, Madeleine beamed. The contrast between the bright sunshine and the shade provided by the hat made the startlingly white of Madeleine's teeth something to behold.

'Buenos Aries, amigo!' She waved an envelope that looked suspiciously like flight tickets. 'Well, aren't you going to ask me in?'

Another glint caught Ros's eye.

'Oh, you've got a ring!' shrieked Ros, ignoring the envelope. 'Come in, come in.'

Madeleine positively danced into the room and spread the fingers of her left hand for Ivy, Nia and Ros to see. It was evident that keeping the news to as few people as possible was now a thing of the past.

Ros made a grab for Madeleine's hand to get a proper look. 'Oh, it's lovely! Is it white gold or platinum? How long did you take to choose it?'

'It's a heck of a lot smaller than I was expecting,' said Ivy, draining her glass. 'Did he give you a budget you had to stick to this time?'

'Gosh, no,' said Madeleine, glistening from all angles. 'I'm just not one for ostentation, as you know.' Ivy snorted and missed the glass she was hastily topping up. Madeleine ignored her and went on. 'We went to Haroldson's, predictably. But nothing really took my eye. I wanted something simple and unique. I mean, anyone can have a Cartier! I was actually about to give up when I spotted a wonderful little jewellery maker on Evelyn Street. Totally exclusive, one-off pieces – fab! She's new. Her range of rings wasn't huge but this one caught my eye. It's white gold; she's going to make me matching earrings for the wedding.'

'Does Hayden like it?' asked Ros.

'Of course! Anyway, it's up to me as I'm the one who has to wear it! Is that champers?'

Nia wrested the bottle from Ivy.

'I'll get another glass,' said Ros. 'We weren't expecting you until tomorrow. You are coming, aren't you? For the Men's Final? They're both Spanish, you know.'

'Fab, thanks, Nia. Cheers,' said Madeleine, taking the offered glass. 'Not sure yet, I might have another Spanish lesson.'

'On a Sunday! That's keen,' said Nia.

'Well, actually it could be to your advantage,' said Madeleine cryptically. She put her glass down on the mantelpiece. Ros frowned and moved it to a mat on the coffee table. 'I'm going to need extra practice because...' she beamed like an excited child, 'for my hen do Hayden has...' Pausing again for even more dramatic effect, she waved the envelope still clutched in her ringless hand but obviously not forgotten. '...bought me a return ticket for a long weekend in a gorgeous hotel in Málaga, *Las something-or-other...* he's booked a suite – sleeps four, for my hen do! Flying out on September fourth and coming back the following Wednesday... so if you want to join me, all you need to do is book the flight!'

Saturday, 5th July 6.50p.m.

Hayden studied the pack on the hall table for the fifth time since returning home. Addressed to Madeleine, it certainly looked large enough to contain a box that might contain underwear. It was light, too. Not that Hayden had much experience of ordering underwear but Carla had been a fan of Victoria's Secret (one of the few things that Hayden had liked about his ex-wife) and this package was tantalisingly similar; tastefully luxurious – even the black tulip logo in the bottom right hand corner hinted at some delicious hidden delight.

He held the package to his ear and gave it a gentle shake. Whatever was hiding inside rustled. He put it back on the hall table, sipped his scotch and sucked the fiery liquid over his tongue.

'Right, Dad, we're off,' said a voice behind him. He jumped, inhaled sharply and choked. 'Dad, are you OK?'

Saffy banged her father's back and offered a tissue hastily retrieved from her pocket. 'Here, it's only been used once... I think.'

'Are you awright, Ba Ritten?' said a little voice behind his leg.

Hayden coughed into the tissue and blew his nose.

'Thanks, love. Yes, Ben, I'm fine,' he said, eyes still watering. 'Gosh, you took me completely by surprise. I thought you'd gone.'

'No, Ben took ages in the bath. I decided to put him in his

177

PJ's so he'll settle down quicker when we get there. Although I'm still not sure this is such a good idea,' said Saffy with a frown.

'Well, it's not as if he's going for a sleepover on his own,' said Hayden, clearing his throat again.

'I know' said Saffy, with a pensive look. 'But Helen's little boy can be a bit of a handful sometimes and he's nearly two years older than Ben,'

'They'll be fine.' Hayden wiped his eyes and sniffed. 'Just relax and have a nice evening. You haven't had a proper night out with Helen for a very long time – or indeed anyone for that matter.'

'You're right, Dad, I know. And I've got Brian's number if there's a disaster. I just wish I hadn't failed that damn theory test.'

'Oh, it's not the end of the world. You'll be fine next time. And in the meantime you know Brian's available.'

'I know, Dad, and thanks. But I have to admit, it would be nice to be a bit more independent now, you know…'

'I do, love. When's the next date?'

'A week Tuesday,' replied Saffy with a grimace. 'But I'll fail again, I know it,'

'You will with that attitude! We could sit down next weekend and I'll test you, if you like?'

Saffy put an arm around his waist and squeezed gently. 'Thanks, Dad.'

'Right,' said Hayden. 'Now off you go or you'll be late… and try not to call Brian after eleven unless it really is a disaster. He's bringing Maddy home later so–.' The sound of tyres on the gravel outside stopped Hayden mid-sentence. 'Oh, that's him now. Looks like Maddy's home already.'

Hayden's heart rate kicked up slightly. The package on the table behind Saffy positively glowed with promise. He put his arm around his daughter's shoulder and gave her a gentle squeeze.

'Have a lovely time darling, and,' he said turning to Ben, 'You look after your mum for me, young man. And go to bed when she tells you. Best behaviour now and if a good report comes back I might just take you swimming tomorrow afternoon.'

Now anchored firmly by Saffy's outstretched hand, Ben shouted, 'Yeah!' and jumped up and down, Madagascar wedged under his free arm.

'Right, come on then. Helen'll be waiting... and Max!' said Saffy. The sound of the front door catching on the tiles announced Madeleine's entry into the house. Saffy pecked her father on the cheek and made for the gap before Madeleine could close the door. 'Bye, Dad. Hi, Maddy, have a lovely peace-filled evening. Bye.'

And with a skywards glance, she and Ben disappeared into the cooling twilight.

'Gosh, if I'd known it was that easy!' said Madeleine, almost in passing.

'They're off to Helen's for a sleepover,' said Hayden. He leant on the front door until it clicked shut then threw the deadlock.

'Both of them?'

'Yep. Hence Saffy's reference to a peace-filled evening. Drink?'

'Mmmm, any champagne? Just had a glass at Ros's. Another'd be fab.'

'I think there's one in the fridge... Oh, I nearly forgot,' Hayden lied. 'There's a parcel for you, there on the hall table.'

He nodded towards the package of promise.

Madeleine gave it a cursory glance.

'Oh, that. Fab. I'll have a look later. Right now my feet are killing me. Where's that champers?'

'So you know what it is then?' asked Hayden, unable to stop himself. The parcel had been thrust into his hand by a surly van driver earlier, just as Hayden was leaving to meet Madeleine in town. The uninitiated driver had fallen foul of the minefield of potholes that, linked together, formed the long perilous driveway from the main road. He had made it patently obvious that he wasn't impressed. But as the dust settled on the parched drive Hayden was already eagerly anticipating the hidden delights of the parcel he had been left holding. The image of the black lace basque in the magazine (*the Basque of Engagement*) had haunted him ever since his proposal; the word 'peephole' had certainly been a major influencing factor of during the purchase of the ring – the most expensive item of jewellery Hayden had ever bought – and had served Madeleine well in prompting Hayden's impulse purchase of her hen weekend in Málaga.

After the purchase of said ring, however, to Hayden's already simmering frustration, Madeleine had insisted on calling by Ros's house on the way home – to show off the ring, no doubt – leaving Hayden to return to Landsmere Grange alone.

On his solitary arrival he could have sworn he'd heard the package's mocking giggle and so, in an effort to distract himself while waiting for his future wife's return, Hayden had taken Morris for a long walk, had a shower and even clipped his nails (fingers *and* toes). Now, the scotch he was sipping was definitely refreshing the parts other drinks might not have reached quite so rapidly.

'Can I smell Christian Dior?' asked Madeleine. Hayden watched her run a finger over the package, unable to answer. She tapped it once, hard. Then, to his utter disappointment, she walked into the sitting room.

Hayden moved to follow.

'What about my drink?' Madeleine said, her bottom lip in a pout.

Temporarily defeated, Hayden retreated to the kitchen and popped the cork from a bottle of Dom Perignon. It had been chilling in the fridge since the garden party – Hayden's plan being a private toast to Madeleine once the guests had gone. But of course events had taken a different turn (and Hayden had momentarily toyed with offering the ice cold bottle to Nia, that evening, for her black eye).

There had been another opportunity to open it the day Madeleine had accepted Hayden's somewhat offbeat proposal, but the arrival of Brian and yet another meeting had put the mockers on that. So now, with the ring firmly planted on Madeleine's finger, Hayden was determined to get his own fingers on the rest of her before much more of the evening had passed, and Dom Perignon seemed an ideal apéritif.

Armed with two champagne flutes and the bottle, Hayden headed back through the hall. The package was sitting neglected where he had left it. Hayden's throat tightened, his thoughts consumed with the image of Madeleine in black lace – well, a little bit of Madeleine anyway.

He nudged the sitting room door open with his foot.

'As I'm going to Málaga I've booked some extra Spanish lessons – one tomorrow and another two next week,' said Madeleine. She was reclining in one of the armchairs next to the fireplace, barefoot now, and wiggling her toes in obvious relief. She reached for the offered champagne flute but Hayden raised it just out of her reach.

'Hmm, well with all these lessons and almost a whole week in Spain, what will you do if I forget what you look like and change my mind about the wedding?' His voice bore just the faintest hint of mischief.

A trickle of condensation ran down the side of Madeleine's glass, wetting his fingers on its journey to the floor. 'Oh, I'm sure you won't do that,' she said pulling his hand towards her mouth and slowly halting the drip with the tip of her tongue.

Hayden recognised this game and savoured every increased heartbeat. 'A confident Miss, aren't you?'

'Mmm,' nodded Madeleine, taking the glass.

'And so, Miss Edwards, how exactly *do* you intend to make sure that I don't forget you?' Hayden moved to the opposite armchair, sat back and crossed his legs (no mean feat as the tension wasn't the only thing rising in that room).

Madeleine stood but made no move towards the door as Hayden had anticipated – no – *hoped*! Instead she stood up, placed her glass on the mantelpiece and with her back to him slid her arms out of the linen jacket she had been wearing all day. Then she undid her linen trousers and let the satin lining take them effortlessly down over her hips and on to the floor.

'Panties just aren't your thing, are they?' observed Hayden. He sipped his scotch and drank in the view of Madeleine's naked milk-white bottom barely contained behind two thin black suspender straps.

'Overrated,' said Madeleine, still facing the fireplace.

'So what *is* in the parcel in the hall?' asked Hayden. Although part of him – a key part – really didn't give a shit right now.

Madeleine didn't answer immediately. She slowly undid the buttons of her blouse, slid the shirt back off her shoulders and turned as it too floated to the floor. The black lace basque supplied everything Hayden had been torturing himself with all afternoon, and more – and, he mused, was definitely worth the hen do in Spain.

'Not what you thought,' she grinned.

Hayden uncrossed his legs and put his own glass on the floor, tucking it out of the way under his chair.

'Then come here,' he said, 'and make sure I remember you.'

***

Saturday, 12th July 11.05a.m.

Nia sat and glared at the number that had just appeared on the calculator in front of her. She pressed her index finger on the cancel button and started again. Taking each of her credit card bills one at a time, she punched in the amounts due rather harder than was strictly necessary. Then, after a moment of hesitation, she reluctantly added in the electricity bill that had been lying in wait on the doormat that morning. With a gulp of her rapidly cooling tea she pressed the equals button… the figure that appeared was stubbornly the same as the first, second and third times she had done the calculation. Nia sat back, took a shuddering breath and swallowed hard.

OK, she thought, *time to take stock and face your fears.*

She had the job with Cornerstone, which promised to occupy her almost full-time by Easter next year – if not sooner (*please, sooner*); and John Cavendish really was being very forthcoming with projects, large and small – although mostly small. But even with all of that, she still owed nearly three times what all that work was worth over the next twelve months (actually it was nearer to eighteen but there were only so many fears a girl could face at one sitting).

Nia's immediate problem was that while not quite as bleak as they had been several weeks ago, 'things' were not boding well for a trip to Málaga anytime soon. She was also aware that as Ros's charity fashion event clashed with Maddy's hen weekend, she would have to be more generous than she had planned in any cheques she handed to Ros on her way to the airport. And, again based on the 'fears' count, Nia quickly shelved any idea of a new outfit for the subsequent wedding.

Staring at the calculator as if it might suddenly have a change of heart, Nia wondered why Madeleine had picked that particular weekend. It wasn't as if they'd set the date for the big day yet, although late autumn had been mentioned more than once – something about the colours matching Madeleine's hair, Nia hadn't really been paying attention. Surely even Madeleine couldn't have just forgotten about Ros's event – especially after Ros had given so much time to the Cornerstone garden party?

Wondering how difficult it would be for Madeleine to change the booking, Nia resolved to have a quiet word with the bride-to-be some time over the following week. After all, the Treddies launch would also be done and dusted by the beginning of September, too; so if the trip could be put back she might just be able to stretch the pennies and book a last minute flight. Failing that, Nia concluded, looking at the number still shining out of the calculator, she would have to feign a heart attack or contract something terribly contagious.

Wednesday, 16th July, 4p.m.

Madeleine stomped into Martha's with a face like thunder. For a fleeting moment Nia clung to the hope that the wedding (now set for Saturday 18th October at three-thirty p.m.) had been called off, thus averting the need to have the conversation she had spent the last three days rehearsing.

'Gosh, all not well with love's young dream?' she asked, making a huge effort to sound concerned rather than optimistic.

Madeleine advanced and threw her bag onto the table – a very smart, very new Mulberry, Nia noticed with envy.

'Bloody no!' spat Madeleine. She plonked down in the chair and grabbed at the arm of a young lady walking past the table.

'I'll have a cappuccino, heavy on the sprinkles.'

'I'm so sorry,' smiled the girl. 'But I don't work here.'

'Oh,' said Madeleine, adding, with barely a breath, 'Well ask someone on your way out.'

And without another second to spare for the surprised girl, Madeleine turned back to Nia.

'I've just been fucking done!' she said, sounding exceptionally high-handed – even for Madeleine. 'There I was, minding my own fucking business at the lights on Cecil Street – you know that fucking awful junction where the lights take an age? Well, I'd already been waiting far too long and this fucking idiot on the inside lane decided to change lanes just as my phone rang. It was Sebastian so I had to take it. Luckily I just spotted the car as it swerved in front of me and I slammed on my brakes. Suddenly there's a blue flashing light in my rear view mirror!'

'Oh, no,' interrupted Nia. 'What did you do?'

'Well, naturally I assumed it was after the fucking prat who had just cut me up, so I pulled in.'

'And did you get off the phone?'

Madeleine looked genuinely amazed.

'Of course not! Sebastian is having terrible problems with his girlfriend! He needed to talk. No, I made way for the police car and next thing I know there's a knock on my window and *I'm* the one being booked! Six fucking points! *And* a fine. Lucky I had my credit card. Honestly, haven't they got anything better to do! Where's my coffee!'

She looked around angrily.

'I don't think that girl passed on your message,' said Nia, in what she hoped was a helpful tone. She couldn't recall a Sebastian, but life was just too short. 'Don't worry, you stay there. I'll go and order it.'

'Right, well I'll nip to the loo then. Honestly, they kept me there ages! It was absolutely mortifying. We were right on the junction. Poor Sebastian. You know, the officer wouldn't even let me finish my call!'

Nia decided to step away from the obvious and when she returned with the coffees Madeleine had calmed down.

'It's OK, I've just spoken to Seb again, to apologise for cutting the call short.' She took a sip from the frothy drink. 'I'm having another lesson later so we'll have a good chat then. So, have you booked your flight?'

Nia took a deep breath and tried not to look guilty.

'Well, not exactly.'

'Oh, come on, Nia! If you don't book soon you'll miss out. First class obviously. If we all check in at the same time we'll be able to sit together.'

As Madeleine took a breath, Nia took a deep one of her own and waded back in where she had left off.

'The thing is Maddy, well, it probably slipped your mind with everything going on, but Ros's charity fashion show is that same weekend.'

'Is it?' said Madeleine without a shred of remorse. 'Well, that explains why Ivy's not coming! That's OK, I'll ask Kaz instead. You, me and Kaz. It's going to be fab!' She wrinkled her nose as she smiled – the effect was quite some distance short of cute. Nia had no idea who *Kaz* was either but pressed on.

'But don't you think Ros might want to come? You know… if you postponed by a week? Ivy might come then, too.'

'Postpone? No, absolutely not. Hayden's been given tickets for the annual Grouse Supper at the club. Obviously I'll be going with him – as the future Mrs Elliot. No, I'm afraid that if Ros can't come that weekend, she can't come. Honestly, if I started trying to fit in with everyone's little whims I wouldn't only *not* be going on my own hen-do but I wouldn't be getting married at all!'

Nia sipped her very strong, black coffee and parked any mention of her own financial woes – maybe she'd get paid early for the Treddies work after all?

Friday 18th July 12.05p.m.

'Oh, Saf, I'm so sorry about that. What went wrong, not your nerves? You were great last night.'

Hayden looked out over the wind-chopped sea of the bay, holding his mobile to his ear as his daughter cried silently on the other end. Eventually she spoke again.

'I'm so sorry, Dad. I… really thought I'd be OK… But just before… I went in I…' Saffy sniffed loudly and took a deep breath. 'I got a text from Alistair. He wants to come over for Ben's birthday.'

'Well, that's not so bad, love. He's got the right to see his son,' Hayden said, far more generously than he felt, 'and I'm sure Ben wants to see his father. It's been a long time for a little boy, Saf.'

'Yes, Dad, I know. And you're right, but…'

Whatever Saffy said next was lost among renewed sobbing.

'Look, love, I'll jump in the Landy and come and get you. Morris and I could do with some fresh air. We can go for a walk on the cliffs – Maddy's gone off in search of the perfect wedding invitation so I'll treat you to a latte in Pinero's if you like. Hang on; I'll be there in twenty minutes.'

***

Friday, 18th July 5.50p.m.

'Wine?' spat Madeleine. 'I need a double gin! God, Nia. First he tells me she's failed her driving theory yet again, so any hope of getting rid of them before the wedding is rapidly disappearing! Then he casually breaks the news that I've got to play host at a fucking birthday party… for a four-year-old… *fifteen* four-year-olds, to be precise!! Christ, I only went out for a few fucking hours for a sodding bag!'

'I thought you were looking for wedding invitations, now you've set the date?' Nia nodded at Travis, who was hovering at a safe distance. 'And a large merlot for me. Thanks, Travis.'

'Oh, those. No, I'm going to have them professionally made. Do you know how difficult it is to get hand-woven silk paper wedding invitations off the shelf? I was in John Lewis when Hayden rang. They were less than useless! The signal in there's *terrible*. I had to go out into the street!'

As Travis beat a hasty retreat back to the safety of the bar, Nia concentrated on not looking surprised about the shortage of hand-woven silk paper anything in their local John Lewis. She also chose not to comment on the new bag – to her knowledge the second in a week – or her lack of knowledge about wedding invitations of any kind. In her current financial dilemma, however, the birthday party looked fair game.

'Well, a birthday party at Landsmere might be fun. Children are just lovely at that age. My sister's daughter was an absolute tr–'

'Fun! There's absolutely nothing fucking fun about fifteen children rampaging around my house! It's bad enough with one! There's a reason I haven't had the play room done out, you know! It's earmarked as my studio, to be transformed the second that woman and her brat child finally vacate the premises!'

'Studio?' said Nia, taken aback.

'For my painting. I'm going to have lessons when we come back from Mauritius. I've always wanted to paint. I'm going to record my honeymoon in oils.'

'Oh! And what does Hayden think of that?' asked Nia – the words 'painting' and 'Madeleine' not being an automatic link in her mind.

'He doesn't know yet, it's going to be a surprise. I've already decided I'm going to give him my first piece as a Christmas present.'

'Well, it'll certainly be a surprise,' breathed Nia. Madeleine didn't hear – the drinks were on their way.

'So Hayden has agreed that Saffy and Ben are going to move out then?' Nia asked as Travis once more retreated.

'Not yet, but I'm working on it,' answered Madeleine. She gave Nia a conspiratorial nod. 'You see, the only glimmer of sunshine in this birthday fiasco is that apparently Alistair is coming over.'

'Really?' said Nia. 'Gosh, and Hayden has agreed to have him under the same roof?'

'Well, no actually, he hasn't. No, Alistair's going to stay at Amrose Street – I think that's the only reason Hayden called, to ask if Alistair could use the house. I thought it was a bit of a cheek but anyway, I've decided to look on it as an opportunity. I'm going to move heaven and earth to get them to play happy families there. Honestly Nia, from what I've heard, that thing between Saffy and Alistair was a storm in a tea cup. She's such a drama queen! No, once they spend some time together Saffy'll realise what she's missing and they'll all be jetting off back to Hong Kong before the end of August.'

She raised her glass to her own brilliance and downed half her double G and T in one.

***

Tuesday, 22nd July 9.45a.m.

Madeleine was flicking idly through a pile of magazines on the breakfast bar when Hayden pushed the kitchen door open. Morris wandered in and headed straight for his bed.

Madeleine glanced briefly at the old hound and then at Hayden.

'That was quick. I want to have a bath before we go.'

Hayden frowned.

'He just wasn't interested today,' he replied. Hayden's expression suggested that Morris wasn't alone and what he said next confirmed it. 'And to be honest, my heart wasn't in it either. I thought the morning sunshine might liven us up a bit and help me take my mind off this Alistair business but we got to the end of the drive and Morris just stopped and stood there looking at me.'

'Well, why didn't you just use the lead and insist? You're supposed to be the master, after all!' said Madeleine. A very elegant Mouton lace over luxe crepe 1950's wedding dress had just caught her eye; it was almost exactly what she had pictured herself wearing (although the bow thing in the model's hair was a definite no-no) and at only two thousand seven hundred she was very tempted. She'd have to find the right bag though for the evening, to replace the bouquet once the formalities were over. And she did like that antique white…

'…been concerned for a while now. I mean, I know he's getting on and obviously he's not going to go on forever.' Hayden's voice drifted through Madeleine's wedding attire plans.

'Who? Alistair. I didn't think he was more than thirty-five!' said Madeleine, dragging her gaze from the magazine pages.

'No, the dog, silly! God, Alistair! Saffy spoke to him again this morning. I just wish he'd– '

Madeleine had gone back to her magazine.

'So what's wrong with him then – the dog? He's eating, isn't he? And he's certainly farting! God, the smell in here this morning! Have you been giving him All Bran again?'

'It's good for him,' said Hayden, on the defensive. This was not the first time Madeleine had aired her dim view of his beloved wolfhound. 'I think it's his back leg. Did you notice when he came in? He's walking short on it – the right one.'

'Looked OK to me,' said Madeleine, turning the page of her magazine. An olive-skinned model was draped in the most beautiful lace veil... now she hadn't really thought about a veil...

'No, he's definitely not right.' Hayden paused and stood watching his old friend snoring gently, wedged up against the wall beside his bed, his favourite sleeping position. 'We'll see how he goes over the weekend. If he's still limping on Monday I'll take him down to the vet. Probably a bit of rheumatism.'

Madeleine turned another page. Sand-washed silk... ooh, that was an idea...

'Mmm,' she offered and then looked up. 'Oh, that reminds me, I'm having a massage after my Spanish lesson this afternoon. Saffy's been so wound up over this driving test failure. I think the tension's getting to me – my shoulders are really stiff. I'll need Brian to pick me up at four-fifteen.'

'In fairness, I think the news about Alistair has had rather more to do with it, darling. Anyway, I've got a meeting with Nia this afternoon.' Hayden studied the clock on the kitchen wall. 'I could have made it earlier but what with the vicar at twelve and I wasn't sure how long we'd be...'

Madeleine's eyes flashed from the magazine.

'Well, it's not as if you haven't done it before. I'm surprised you can't remember from the last two times? I'm the novice here, remember!'

Hayden returned her mocking look with a measured gaze.

'As you are well aware, my love, it's an awfully long time since Georgina and I went down the aisle and as you are also well aware my marriage to Carla was in Barbados so, no, I can't remember. My meeting with Nia is at two and with me being away so much over the next three weeks we've got a lot to discuss. So I suggest you get a taxi if you don't want to be kept waiting.'

Madeleine caught the tone, slid from her stool and headed for the door to the lobby.

'Right, well I'll just go and have a quick shower. I was going to have a nice relaxing bath but I'd hate to make you late for your marketing guru.'

The kitchen door closed rather louder than was absolutely necessary.

'Or *your* vicar,' muttered Hayden.

Thursday 24th July 3.45p.m.

'Right, Grace, can you put that lot in an email to Jackson? Copy me in and I'll put them all in my diary here. Goodness, I'm going to be in the air more than I'm on the ground over the next three weeks – I just wish there weren't quite so many landings! See you Tuesday. Thanks.'

Hayden put the phone back on the hook in his peace-filled study and sat back to admire the view. No matter how many times he looked out over that seascape it was never the same twice. Today a flock of gannets were plunging into the waves off the head; climbing high into the air they were taking turns to wheel and plummet into the water far below. The cleanness of their dives and the length of time they remained underwater never ceased to impress Hayden.

Downstairs the front door scraped open and the patter of welly-clad feet up the stairs gave a hefty clue as to whom had just arrived.

'Ben! Ben! Come back here at once! I've told you before about going upstairs in your wellies,' Saffy's voice called.

'But I want to thow Ba Ritten my thstick,' said Ben, whose continued footsteps showed no sign of stopping.

'No, not on the banister! Ben, come here at once!'

More advancing footsteps.

'Ben! Ooh, sorry, Dad. He's muddy!'

Ben burst into the room, the soles of his wellies now clean – the carpet behind him now not so.

'Look, Ba Ritten, my thstick's got a cliff in it! Mummy thaid it was a thpethial thstick for finding water!' He waved the grubby stick at his grandfather, scraping one end along the wall as he did so. Saffy ran in just too late.

'Oh, Ben! I can't believe you've just done that! Look at Grandpa's wall! Dad, I'm so sorry. Can you grab him and I'll get a cloth – or a noose! Honestly!'

Saffy marched back out. Seconds later Hayden heard the tap running in the guest bathroom – the nearest to his study.

'It's OK, Saf. Morris has made far more mess in the past. When that tail wags it's all hands to the pumps!'

Saffy came back with a dripping cloth.

'No, Dad, it's really not alright. Ben, you really must learn to listen to Mummy when she tells you something!' She grabbed at the boy's arm and wiped his muddy hand in the cloth. 'Give me that stick. No, don't give it to Grandpa! Dad, no, it's covered in mud!'

Despite his daughter's protestations, Hayden took the offered stick and turned it around in his fingers.

'Hmm, and did Mummy tell you what a water-finding stick like this is called?' he asked, laying yesterday's copy of *The Financial*

Times out across the floor, one long edge touching the tips of Ben's wellies. Ben shook his head. 'Well, it's called a divining stick,' said Hayden. 'Right, one step forward onto the paper and then we'll have those wellies off.'

'Thanks, Dad,' said Saffy, dragging her son's anorak off his arms. 'And everything else, young man. You might as well go straight in the bath!'

'Well, I hope you had a good time getting this muddy?' said Hayden, brightly. He loved that Saffy and Ben spent so much time in the woods around the Grange. It really was good to see the house being used as a proper family home again, and the mud was all part of it.

'So, talking of muddy tails, where's Morris, Dad? He's normally up here if you are.' Saffy looked over at the grey hair-coated mat lying in front of a battered settee that had long ago been relegated from the sitting room into Hayden's study. Its front edge was also matted with dark hairs – the tell-tail sign of an Irish wolfhound whose favourite place to lie was with his long back right up against the base of the sofa.

'Downstairs sulking,' said Hayden. 'The vet said to avoid stairs for a while.'

'Oh, but he's OK, isn't he?' asked Saffy, searching her father's face. 'He's walking much better this week.'

'Oh, yes,' said Hayden, a little too cheerfully. The news at the vet had not been the best but the prescribed twice weekly pain relief injections seemed to be having some effect. 'He's perked up considerably. I feel a lot happier about leaving him now.'

'Gosh, yes,' said Saffy, midway through extricating her son from his impressively mud-coated jeans. 'Wednesday, isn't it? Now you are going to be back for Ben's birthday?'

'Yes… and yes,' said Hayden pointedly. 'Goodness, I take it he found the mud under Pooh-sticks bridge?' Hayden laughed.

The memory of Saffy, aged four, with that same mud spilling into her wellies still made him smile – she had never quite grasped the concept of dropping the sticks into the water from the bridge and insisted she help them through by pushing them.

'Yes, 'fraid so. That rain we had last week wasn't enough to refill the stream. It's a mud-filled child magnet now – he was sitting in it at one point.'

'I was uthing my deafening thstick to find the water,' said Ben.

'A bit of mud never did you any harm, my girl,' Hayden scolded affectionately. 'Is that bath ready yet?'

Hayden scooped up his now naked grandson and headed for the bathroom.

'Goodness me, young man, you're getting a bit big for this!'

'Yes, Dad, I was about to say, you watch your back. I know he's small for his age, but he's still quite a lump!'

'Well I'm not going to see much of either of you for the next couple of weeks so I might as well make the most of it.'

Saffy dragged her hand through the water in the bath and turned on the cold tap. Hayden waited. Ben began to wriggle.

'Put him down, Dad. Ben, do you want bubbles?' Saffy sloshed blue bubble bath into the water before Ben could answer. 'So where are you going after Singapore, Dad?'

Hayden squinted with one eye closed as he tried to recall the itinerary.

'Jackson wants me to go over to New York via Cape Town and then up to Goose Bay in Canada.'

'My God, Dad! That's practically a world tour!!'

'Well, there are some quite exciting opportunities coming off and Maddy's in wedding planning mode so I thought I'd make the most of it. While I'm still a free man, as it were.'

'Hmm, not so sure about the 'free man' bit,' said Saffy with an edge Hayden did his best to ignore. 'You know she's trying to track down someone to design silk invites, don't you? Are you sure you should be leaving her with your credit card?'

Hayden laughed.

'It's alright, we've discussed the invitations – and the budget… By sheer luck I managed to find some online. They've got silk on the cover, so we compromised. Oh, and Paul from Ashcroft's will come up here every other day to check on Morris and give him his injections when they're due. He'll come when Mrs B's here, so don't worry about staying in specially. But if you could just make sure Morris is fed, watered and the occasional walk…'

Saffy nodded and picked up her son.

'Right, Ben, in you get, come on. Mrs B's made you fish pie for tea. Quick, in! No problem, Dad. Can't see Madeleine mucking in though, especially if vets are going to be involved. Oh, that reminds me. We bumped into that Ms O'Reilly when we were up on the common yesterday. Apparently, it's actually Mrs – widowed four years ago. Cancer.' She pulled a face but moved on. 'She's got a really sweet little Westie – Trigger, or Tigger… Ben, what was Mrs O'Reilly's dog called?'

'Tiger,' answered Ben while staring into a handful of bubbles.

'Don't forget to actually rub your hands together in there. The idea is that you're getting clean, remember!' said Saffy, with her hands on her hips. Then she turned back to her father. 'She's really nice actually. Ben certainly seems to like her. I think the dog helped. Ben insisted on telling her all about Morris – apparently her parents had an Irish Wolfhound when she was young.'

'So you're happy with Rockmoore then?' asked Hayden, lowering his voice as if anticipating a negative answer that he didn't want Ben to hear.

'Gosh, yes!' said Saffy. Then she turned her back on Ben and said under her breath, 'Al's a different matter, but… well…'

'Is Daddy coming over to stay for my birthday?' asked Ben

from behind his mother.

'Little ears!' mouthed Saffy and then louder, 'Yes, and if you're a very good boy you might be able to go and stay the night with him at Aunty Madeleine's house. Would you like that?'

'Will you be there, too?' asked Ben, studying another mound of bubbles.

'We'll see,' said Saffy. 'Right, come on. You'll turn into a prune if you stay in there much longer!'

Tuesday, 29th July, 3.35p.m.

'Oh, Ros, hi!' Madeleine's overly cheerful reply to Ros's, 'Hi, Madeleine,' suggested that she hadn't expected to hear Ros's voice on the other end of her phone. Nonetheless, she ploughed on. 'Goodness, I was just thinking I haven't spoken to you for ages and now you've beaten me to it. Now, the next time we meet up, you must remind me about that money. I haven't forgotten Hayden owes it to you – two hundred, wasn't it?'

'Well, it was two-fifty actually,' said Ros's voice on the other end of the phone. Madeleine inspected her nails. There was a chip in the *Cherie Bow Nail Glow* on her index finger and on closer inspection it appeared the nail was split, too.

'Oh, how annoying!'

'Sorry?'

'What? Oh, sorry, Ros,' Madeleine laughed. 'Just broke my nail and I'm going for my first fitting tomorrow. Wanted to look my best.'

'Oh, I thought Hayden was going away tomorrow. Nia mentioned something. Aren't you going to see him off? He's away for almost three weeks, isn't he?'

'Yes, I am. Brian's dropping him to Heathrow first and then we're going on into Knightsbridge. It'll be so much easier with Hayden away. I'll be doing heaps of running around now so I'm going to need the car.'

'Oh, haven't you got the Audi anymore?' asked Ros. 'Has Hayden sold it? Or the Beetle?'

'God no!' Madeleine sounded genuinely horrified. 'You know what London's like – Brian can drop me at the door. He'll carry everything, too. So much more convenient.'

'Oh, right… Of course.' Ros chose not to pursue Madeleine's wedding shopathon and, instead, turned to the reason for her call. 'Well anyway, I'm looking for a favour actually. As you know I won't be able to come on your hen trip as I'm committed to the charity fashion event–'

'Yes, I heard,' interrupted Madeleine, her voice oozing with pseudo tragedy. 'And it's going to be fab. The apartment is gorgeous and the pool looks stunning. D'you know if Nia's bought her ticket yet? Kaz's bought hers. Have you met Kaz?'

'Doesn't she own Saffron, that designer shop in town?' said Ros. 'Have you bought anything in there? It's terribly expensive.'

'Yes, that's the one. Fab stuff. She's going to order the underwear for my outfit once I've chosen the dress.'

'Oh, I'm surprised you'll be wearing any!' said Ros. But determined to stick to the point of her call, hastily added, 'Anyway, my charity fashion event… I was wondering, as you won't be coming, if you could give me the guest list that you used for the garden party? I've got heaps of my own contacts obviously but a lot of them are the same old faces. I thought it would be really lovely if I could introduce some new blood… and some new money, of course, as that's what it's all about. Could you email it to me? Or do you want to give it to me when I pop over with a donation form for you? Now don't forget to sign the Gift Aid bit.

I could collect the two hundred and fifty pounds at the same time.'

'Oh, well, my email's down at the moment. Tell you what, pop over tomorrow morning; Mrs B will be here with the vet. I'll pop into the bank before we go and leave it with the list for you.'

'Vet? Is there something wrong with Hayden's dog?'

'Oh, it's probably nothing a bullet wouldn't put right! Honestly, that thing is just so old. Hobbling around, breaking wind. It won't be long before it's incontinent, I'm sure. And I'm damned if I'm going to be the one to clean up after it!'

'Well, yes,' said Ros. 'After all, that would involve you finding where Mrs Bosworth keeps the mop. So who's looking after the dog while Hayden's away? Is Saffy helping?'

'The vet calls every two minutes. Saffy runs around after it the rest of the time... when she's not on the phone to Alistair, of course!' said Madeleine testily.

'Oh, so what's happening there? Nia said you're hoping for a reunion. When's he arriving?'

'Flies in on the seventeenth. Hayden isn't back until late on the eighteenth, so apparently Alistair's going to stay up in London for a day or so. For some stupid reason Saffy doesn't want him to arrive without her father here. Honestly, you'd think at her age she'd be a bit more mature! Anyway, look Ros, I'm going to have to go. I'm having my hair done at four-thirty. Hayden's taking me to *La Petite Maison* for a bon voyar treat.'

'And will you be giving him a *bon voyar* treat, too?' Ros enquired mischievously, etching unseen quotation marks at the phone.

'We'll see,' grinned Madeleine.

***

Wednesday 30th July 11.40a.m.

Ros carefully steered her car around the potholes that were now positively yawning after almost daily sudden, frequent and drenching cloud bursts over the last two weeks. She arrived in the courtyard of Landsmere Grange just as another torrential downpour washed down her windscreen.

'Bollocks!'

Pulling her car alongside Madeleine's Audi, Ros glared at the torrent. The proverbial stair rods were now falling with grim determination. She reached under her seat and groped about blindly in the vain hope that a forgotten umbrella might be loitering as if waiting for such a time as this, when it might once more find employment. Her searching fingers quickly located a discarded cream egg wrapper (one of Ros's guilty pleasures), but other than that the space gave up nothing of any use.

A light at the kitchen window of the great house suggested someone was in – as did a small black car that Ros had just noticed, parked on the other side of Madeleine's Beetle. Hayden's Land Rover, Ros could now see, was stationed across the courtyard, facing the open garage doors with its bonnet yawning open. As Ros gingerly opened her own car door a crack, a metallic tinkle from that direction was followed by a muffled but still audible string of choice words. Barry, leaning over the engine, looked up, waved and dropped to his knees, to retrieve whatever it was he had just dropped, Ros assumed. Unable to find any rain protection – not even an old carrier bag – Ros made up her mind to bite the bullet and ran for the front door.

'Oh, hello, Ros,' said Saffy, hauling the door open. The rain had obviously taken its toll on the old wood and it was with some considerable difficulty that she was able to pull the door wide enough for Ros to step through.

'Sorry about this. Come in, sorry,' said Saffy. 'Dad did ask Barry to have a look at this door while he was away, I think it's on one of Madeleine's lists. But Morris isn't looking too good, and the Landy's playing up. The vet's here now but if Morris needs to go in to Ashcroft's it's the only thing big enough to take an Irish Wolfhound. He's fifteen stone, you know! God help us if he collapses before we can get him up his ramp!'

Saffy's face was etched with worry.

'Oh, dear,' said Ros. 'I'm afraid I wouldn't be much help – my car's even smaller than the vet's, assuming that's his?' she nodded to the little black Corsa in the yard, 'and I'm not that partial to animals. Do you know what's wrong with him? Is there anything they can do?'

'I'm not sure,' said Saffy, leading Ros into the hall. Ros dripped onto the parquet but neither of them took any notice. 'Old age, I think. I was hoping he would last until Dad got back – the rate he's going Dad won't have even taken off!'

'Have you telephoned him? Does he know how bad things are?'

'No, not yet. Paul has just given him another steroid injection and a stronger pain killer. He's hoping that Morris'll rally over the next few hours. If not, we'll be taking him in.'

Wednesday 30ᵗʰ July, 1.05p.m.

Ros manoeuvred into the last empty space available in the car park – not easy with the wheels of the car on her passenger side planted, as if staking a claim on the white dividing line. She hauled on the handbrake. The rain had stopped and, as seemed to be the pattern of the weather that summer, the sun was now beating through her windscreen.

A buff A5 envelope lay on the passenger seat beside her. Her exit from Landsmere Grange had been somewhat hasty following the appearance of an extremely handsome vet who had appeared while she and Saffy had been talking in the hall. His expression had not been one of optimism and so, choosing to view the envelope's contents once she had arrived at the bank, Ros had taken her leave (albeit somewhat reluctantly, as the young man had had the bluest eyes she had ever seen).

She picked up the envelope now and recalled to her memory the impressive wad of paper that Madeleine had spent most of June clutching to her breast. The tatty and obviously recycled envelope was taped down with a scraggy piece of crinkled sticky tape. It was also, Ros noticed now she was in the dry quiet, much lighter than expected.

Inside Ros found another, smaller envelope, together with her Gift Aid form to which a rather grubby ten-pound note was paper-clipped on one corner.

'Oh,' breathed Ros. In fairness, Madeleine had completed the form correctly, stating the ten pound donation *and* she had ticked the Gift Aid box. There was, however, no list.

'Oh well,' Ros said to herself. 'She was probably in a rush and forgot.'

The small envelope held more promise – a bundle of ten- and twenty-pound notes, no note from Madeleine, but even so...

Ros popped the money-filled envelope into her bag, retrieved her phone and texted the words '*No list! Don't worry, email is fine x*'. Then she found Madeleine's mobile number in her favourites list and pressed send as she got out of the car.

Radio Gaga was playing over the inter-bank radio station in the bustling banking hall – FM HBS or something, she had no idea what and cared less. She found a quiet corner and withdrew the envelope containing the two hundred and fifty pounds from her bag, along with her paying-in book. Four people were queuing at the counter. There was always the option of using the automated banking machine but as far as Ros was concerned, if there were staff there being paid to do a job she was jolly well going to use them. So she rustled through the twenties, counting two hundred pounds with a nod; completed the paying-in slip by adding fifty pounds to the tens box before she took her place in the queue for the counter.

'If anyone's just paying in, would they like to use the machines?' asked a smiling young lady clad in the navy trousers and white, green and navy blouse that singled her out as Helpful Lady at the Bank. Two people relinquished their place in the queue to accept the offer. Ros took two steps forward to fill the space.

'Good afternoon,' said another smiling face, this time from behind the glass when Ros finally got to the counter. She had just waited five minutes, listening to a debate between the smiling girl and a gum-chewing woman – apparently the cash machine had refused to give her any money. Three times the young girl had patiently explained that this was because the woman had already exceeded her overdraft limit. The overdrawn woman's voice was drowning out Lionel Richie's *Hello* before the manager eventually intervened. There was now shouting from a side room, but at least Lionel had finished singing, and Ros was able to get to the counter.

'Gosh, some people just won't take no for an answer, will they?' said Ros, casting her eyes heavenwards. 'Are you trained to deal with people like that?'

'Oh, she wasn't too bad,' said the girl kindly. She took the money from Ros's paying-in book and swiftly counted the twenties before planting a tick next to Ros's entry. Then she counted the ten pound notes... twice... held her pen poised against Ros's entry of fifty pounds and then said, 'There's only forty here. Do you still have the other ten?'

'Oh!' said Ros, slightly piqued. 'Are you sure?' She peered at the money in the girl's hand – four grubby notes. Realization dawned. 'Ah, sorry, my mistake. Must have miscounted. That'll teach me to rush. Could you change the amount for me? To forty? Would you like me to initial the corrections?'

Friday 8th August, 12.55p.m.

Nia glanced at the menu. Her heart sank. The cheapest item was soup at ten pounds fifty; bread was an extra one seventy-five. She ordered a glass of house red without checking the price.

'Oh, I do love it here,' said Madeleine doing the wrinkly nose, smiley thing again. Nia toyed with mentioning that as cute looks went, it wasn't, but stayed silent. 'The lobster is absolutely fab. Hayden had it when we came here for supper before he went away. I had the turbot.'

'So how's he getting on? What line of longitude is he on now of his *tour du monde*?' asked Nia, while wondering why Madeleine had insisted on them meeting at one of the most expensive restaurants within fifty square miles.

'On his way to Cape Town. Hmm, I think I'll have the mussels in Pernod. An old boyfriend made that for me once – on our first date. Delicious… well worth the effort of all those shells! The sex wasn't bad either, as I recall.' The waiter arrived and offered the drinks menu. 'Right, as we're celebrating me finally finding the perfect dress, I'll get the wine. Champers? I've got Hayden's gold card.'

'Oh, I wasn't planning on a session, I've got the car,' said Nia, disappointed, but at least the mystery was solved. 'I was only planning on having a glass.'

'Oh,' said Madeleine. She beamed at the young man patiently waiting, pen poised. 'Just a half bottle then.' She turned back to Nia as the waiter disappeared behind a heavy walnut swing door. 'I couldn't drink a whole one; we've still got to collect the invitations and I must look for nail varnish.'

'Didn't you buy nail varnish the last time we were in town?' asked Nia.

Another waiter appeared.

'Right, uuummm,' said Madeleine gazing once again at the menu. 'Right, I think I will have the mussels.'

It was Nia's turn to wrinkle her nose. 'Pernod with champagne... is that wise?'

'Oh, it's fine, Brian's picking me up,' Madeleine grinned, missing the point completely.

'*Ça ne fait rien,*' muttered Nia. 'And the soup for me, please.'

'*Voulez-vous du pain, madame?*' asked the waiter.

'*Non, merci,*' Nia replied.

Madeleine's lips tightened as she handed the menu back to the waiter who bowed as he took Nia's. 'It's such a shame we aren't in a Spanish restaurant. Seb is very impressed at my progress, you know. Fab accent, apparently.'

Yet another waiter glided over with the drinks. Choosing safe ground, Nia prompted, 'Anyway, the nail varnish?'

'Yes. I've bought an ivory and a pearly cream but they're not right,' said Madeleine with a shake of her head. 'I'm hoping the Dior counter in John Lewis will have something. God, the rate I'm going, I might have to try Boots!'

'Have you got a swatch of the fabric?'

'Of course. But they all look different in different lights. Honestly Nia, its details like nail varnish that can ruin a bride's outfit if they're wrong! I've been looking at hair extensions, too. The model wearing my dress in the photo had a mane of auburn hair – a bit like Kate Bush but with more control. It was fab. I've shown the picture to Patrick and he's confident he can do it. I've already booked the appointment – Friday the seventeenth.'

'Gosh, the day before?'

'Oh yes.' Glass poised at her lips, Madeleine nodded. 'He's going to set it all up and then he'll be over at seven the following morning to finish it off.'

'Seven! My God, the wedding's not until three-thirty!' said Nia. 'And how will you sleep? You'll have to hover!'

Madeleine halted mid-sip.

'Sorry, I keep forgetting you haven't been married. No, all the magazines say to leave lots of time on the day to make sure you look your best. My hair has to be ready before the manicurist and the beautician arrive. I'll need you there by eight; there's bound to be loads of running around to do.'

'And what about Hayden?' asked Nia, losing her battle with mounting incredulity.

'At Amrose Street. I can't see him before the ceremony – it's bad luck!'

Monday 11th August 6.35a.m.

Saffy lowered herself to stroke Morris's ear. Her knees cricked. Lying flat out, the old hound pressed his head hard into her hand and gave a soft moan of appreciation. Ben was still fast asleep upstairs.

'How're you today, old man?' Saffy said gently. Morris was now on so many tablets that an early start was the only way to ensure his medication was properly spaced out during the day. Saffy didn't mind though, especially as Morris had rallied enough for short walks; in fact the previous day she and Ben had taken him through the woods and on to the cliff. At least the phone call with her father today would be a bit easier.

Hayden had called Saffy every day since his departure to check on Morris, which to her amusement had not gone down terribly well with her father's future wife.

'Well, the next time he calls to check on his dog tell him he can call me on my mobile…, if, that is, he's remotely interested in how *I'm* getting on!' Madeleine had announced on the third day of Hayden's absence. 'It's alright for him, jetting halfway across the world. But I'm the one left here to organised *our* wedding day!' She had flounced out of the room, issuing as her parting shot, 'It won't just happen, you know!'

'We continue to pray,' Saffy told Morris.

Wednesday, 13th August, 11.35a.m.

'Hi, Madeleine, it's Ros,' said Ros. She had been trying for some time to contact Madeleine as the promised guest list had still not arrived but calls to Madeleine's mobile were yet to be returned and Ros was sick of speaking the Madeleine's answer phone. Two email requests had also gone unanswered and so, not one to be beaten, Ros had resorted to the land line at Landsmere. Although it was highly likely the phone would be answered by Mrs Bosworth, at least she would be talking to a human voice. As it was, it was Madeleine who had picked up the phone – after only two rings. Ros continued to speak. 'I've been trying to get hold of you for ages. Have you been having a problem with your mobile? You haven't lost it, have you?'

'Oh, hi, Ros. I was expecting someone else. No, sorry, I had noticed the missed calls but I've just been so busy. With Hayden away there's been so much to do!'

'Yes, I can imagine. How are the wedding plans going? And more importantly, how is Morris?'

'Oh, he's fine. Another one of Saffy's mini-dramas, I'm sure. She's been out walking with him every day! And that vet's here more than he's in the surgery! A lot of fuss about nothing as far as I can see!'

'Oh, well sounds like good news. Is Hayden pleased?' Ros asked, but cut to the chase before Madeleine could answer or, more to the point, find an excuse to end the call. 'I was wondering if you'd had a chance to dig out that guest list yet. You remember, I asked for a copy? For the charity fashion event?'

There was a pause and the sound of the front door scraping. Then Ros heard Madeleine's voice. 'Yes, come in... I'll just be a second... oh, they are lovely... Sorry Ros, the florist's just arrived. I'll email that list as soon as I've finished using it for the invitations.'

Ros did her best not to sound as exasperated as she was starting to feel.

'Oh, er, that's wonderful but I was hoping to get the invitations for the charity fashion event out as soon as possible. It's on the fifth and, well, I really should have sent them out by now.'

'Well, I'm sorry, Ros,' said Madeleine. 'But, as I said, I am very busy organising my wedding. There must be a raft of people you can invite without relying on me. Look, I'll send something over later, I promise. I've really got to go now... oh, that colour is fab–'

And with that the line went dead.

Ros stared at the silent phone. 'Well I just hope it's all going to be worth it!'

Thursday, 14th August 12.55p.m.

'Tomorrow! Gosh, Dad, that's great. But are you sure… if you've still got stuff to do, I mean? Morris is doing well. Paul's pleased with him,' said Saffy, pushing an escaping fish finger back into the pitta bread her son was battling to eat.

'Well, that is good news, Saf. But I'll feel happier once I've seen him. As the vet says, I know my dog – no offence,' said her father's voice over a crackly line.

'I know, Dad, it's OK. Ooh, I just said D-A-D and Morris's ear's pricked up – I think he misses you! So what time will you be back? Shall I tell Brian to pick you up?'

'No, it's alright; Grace has already made all the arrangements. I'm only missing one dinner over here and Jackson's quite happy to stay on for that. He's taken a bit of a shine to our guide – won't last, of course!' Hayden laughed. 'I should be home around four in the afternoon. Can you ask Mrs B to do something light for supper? I'm going to have to watch what I eat for the next few weeks or whatever Madeleine's organised for me to wear for the wedding definitely won't fit!'

Friday 15th August 10.50a.m.

'I'm going, it's for me,' shouted Madeleine, skipping down the stairs to answer the front door.

'OK,' Saffy's disembodied voice came back from the kitchen.

'Delivery for Madeleine Edwards,' said the delivery driver. He offered a shoe box sized package and a pad. 'Sorry, I haven't got a pen, the lady at my last drop must have kept it.'

Madeleine took the package, grabbed a pen from the hall stand and hastily jotted her signature down on the delivery note.

'They're OK then?' said the driver. 'Mind if I hang on to this?'

'Sorry? Oh, the pen, yer... yes. Go on then, it's only a cheap one.'

The driver tapped his forehead with his newly acquired pen and turned back towards his van.

The door wouldn't quite close but satisfied that it was shut enough Madeleine tucked the box under her arm with a smile and headed for the kitchen. Saffy and Paul were sitting at the breakfast bar drinking coffee. Ben was standing on a stool at the sink, bubbles spilling down the unit; his T-shirt bore the tell-tale signs of a four-year-old throwing his all into the washing up. Morris was sound asleep on his bed, as usual.

Saffy got to her feet as Madeleine entered the kitchen. 'Ben, I think Morris's water bowl's clean enough now. That's the third time you've washed it... no, no more washing up liquid.' Saffy wrestled the bottle of bright yellow liquid from her son and scooped him off the stool. 'Mrs B will have your guts for garters if she sees how much you've already wasted! Come on, Paul's going now and before he can leave he needs to make sure Morris has got his water.'

Madeleine put the package on the breakfast bar and reached for a mug. 'Coffee, anyone?'

Paul shook his head and Saffy spoke for them both. 'No thanks... Ooh, what have you got there?' Saffy leant over to examine Madeleine's parcel.

'Invitations,' answered Madeleine. She reached for the bread knife and sliced through the tape holding the box secure. 'Just arrived, thank God. I'll be sending them out this weekend. And now he's finally finished swanning around the world, I'm going to insist your fa–' Madeleine stopped so suddenly even Ben looked up. 'What the f–'

'Anything wrong, Madeleine?' Saffy interrupted. Madeleine's expression had gone from beaming to boiling in a nanosecond.

'Has that bloody driver gone yet?' Madeleine said to no one in particular before charging into the hall and out into the courtyard. In the distance, a white van disappeared behind a dust wake and turned out of sight. 'Fuck!' said Madeleine. 'Fuck, fuck, fuck!'

Friday, 15ᵗʰ August, 11.55a.m.

Madeleine was on the phone. She had been on the phone for the last hour. Mrs Bosworth was maintaining a low profile in the kitchen; so far she had made a gooseberry crumble and a Victoria sponge. She was now baking a ham and wondering if she had enough sugar to make some more blackcurrant jam. Paul, the vet, had long since run the gauntlet of the potholes, and Saffy and Ben had made a very hasty welly-clad exit, with Morris in tow – and even he looked grateful to be leaving the scene. The sense of foreboding in the house was palpable.

'Yes, and as I've said to the other two people I've spoken to so far this morning; I agree that I did sign for the damn package, but that was rather based on my belief that you could get such a fundamental detail right!'

'…'

'Well, even if you couldn't read my handwriting, which incidentally I'm struggling to believe, surely it might have occurred to even someone of fairly limited intelligence that 'The marriage of Helen and Madeleine' might not have been quite correct?'

'…'

'Yes, I have heard of civil partnerships, dear, but this most definitely is not one!'

'...'

'No, that's not what I said and I hope you're both very happy but the fact here is that *my* invitations for *my* wedding are wrong and I simply refuse to accept that it is my fault!'

Mrs B tried not to bang the pots during another brief silence. Madeleine gave a snort. 'I don't think so! I insist that you put this right and send me the correct version today! All this has taken far too long as it is!'

A slightly longer silence followed. The housekeeper peered through the barely open kitchen door. Madeleine had one hand on her hip, listening. Then, as she moved to speak, she jabbed the air with her index finger to reinforce her words.

'Right, you do that. Although I really can't see the point! I am certain that my original order showed my future husband's name quite clearly! My email address? Capital M, capital E @ landsmeregrange.co.uk. Are you sure you don't want me to spell that for you? And don't think I'll be recommending your company anytime soon! Goodbye!'

Saturday, 16th August, 6.05a.m.

As soon as Hayden walked into the kitchen he knew something was wrong. Morris was on his bed. His breathing was all wrong. At the sight of his master the great hound hauled his huge frame to a sitting position and gazed at Hayden. His tongue lolled out of his mouth and his breath was coming in great gasps.

'You alright, old man?'

Morris made to stand but his legs didn't seem to have the strength, and after raising his bottom only an inch or two he slumped back and lowered his chest back onto his bed with a groan.

Hayden was at his old friend's side in a second. Gently stroking Morris's lion-like mane, he too struggled to find a breath.

'You waited, didn't you? You waited for me to come home so I could...' A tear trickled unchecked down Hayden's cheek and plopped onto the soft grey blanket of Morris's bed, '...say goodbye,' he finally whispered, forcing himself to say the last word before it was too late.

For a long time Hayden crouched, tears dripping on to Morris's coat while he waited and waited for Morris to take just one more breath. Stretched out in his usual repose; his warm brindle coat as soft as ever. Looking thick and coarse as it did from any distance, it always surprised people when they touched him; the silky softness of the hound's hair was anything but what they expected. Hayden fondled one of the hound's soft, velvety ears. It was still warm. But Morris's eyes, half-closed now, no longer shone amber-bright and the long awaited breath didn't come.

Behind Hayden, the door opened. He didn't look up.

'Dad? Is Morris... oh.' Saffy's voice faded. She padded barefoot across the kitchen and stood beside her father.

'He waited, Saf. He knew he was going and he waited...' Words failed him and together they wept silently, and, as if something knew to keep them away, neither Madeleine nor Ben disturbed the sad farewell for a very long time.

***

Monday, 18th August 5.50p.m.

'Honestly, Nia, it's all become rather trying!' said Madeleine with a tragic look. Horton's was surprisingly busy for a Monday evening and they had only just managed to squeeze themselves into a cramped table in a corner, which had done nothing to improve Madeleine's mood. 'What with that fucking birthday party of Ben's, the imminent arrival of his father which seems to have turned his mother into a gibbering wreck, *then* the cock-up with the invitations!' (On his return on Friday evening Hayden had taken one look at the emailed scan of Madeleine's handwritten order and agreed that it did indeed say 'Helen and Madeleine' – Madeleine was still livid.) 'And to cap it all the bloody dog dies!'

'I know, Maddy. Saffy told me when I rang earlier,' said Nia. 'I'm so sorry. Hayden must be devastated.'

'Oh, for goodness sake Nia, it was a dog – an old dog, at that! How people get so attached to them is beyond me! Do you know he's actually had a private cremation? When he told me I thought we were all going to have to dress up in black and sing hymns. At least I look good in black!'

'So what is a private cremation?' asked Nia, her face showing more than enough concern for the both of them.

'Oh, I don't know. God, where's Travis, I need a glass of something chilled! They do them on their own or something. So you don't get someone's hamster mixed up in the ashes, I assume. Anyway, that's where he's gone today – to collect the urn, or whatever it is they put them in. Saffy's gone, too. Well, there was no way I could go; I've got far too much to do. And they keep bursting into tears – God, it's so depressing! Have you booked the flight yet?'

'Well actually, yes,' said Nia, brightening. 'I'm afraid I've had to book economy but at least I'll be there.'

Madeleine's stony expression took Nia by surprise.

'Economy class?'

'Yes. It was the last seat on the same flight as you. Actually it was a good job I left it until now, they were a hundred pounds more expensive two weeks ago when I first looked!'

Madeleine's expression set.

'Well, don't think we'll be popping out with the champers. Would rather defeat the point of flying first class!'

'Oh, that's alright,' said Nia, determined not to fall out. She could see that Madeleine was stressed with everything that was going on. 'I'll be fine. Might even treat myself to a glass.'

'Oh, I doubt they'll serve anything like that! It'll be tins of warm lager and a gin and tonic in a plastic cup – it's called economy for a reason, you know!'

Nia pressed on.

'And, you'll be pleased to hear, that with the money I've saved on the flight I've bought my outfit for the wedding! There was a sale in the shop two doors down from Kaz's. You know, *Miss P*? I've got a really lovely cream dress–'

'Cream?'

'Yes, I'm really pleased with it – it's a fairly heavy silk with a dropped waist, very flattering *and* it was fifty per cent off,' Nia beamed.

'Well make sure you don't stand too close to me on the day, won't you?'

'Oh, why?' said Nia, her smile fading.

Madeleine shot Nia a rigid-jawed look. Travis appeared with an oblivious smile.

'Because everyone knows that you aren't supposed to wear white or cream to a wedding in case you detract from the bride! Are we having a glass of wine?'

***

Wednesday 20th August 4.05p.m.

Madeleine lowered herself into her bath and took a deep, luxurious breath. Everything was set. She had given Mrs B strict instructions to make up the double bed at Amrose Street with one of the prettier sets of bedding that Madeleine had stored away with no intention of ever using again. On her insistence, the bed at Landsmere Grange was only ever to be covered in silk or linen, all brand new, of course. She had also suggested that Mrs B 'borrow' Ben's favourite Thomas the Tank Engine bedding to make up the single room, together with some of his toys (and if her plan was successful these items would only be making that journey one way). Flowers had also been ordered and Ocado had delivered a fortnight's supply of groceries only that morning (and Madeleine had made quite sure there would be plenty for three).

She had even called into the house herself (a first since she had met the agent there as a prelude to the erection of the now very weathered For Sale board) to add some final little touches that she knew Mrs B wouldn't think of, including scented candles for the bathroom, two new towelling robes that she draped casually across the newly made bed, and a stock of CDs to melt even the hardest of hearts.

The plan was that they were all meeting at a new Italian restaurant in town at six-thirty that evening – early enough for Ben to eat with them. Ben was beside himself with excitement and apprehension – Saffy, Madeleine had noticed, was just beside herself.

Madeleine's plan, however, was to feign illness just as they got to the restaurant. She would then insist that Saffy and Ben go to join Alistair while she and Hayden went home. That would give Saffy plenty of time to renew her acquaintance with her husband while Madeleine reminded Hayden just how good it would be to have

Landsmere all to themselves. Not one to miss a trick, the basque had been professionally cleaned for the occasion (it had chafed a little the last time but she wasn't planning to be in it for long).

Madeleine sank lower into the bubbly water, satisfied with a plan well executed. It was obvious that once Saffy and Alistair spent time together again with Ben, Saffy would realise what a terrible mistake she had made to leave in the first place – and Madeleine was going to make sure they spent as much time together without her and Hayden as was humanly possible.

Wednesday 20th August 6.20p.m.

Brian slowed the car to a halt, pulling onto the double yellow lines outside the restaurant and unclipped his safety belt.

'It's OK, Brian, you stay there. I'll let the ladies out,' said Hayden, reaching for the door handle on his side. He didn't often travel in the front seat of the Jag but with Madeleine, Saffy and an uber-excited soon-to-be four-year-old in the back, it seemed the wisest move. He opened the rear door onto the kerb. Ben bounced out but stopped dead. Hayden gave him a reassuring grin. 'It's OK, Ben. Daddy's probably in there already. I bet he can't wait to see you!'

Ben didn't seem convinced and backed into his mother as she was exiting the car.

'Oh, Ben! For God's sake, that was my foot!' Saffy said rather more sharply than was necessary. Ben's lip trembled.

'Oh, no harm done,' said Hayden brightly. He clutched his grandson to his leg and squeezed Saffy's hand. 'It's alright, love. It'll be fine.'

'Is anybody going to help *me* out?' Madeleine asked testily from inside the car. Hayden leaned in and offered his outstretched hand.

'Sorry, darling. Saffy's just a bit nervous, you know… meeting–'

'Oh!' Madeleine made a grab for Hayden's hand but missed and dropped back into the seat. 'Oh, Hayden, I suddenly feel very strange… I… don't think I'm going to be able to make it, you know.'

'What!' said Saffy from the pavement. She was now bordering on hysteria. 'But you've got to. I can't do this on my own! Dad!'

'Mummy!' said Ben. He grabbed his mother's hand. Hayden touched his daughter's shoulder.

'It's alright, Saf. Calm down. I'm not going anywhere.' Then he leant into the car and studied Madeleine's face. Very quietly he said, 'Unless you are close to death you are going to get out of this car now and join me and my daughter to meet her son's father and his future wife.'

Madeleine really did feel the colour drain from her face. The raw silk dress she had chosen was already rubbing her exposed nipples and it was fairly obvious that she had put on a pound of two since the last time she had worn the peephole basque. But Hayden's set jaw said it all.

'Future wife?' she said feebly.

'That's right. I knew you weren't listening when I phoned you! Now get out of the fucking car and smile!'

***

Friday, 22nd August 8.05p.m.

Hayden gazed unseeing out over the dark sea. The bench that normally held such comfort on a warm summer evening supplied little pleasure today. Just in front of him, lit now by the lights shining from the lounge, he could just make out a wolfhound-sized patch of almost bare earth; what grass there was, was flat. Only a week ago, Hayden had sat looking out over his favourite view with his favourite companion at his feet. Like so many tears that had fallen that past week, he let another trickle unchecked down his cheek.

'Shall we give him a toast?' said a gentle voice behind him.

Saffy handed a simple glass flute over her father's shoulder and poured while he held it steady.

'It was his time, Dad,' she said softly. 'And goodness me, he couldn't have been loved any more.'

Hayden opened his mouth to speak but there were no words so he simply lifted his glass in salute. With a wobbling chin, he took a sip, pressed his lips hard together and swallowed.

'To Morris,' Saffy whispered.

It was some time before Hayden broke the silence. He patted the empty space next to him by way of invitation for Saffy to sit.

'Well, at least I know one young man who enjoyed himself today,' he said with a sad grin.

'Yes, thank goodness,' said Saffy. Her tired eyes told of the strain she had been under for the past few days and Hayden knew his relief would be more than matched by his daughter's when they said a final goodbye to Alistair and Charlize the following morning. There had been a difficult moment the previous day when Charlize had voiced the idea that Amrose Street would be an ideal holiday home for her and Alistair, being so near to Ben (although Hayden was also sure that access to Brian and the Jag for the past few days might also have coloured her judgement). But to Hayden's relief, Madeleine had sounded positively negative and a brief mention of a dry rot problem that Hayden was hitherto unaware of had quashed that idea in its infancy.

'He certainly did well for presents – two bikes!' said Hayden, with more of a genuine grin.

'Yeees,' said Saffy. 'I did tell Al that I was getting him a bike. But I guess he forgot. It's alright, though. I can take the one I got back, I called the guy earlier. He was lovely. I promised to get the next one from him – which at the rate Ben's growing, won't be too long at all!'

'It's the sea air and the influence of a wonderful grandfather,' said Hayden with a sage nod.

'Of course,' agreed Saffy. She sipped her drink and threaded her arm through her father's. 'Thanks for this, Dad. For the party today… and for giving us a home.' +She grinned. '*And* for putting up with Madeleine's obvious displeasure! Do you think she'll ever get used to us?'

'Oh, yes. She'll be fine. She gets wound up when she's got a project on, that's all it is.'

'What? And the latest project is your wedding! Goodness me, Dad!'

Hayden shrugged.

'She just likes to be busy. She'll be fine when we're married. More secure.'

'Likes to spend money more like – yours!' sniffed Saffy. 'Honestly, Dad, did you see how much those invitations cost?'

'That did include VAT,' said Hayden. 'And they threw in the place settings for nothing after the… cock-up. If you'd seen what she was originally looking at, three hundred-odd pounds was on the light side!'

They both took another drink and Hayden took the

opportunity to change the subject back to his grandson.

'So, aside of the two bicycles, did Ben get everything he wanted for his birthday?'

Saffy took another sip of her wine before she answered.

'To be honest, Dad, I think he would have been happier just to have Morris back. He misses him so much. I'd never really realised… well, I suppose you don't, do you, until they're…'

Her voice tailed away into the evening darkness.

'I know, love. And God knows I miss him too. But you said it yourself. It was just his time.'

Saturday 23rd August 11.20a.m.

'Stay! God, no! I managed about twenty minutes but the screaming was just too much. Thank God Kaz had already invited me over for supper – fab house, huge! No, honestly Nia, there are many reasons why I haven't got children and volume is up there with stretch marks and sleepless nights! Hang on.' Madeleine tucked her phone under her chin and changed gear. 'Can you still hear me?'

'Are you driving, Maddy?'

'Yer. It's such a bloody nuisance; Hayden had to help Saffy take bike number two back, then he's dropping her off for her theory test – her third, of course!'

'So where's Brian? I was under the impression he was at your disposal these days?'

'Day off – funeral, wedding… something like that. And anyway, now Hayden's back I'm hardly getting a look in! Thank God Jackson's still away!'

'Well, look, I won't keep you; you don't need any more points! Where are you going, we could meet up?'

'Nail varnish. CD's winter colours are in at John Lewis. I'm going to have a look and then I'm meeting Kaz for lunch so I'll have to take a rain check. I told you about her house, didn't I? Couldn't believe she lives there all by herself. Anyway, sometime next week'll be fab. I'll give you a call.'

'Oh, OK. Well, good luck with the nail varnish hunt.'

There was no answer from the other end of the phone. Madeleine had already hung up.

Wednesday, 27th August 9.20a.m.

Madeleine poured herself another black coffee and sorted through the post.

'So now that Saffy's finally passed her theory when's her test?' she asked. An unused breakfast bowl sat in front of her. 'It'll be good for her to be a bit more independent.'

'Oh, there's no rush,' said Hayden, pausing mid-spoonful of All Bran. 'I think she's hoping for sometime in September. Mmm, this really is rather good with banana.' He shovelled the loaded spoon into his mouth and nodded appreciatively.

Madeline opened a gold envelope – one of three in that morning's delivery. 'Oh good, Kaz's coming to the wedding. Did you know she lives in that huge house opposite Ben's school? That reminds me, I must take another look at the seating plan. She'll be on the top table next to me – I'm going to ask her to be my maid of honour. Jackson will be next to you, of course, as best man. Obviously Saffy won't be on our table.'

Hayden stopped mid-chew. 'Why not?'

Madeleine did the wrinkly nose thing.

'Ben, silly. We can't have a four-year-old on the top table.'

'Why not?' repeated Hayden.

'He's a child, darling. It's just not appropriate. No, he and Saffy can sit on Table Five with my Aunt Jess. You'll like her. And the chap from the bank. What's his name?'

'Gregor.'

'That's it. He's bringing his partner, Chris. I'll find someone else to sit with them when we've had a few more replies.'

Hayden had now stopped chewing altogether.

'So it's not appropriate for my grandson to sit on my table at my wedding, but it's alright for him to sit with a couple of gay guys and a batty old woman, none of whom he's ever met before?'

'Don't be silly, darling.' Cue even wrinklier nose. 'Saying it like that makes it sound sordid. After all, Gregor is your bank manager. Oh, and by the way, I hope *that's* going before the wedding.'

Madeleine was pointing towards Morris's bed, still in the corner exactly the same as the last day he had lain on it – the only difference being that now Morris's beech casket was there in his place, together with a simple sprig of dried flowers and the certificate of cremation (Hayden had been a little taken aback when he had discovered the contents of the plain white envelope that had come with the casket – it was so final. But filing it just didn't seem appropriate).

'No,' said Hayden simply.

'What?... But... you can't... what will people think?' spluttered Madeleine.

'Well, as it seems almost everyone on the guest list is a friend of mine and knew Morris, I suspect they will think it fitting – just like they will when my daughter and my grandson are sitting next to me in my dining room on my wedding day.' He scraped out the bowl, popped the last spoonful into his mouth and said, 'And now I'm off to help said daughter buy her son's school uniform. Happy planning!'

Saturday, 30th August, 2.40p.m.

'Paolo? Well, I'd love to invite him but I never know if he's in or out of a relationship,' said Madeleine. After two false starts she had finally agreed to meet Nia in town, under the pretext of buying a new bikini because she had lost 'so much weight'.

'Oh no, he's still with Jonathan. I think he might finally have met the man of his dreams,' said Nia.

'Jonathan?'

'Yes, you know, Paolo met him in June. You were quite bitchy as I recall.'

'No idea,' sniffed Madeleine. 'But anyway, Paolo's never had much luck with the boys, has he? God, haven't seen him for ages.'

'It hasn't gone unnoticed,' said Nia. 'Jonathan is very nice, actually. A dentist. Bit older than Paolo but they really are very good together. Wouldn't be surprised if I'm not buying another hat very soon!'

'A dentist – sounds a bit dull! Well, the guest list's done now anyway. If I have a last minute decline, I'll give him a call.'

'So, have all of the invites gone out now?' asked Nia with a sudden frown.

Madeleine stopped and peered into a shop window; Nia took one look at the price tags and winced.

'Gosh, yes. All the wedding guides tell you to send them out as early as you can. To get the maximum number of acceptances. Some of my guests have very busy schedules. Some will be booking flights, of course. You've got yours, haven't you?' Madeleine wandered across to the other window.

'Yes,' said Nia, still frowning. 'But Ros hasn't had hers yet.'

'Oh,' said Madeleine. She pointed at a very skimpy item draped over the hips of a size 6 mannequin in the window. 'Oh, now that one is fab. Come on, I have to try it on. Only don't laugh, I'm going for a top-up on my tan on Tuesday.'

Tuesday, 2nd September 11.15p.m.

Madeleine stepped into the shower and let the rainwater effect soak her scalp.

'Oh, this is so nice,' she called over the running water.

'Sorry?' said Hayden, from the bedroom.

'This new shower. Feels like a waterfall. It's absolutely fab.'

Hayden's head appeared around the beautifully tiled wall that now created a walk-in wet room where the bath had been only a week before. Brian had not long dropped him home from a meeting at the club and now that third brandy was drifting through him nicely.

'Is that a new tan, the future Mrs Elliot?' he said, unbuttoning his shirt.

Madeleine did a twirl under the water. Soap suds drifted over her bronzed thighs on their way to the floor. Just level with her hips was a wide shelf.

'That's a bit big for a soap dish?' observed Hayden.

Madeleine giggled.

'It's not a soap dish, silly.' She hooked her finger into his belt and slid the zipper of his fly down very slowly. 'Come here and I'll show you.'

Wednesday 3rd September 6.50p.m.

'Well, to be honest, Ros, I'm beginning to regret booking the flight anyway. And now Mum's not well again. I wish I'd delayed a bit longer.' Nia had just ordered a small glass of Merlot but knew as she spoke that it wouldn't be her last.

'Oh, I'm sure it'll be fine. What did the doctor say?'

'It's her heart. They can't regulate the beat. Looks like she's going to have to have a pacemaker.'

'That won't be too bad,' said Ros. 'My mum had one for years. It was great once she'd got used to it – forgot it was there half the time. When will they fit it? Will you need to be there?'

'Not yet, they want to do more tests first. Looks like the week after next at the earliest.'

'Oh, in that case you should go while you've got the chance. The rest of the family are with her, aren't they? And the hotel does look lovely; did you see that link I emailed over? And did you see the prices?' said Ros, eyebrows heavenwards.

'Mmm, had a quick look today. It's certainly grand. I'm going to be the poor relation,' said Nia, gloom descending again.

'What do you mean? Why do you feel like that all of a sudden?' asked Ros.

'Oh, it's Maddy's friend Kaz. She's just so… upmarket. I looked at a scarf in her shop the other day. It was fifty quid! And when we're out she's so keen to splash the cash. Honestly, Ros. We all went out on Sunday evening, you know for a pre-hen night supper, and to be honest I was glad when I got the call from the hospital. I'd have spent all my holiday money that night if I'd stayed!'

'Oh, you know Madeleine, Nia. Kaz'll be her new best friend until she gets bored. I mean, where's Emma Jenkins nowadays? And as for that Josh guy.'

'Who?'

'Exactly! To be honest I'm half-surprised she's stuck it out with Hayden! How is he, by the way? Is he going to get another wolfhound?' asked Ros, her brain doing its usual butterfly flip between subjects.

'Not great by all accounts, although that does depend on who you talk to. Madeleine says he's being awkward and is refusing to move Morris's bed – apparently the casket is on it at the moment. Saffy, on the other hand, says her dad's really upset. He got Morris not long after Georgina was killed.'

'So do you think he'll get another? More's the point, d'you think Madeleine'll allow it?'

'Not sure. One minute she seems to have him wrapped around her little finger and then… you know they had a terrible row about the seating arrangements for the wedding?'

'Really?' said Ros, leaning in to share. 'Who won?'

'Well, Madeleine was really upset actually – apparently she was worried that Ben might be a bit daunted sitting on the top table but when she tried to talk to Hayden about it he got really angry!'

'Goodness!'

'Yes. Apparently, all poor Madeleine had done was suggest that Ben might be more comfortable sitting next to her Aunty Jess rather than on the top table and Hayden hit the roof!'

Ros looked at the ceiling as if trying to recall some long forgotten detail.

'Oh, I think I've met Aunty Jess – stale sherry and tobacco, if that's the right one? God, is she still alive? What on earth has Madeleine invited her to the wedding for?'

'That's the one. The spinster aunt – pots of money.'

'Wasn't she at Madeleine's brother's fiftieth? God, she was about a hundred then!'

Both women guffawed.

'Oh, I can't wait to see this lot,' said Ros. 'Have you got your outfit yet? Did you go for a hat?'

Nia hesitated under the pretext of having a glug of Merlot and then said, 'So your invitation's arrived then?'

'No,' said Ros, not remotely perplexed. 'I checked to make sure it hadn't arrived and slid under the unit in the hall yesterday but I couldn't see it. Has yours? Do you think I should wear a hat? I could get a really extravagant one!'

'No, mine hasn't come yet either,' Nia lied. 'Apparently there was a mistake in the first lot, something to do with the names. She's probably been a bit delayed because of that.'

'Gosh, I haven't seen Madeleine for weeks – our diaries've just been too busy,' said Ros. 'At least I won't be so manic after Friday, once the charity fashion show is over. Do you want to meet up when you get back?' Ros delved into the handbag for her diary. 'Or will you be going straight off to see your mother?'

'Probably, I'll let you know,' said Nia. 'How's the event going, by the way?'

'Oh, really well, actually. A lot of people from the garden party are coming – apparently my umbrella distribution made quite a good impression… Although getting the list was a bit of a pain. Madeleine kept forgetting to send it over. In the end I asked Hayden,' said Ros, with a tiny sparkle of triumph in her eye. 'I should've realised it was his list anyway!'

***

Friday, 5th September 11.25a.m.

Nia picked her way through the half-dozen sun loungers that lay empty in the hot sunshine before she reached Madeleine, who was already ensconced on her own lounger in her own sunny corner of the quiet poolside. Kindle in hand, she did not look up when Nia approached.

Nia scanned the pool.

'Where's Kaz?'

'The bar. We're going to have Buck's Fizz. Give her a shout if you want one,' Madeleine replied without lifting her eyes from her Kindle.

Nia noted the sunbed next to Madeleine's was draped in one of the towels from their room, and underneath it she recognised Kaz's beach bag (Marc Harrison – but she only knew that because of the label). There was a vacant bed a few feet away; Nia grabbed the nearest end and dragged it forward noisily.

She grinned and tucked her own unlabelled beach bag under the newly claimed bed. 'Gosh, it's lovely and quiet, isn't it? Eat your heart out, Benidorm!' Squinting in the brightness, Nia looked out over the glistening pool and undid her sarong. 'Think I'll have a swim before I start drinking.'

Not expecting an answer, she wasn't disappointed. So, leaving the thin fabric behind, Nia stepped to the edge of the pool and dived neatly into the cool blue water.

Coming up for air on the far side, she called out to Madeleine, 'Oh, this is lovely. Are you coming in?'

'Not yet,' Madeleine replied without even the briefest glance over her Ray Bans. 'Maybe this afternoon.'

From her side of the pool Nia could see Kaz at the bar. She was talking with another woman. She gave Nia a friendly wave and resumed her conversation.

Nia did a few gently laps of slow, deliberate breast stroke, taking in the gorgeous façade of the elegant hotel with its textbook trailing bougainvilleas and palm trees swaying obligingly in the warm breeze. By the time she got out she had almost forgotten her worries about money, about her mother and about how she was going to get around the fact that Madeleine appeared to have no intention of inviting Ros to her wedding – almost.

'That was wonderful,' she said, sitting at the end of her lounger dabbing herself dry. The population around the poolside had now grown considerably and she was grateful she'd grabbed a sunbed before her swim.

'Gosh, where's Kaz got to?' said Madeleine, sounding slightly piqued. 'I was hoping to be on at least my second by now!'

Nia crawled up her sunbed and lowered down onto her stomach. 'Talking to someone at the bar.'

'Oh fab, she hasn't copped on already, has she? She mentioned something last night about keeping her eye out for a bit of totty!'

'Wouldn't have thought so,' replied Nia. 'She's chatting to some woman.'

'Oh, right,' said Madeleine, no less piqued. 'Well, I hope she's not planning on being long!' She scrolled a page of her Kindle and continued reading.

'Right, book…' said Nia to herself, and clambered up the sunbed in order to reach her bag.

Looking back on what was to become a lasting memory, Nia couldn't quite see why she had chosen such a manoeuvre. After all, she had always considered herself to be a genuinely bright girl who had grasped rather more than the basic laws of physics at school… So what made her put all of her weight on to the quite obviously unsupported end of her sunbed was a complete mystery to her; but that's what she did.

The choreography of the fall, however, was to forever remain just a blur of passing canvas, a clutch of helping hands, and the voice of someone offering a towel – as it turned out, to staunch the blood from a rather nasty graze on Nia's temple… And the reason for this lasting mystery? Because despite the crash of tubular steel on terrazzo, the yelp of an injured friend and the rush of concerned bystanders, not once did Madeleine look up from her Kindle – not once.

Sunday, 7th September 4.35p.m.

'Hi, Ros, it's Nia,' said Nia unnecessarily.

'Oh, Nia, hello,' said Ros. 'How's it going? Are you having a good time?'

'Well, it was going OK but I had a call at lunchtime. Mum's really not well. I'm at the airport now. Can you do me a favour? The first flight I could get goes to Cardiff but my car's in Bristol–'

'Oh, so how are you going to get your car? Is there anything I can do?'

'Would you be able to come and collect me – the flight gets in at eighteen-twenty? I'll have to see if I can get a train over to Bristol. God, this has to happen on a Sunday!'

'Oh, that's fine. I'll come and get you, and take you to get your car.'

'Oh, gosh, that's very kind, Ros, but it's a heck of a haul. No, there'll be a train, it's fine.'

'Don't be daft, Nia. Anyway, I'm looking online now. You'll be pushed to get that last train. No, I'll come over and get you, haven't been to Wales in an age. Anyway, it's all been rather quiet here since the charity fashion show on Friday. I'll be glad to get out.'

Monday, 8th September 3.35p.m.

'Oh, hi, darling. Is everything alright?' said Madeleine, suddenly concerned. As the dog was done and dusted, was there a crisis with Saffy or Ben? Or, and then she did start to worry, had a key guest sent a declining RSVP? She swapped her phone into her other hand and pressed the call button for the lift.

'Yes, darling, everything's fine,' replied Hayden. 'Just waiting for Saffy to come home with Ben. She passed her test today and I let her go and get Ben all on her own. Quite fitting for his first day.'

'God, was that wise? You haven't let her use my car, have you?'

'No, darling,' said Hayden patiently. 'She went in mine. She's due back in about half an hour so I thought I'd give my future wife a call to find out if she's having a good time on her hen weekend. So, are you… having a good time?'

'Oh, yes. Fab. Nia had to go home yesterday – her mother's had another turn.'

'Oh, no,' said Hayden. 'Have you spoken to her today? Is everything alright? Can I do anything?'

'Don't think so, darling. No idea if she even got a flight. She hasn't called. But she wasn't there when we rolled in last night, or this morning, so I can only assume she's back in the UK.'

The lift doors opened and the bellboy silently guided her in. She held up four fingers. He nodded, pressing the button for the fourth – the top – floor.

'Oh,' said Hayden. 'Well, let me know if you do hear something. Gosh, that's bad luck for her… and you!'

'Weeell, not really. To be honest she was being a bit of a pain. Didn't want to go shopping on Saturday and when she did finally agree, she didn't even try anything on. And she drank soda water all the time we were out! It was all a bit dull.'

'Oh dear. So, how's Kaz? How're the two of you getting on?'

'Oh fab! She bought me a gorgeous Louis Vuitton weekender bag as a thank-you for inviting her – and I haven't even broached the subject of maid-of-honour yet! We're talking about staying a few more days, if that's OK with you?' The lift doors opened and Madeleine stepped out, still talking. 'We sat around the pool drinking Buck's Fizz all day on Friday. She's so friendly. She was chatting to one of the other guests at the bar who came over to join us – Justine. Really nice girl. Ended up staying with us all afternoon and joined us for supper, too. Last night in the bar she was telling us some of the rudest jokes I've ever heard – would have made Jackson Tranter blush!'

Hayden listened to the sound of Madeleine's relaxed laughter and smiled.

'If you want to stay on until the end of the week that's fine with me, my love. You're obviously having a good time. What's the suite like?'

'Fab… well, the one we're in now is.' Madeleine rushed on before Hayden could quiz her. 'There's a walk-in shower and a huge sunken bath. Gorgeous view from the balcony. The staff are fab, too. I'm on my way there now. We hit the tequila last night – Justine's idea – and poor old Kaz was a bit worse for wear this morning. She went up for a lie down a while ago. I'm just going to pop up and see how she is. Poor Justine hasn't made it out at all yet – mind you, she was downing tequila slammers like I've never seen! Said we were like coiled springs – well, we were certainly uncoiled by the end of the evening!' She laughed again. 'Look, darling, I'd better go. I'm back at the suite now. I'll give you a call when I know what flight we'll be on. See you soon. Hugs, bye.'

Key card already in her hand, she swiped the entry pad.

'Hi, Kaz, how're you doing? Did your lunch stay down aft–'

Kaz, on her back, naked and spread-eagled on the vast marble coffee table, turned her head.

'Don't stop,' she snarled through gritted teeth, grabbing the head of the naked girl kneeling between her legs. 'Arghhh, fuuuuuck... Yeeeesssssss...'

Madeleine stood as if petrified while Kaz shared the loudest orgasm Madeleine had ever heard.

Finally Justine came up for air. Kaz grinned, sweat gleaming... all over.

'Well, thank Christ it wasn't only my lunch that stayed down. Fuck me, that was good. Want to join us?'

Tuesday, 9th September 1.10p.m.

Madeleine marched through the Departures gate. Slightly thrown by the dark glasses and scarf tied sixties-style around his wife-to-be's head, Hayden drew his arms wide. The cream raincoat briefly brought to mind Audrey Hepburn but it was fairly clear that Madeleine's thunderous expression wasn't going to inspire anyone to break into *Breakfast at Tiffany's* any time soon.

'Darling, are you alright?' he said, hugging her close. 'Flight OK? Where's Kaz?'

'Er, oh, she decided to stay on after all. Don't worry, she's picking up the bill for the suite,' replied Madeleine, returning the hug with a very half-hearted, one-armed clutch. 'Where's the car? I hope it's not far, I'm exhausted.'

'Oh, so... it wasn't a good flight?'

'The flight was fine. Just didn't get much sleep last night. Kaz and Justine were... er, talking... 'til about four this morning.'

'Oh, you should have joined them – you know, made the most of your last night... all girls together. It sounded like you were all getting on like a house on fire yesterday. I still can't believe you decided to come home.' Hayden took Madeleine's bags.

'No, they were... um..., well into it without me,' said Madeleine. 'No, after I'd spoken to you I just felt so terrible about Nia. She needs me here in case anything awful happens.'

Hayden put his arm around his fiancée.

'Well, I think that's really lovely,' he said, giving her another hug. 'And you're sure Kaz was alright about you leaving her on her own? Mind you, if it was Jackson he probably wouldn't have even noticed – would have been too busy fucking some bit of totty in the next room!'

Thursday, 11th September 4.20p.m.

'God, Dad, I was just beginning to get worried!' said Saffy as Hayden shouldered the front door open.

'I really must get that door looked at, I swear it's getting worse!' he said as Ben charged past him, threw his school blazer on the bottom stair and raced into the kitchen.

'I'm tharving, Mummy. Whatth's for tea?'

'Ben, come back here at once and pick up your blazer!' Saffy shouted at the closing kitchen door. 'Ben!'

'It's OK, love, I've got it,' said Hayden.

'Dad! I told Ben to pick that up. He's got to learn that he can't just charge in treating this place like a hotel!' Saffy's cheeks flushed.

'Oh, it's alright,' said Hayden. 'I don't mind, he's only little.'

'So why were you so late back?' asked Saffy, her pink cheeks now calming down.

'I was talking to that Mrs O'Reilly. Ben had told her about Morris... you know... She was a bit concerned. Apparently Ben did a picture today of a black box and kept saying it was Morris.'

'Oh,' said Saffy. 'What did you say?'

'I just explained that it was probably the casket on Morris's bed. I guess I should move it really.' Her father's face was suddenly sad.

'Did Mrs O'Reilly voice any real concerns once you'd explained?' asked Saffy, her voice gentle now.

'No, she laughed actually. Said she'd try to get him to use yellow next time - I told her the casket's beech. It's just, well, you know... don't want people thinking we're odd or anything.'

He shrugged and hung the blazer on a vacant hook in the hall way. Saffy put her hand on his shoulder.

'Well I don't think you should do anything with Morris until you're ready,' she said. 'And I don't think you're ready yet. Ben understands that Morris is gone and if Mrs O'Reilly doesn't have a problem with his choice of art subjects then why should we?'

'Thanks, love,' said Hayden.

'Maddy'll be pissed off though,' she grinned. 'I'm sure she'd have seized the opportunity if you'd told her first!'

Friday, 12th September, 3.45p.m.

'Oh, that is great news, Nia,' said Ros. 'I'd say we should go out tonight and celebrate but I suspect it would take you a few hours to get back here, especially on a Friday evening. So have they said when she can go home? Will you stay long?'

'Well, it's still early days but all the signs are good,' said Nia's very relieved voice on the other end of the phone. 'I'll probably stay until Monday. I don't want to leave until she's back at home. I do feel guilty though; I haven't done any work for Cornerstone for weeks!'

'Oh, I wouldn't worry too much. Madeleine'll be charging around in a blur of credit cards so Hayden probably hasn't even noticed. Ooh, my invitation arrived, by the way.'

'Oh, that is good news,' said Nia. 'Have you seen Madeleine at all?'

'No. I sent her a text about meeting up tomorrow night but I forgot she's got the grouse supper thing at Hayden's club.'

'Oh, I was just wondering if you'd heard anything about last weekend… Spain?'

'No. I just got a brief text saying she was back. Why, what happened?'

'I don't know. Madeleine phoned me yesterday to ask me to be her maid-of-honour – I'm very chuffed. I asked her how the rest of the weekend had gone, you know, after I left… but, well, she didn't really answer. It was a bit odd.'

'Oh. Well, Kaz's shop was closed when I went past today. I don't really know her that well but I might call in on Monday if she's there and ask how it went.'

'Do you think she'd tell you if something happened?'

'Probably not but… well,' Ros laughed impishly. 'It depends on how horrendous it all got, doesn't it!'

Saturday, 13th September 7.45p.m.

Madeleine swept the room with a critical eye and smiled. Wall-to-wall evening dresses and not a Katherine Dane in sight.

She breathed an audible sigh of relief. Now Kaz was off the list (in more ways than one) Madeleine had been forced to resort to a hasty order from Harvey Nic's, and although she had been assured that the gathered metallic weave lace gown with leather shoulder straps and leather waist belt had not been delivered to anyone else within a fifty mile radius, she still needed to see the proof for herself. The peephole basque was a bit of a no-no though – her new acquisition sported a fully lined lace internal boned bodice; but as her nipples had only just recovered from the last raw silk outing, it was probably for the best. Instead she'd gone for the failsafe – no underwear at all. She would mention this to Hayden when she got bored later, as she was sure she would.

'Champagne, Madame,' offered a passing waiter.

'Please,' said Madeleine. She took a glass and turned to where Hayden had been standing only seconds before. The space was empty.

Slightly miffed, she sauntered much further into the room before she spotted Hayden talking to a tall, exceptionally handsome man, and a woman.

'I thought I'd been abandoned,' said Madeleine, gliding up to the group. She flashed a broad smile at the handsome man. Hayden stopped talking as she approached.

'Darling, I was just telling Alfredo here about how well you're doing with your Spanish lessons. Alfredo, this is Madeleine, my fiancée. Madeleine, this is Elaina O'Reilly, Ben's teacher at Rockmoore School.'

Alfredo and Elaina both nodded politely and raised their glasses. Then, beaming at Madeleine, Alfredo launched into a babble of Spanish that lasted several seconds, turning from Madeleine to the woman, who smiled and nodded. Suddenly he stopped speaking and both he and his sister turned to Madeleine expectantly – as did Hayden.

Madeleine gave a vacuous smile but having not understood a word said nothing. The expectant party held their gaze.

It was several more seconds before the idea that a response was expected crept into Madeleine's mind. Elaina came to the rescue, eventually.

'I am so sorry, I think my brother might have spoken a little too fast for you. He gets so enthusiastic at any opportunity to speak in our mother tongue.'

Madeleine waved her hand as if to dismiss the idea that she may have been caught out.

'Oh, gosh no. Out of context that's all, it just took me a moment... anyway, if we chat away in Spanish my darling husband-to-be,' Madeleine linked her arm through Hayden's, 'would be left out... Oh, look, darling, Jackson's just arrived. We'd better go over and hello. See you both later, *buenos nachos*.'

Never more relieved to see Jackson Tranter in her life, Madeleine positively dragged Hayden away across the floor.

'Well, I'm surprised you didn't want to stay to practise—' Hayden began, but changed tack mid-sentence. 'Well, I'll be. He's brought Lily!'

'Wh–. Oh!'

A tall and very slender (size 6 if she was an inch) woman took a glass offered by Tranter and as she turned Madeleine's worst fear was realised. What was more, it was very difficult for Madeleine to ignore the fact that Lily looked absolutely fabulous in the Katherine Dane. 'Well, goodness me,' she beamed, silently vowing, *I am going to sue Harvey Nichols.*

***

Sunday, 14ᵗʰ September 9.45a.m.

Madeleine was not happy. Her grand entrance at the County Club Grouse Supper as the future Mrs Elliot had not gone entirely to plan. For some inexplicable reason Hayden, normally one for a quiet brandy in the bar and home by eleven, had suddenly turned into Britain's answer to George Clooney – all smiles, charm and banter – and it had taken her rather longer to exit than she had planned. She was also livid that someone else had turned up wearing exactly the same dress as her (apparently Lily's decision to accompany Jackson had all been rather last minute and so they had "just nipped into the City on their way from the airport"); and, even this morning, she was still smarting from the *Spanish* incident which had been exacerbated by Hayden insisting that Alfresco, or whatever his name was, and his sister join their table for the meal!

Even their arrival home had not been without disaster. The front door jammed *again*. This did create the perfect opportunity for Madeleine to reinforce her own attributes; but while Hayden was making the most of her pantie-free state, the repeated and vigorous bumping of Madeleine's bottom against said door, freed it at just the wrong moment. Madeleine had broken a nail in the fall.

Oblivious of her dilemma, Hayden had insisted on finishing in the porch, with a repeat performance not twenty minutes later in the new en suite (the Katherine Dane once again raked up around her waist, but minus the fall, thank goodness). And so, to make absolutely sure Hayden remembered the evening – and the dress – for all the *right* reasons, Madeleine had spread her legs once more for the finale on the chaise longue.

By this time though, Hayden was a tad slower off the mark. So, to give him a breather while still keeping up the momentum, she had put just enough pressure on his shoulders for him to get the message. But just as he sank his face beneath the hem of her dress the vivid image of Kaz splayed out on that coffee table flashed into Madeleine's mind and a gushing climax had overwhelmed her completely. Desperate to stifle the desire to yell, 'Jesus Christ, fuck me, fuck me!' (at the risk of waking anyone in a five-mile radius) Madeleine had gripped the edge of the chaise until her knuckles went white – it was quite a bit later before she realised that she'd broken another nail.

Now, from the bed, vacated by a whistling and *very* cheerful Hayden some twenty minutes earlier, Madeleine could see in the morning light a large stain on the petrol blue satin of the chaise. It had only been delivered by the upholsterer the week before – she was going to have to get him to collect it again.

And successful though it was, the Katherine Dane would also need to be dry-cleaned before being packed away for their honeymoon. So much to do and the days were racing by.

Madeleine studied her ragged nails and scowled. It had taken months of painstaking manicures to achieve perfection in time for her wedding and now, with little over a month to go, there was no way they would grow back in time!

Tuesday, 16th September 8.25a.m.

Saffy hauled her coat across her shoulders.

'Right, Dad, thanks for this. I promise I won't make a habit of it. Once I'm into a routine I'll be able to drop him off on the way.'

Hayden drained his coffee cup.

'Oh, don't worry, love. It's a pleasure.' He glanced around. 'Where is he, by the way?'

'Brushing his teeth – I hope! Could you just nip up and check his brush is at least wet? I'm trying to get him to do things on his own but it's not that easy. He's *so* easily side-tracked!'

Hayden grinned.

'Oh, and who do you think he takes after there?'

'Oh, come on, Dad! I was never that bad! If it's anyone it's his father!'

Ben pushed the kitchen door open just as she finished speaking. He was clutching a yellow tow-truck. 'Daddy – where? Is he here?' Ben went up on his tiptoes to get a better look out of the kitchen window. A sad look flashed across Saffy's face.

'I'm sorry, darling, he's not. I was just talking to Grandpa about how you don't do things when I ask you to… hmmm?' She put her hands on her hips and gave her son a mock glare.

Ben pushed the little truck across the edge of the breakfast bar, suddenly deaf.

His mother threw her gaze heavenwards and shook her head.

'Right, well, Ba Ritten is going to take you to school. Mummy's going to work. I'll pick you up this afternoon. OK?'

'Why can't Ba Ritten pick me up?' asked Ben, suddenly sulking.

'I can if you want?' offered Hayden brightly.

Saffy looked tempted but shook her head.

'No, it's alright. I'm going to have to work this out for myself. But thanks, Dad.'

'Well, just remember, if I'm here it's no trouble. And to be honest, with Maddy's whirlwind of planning for the next month I'll be glad to get out of the way!'

***

Thursday 18th September 5.55p.m.

Madeleine glanced at her watch and frowned. She had agreed to meet Ros at five-thirty for an early glass but as yet there was no sign of her. Madeleine was miffed. After all, it wasn't as if she didn't have anything to do! The redecoration of the dining room at Landsmere was turning into a complete nightmare and as for the caterers… a very troubling conversation she had about monkfish tails earlier that day had resulted in rapid flicking through the Yellow Pages in the search for a competent alternative.

She drained her glass and reached for the bottle chilling in an ice bucket next to the table – Chardonnay (far easier to get a bottle especially as she was fairly sure Ros only drank white anyway).

Another ten minutes ticked away while Madeleine quietly fumed about the debacle this morning in the dining room – and that was *before* the conversation with the caterers. Surely any idiot would have known she would be in and out of that room? So why they had chosen to erect the scaffold tower right behind the door was beyond her! What had really piqued her though was the total lack of an apology from the foreman while they were waiting for the ambulance. Was it her fault that the lad had knocked himself out and dislocated his shoulder? Definitely not! She'd only moved the ladder for a second to check the paint chart – and a good job too. That cream was a lot darker than she'd expected! If it had clashed with her dress… she shuddered and did her best to banish that scenario from her mind.

Her phone beeped, announcing the arrival of a text.

The text read, 'Sorry Maddy. Dad not good. Can't come. Will text soon. Ros ☹.'

'Great!' said Madeleine and with an intolerant sigh, chucked her phone back into her bag and reached for the Chardonnay. Well, she thought, Brian was picking her up and with the day she was having, she deserved a drink!

Saturday, 20th September 10.25a.m.

The phone in the hall trilled loudly. Madeleine grabbed up the receiver.

'Hello!' she barked. She had been waiting for a call from the decorator since eight-fifteen that morning and had got up early especially. The full extent of the lad's injuries had only become apparent the previous day and much to Madeleine's horror it appeared that the work on the dining room was now going to be delayed even more. Madeleine had made her feelings on the subject very plain when the foreman had initially broken the news, and now she was fully expecting to hear that the injured boy had been replaced and all would go ahead as planned.

'Madeleine?' said Nia's voice

'Nia?'

'Yes, I—'

'Oh, I was expecting someone else. Won't be able to talk for long. I'm having a nightmare with the decorators. Honestly, Nia, it'll be a fucking miracle if we're not eating the wedding breakfast out of paint tins, the rate they're going!'

'Oh, sorry to hear that. But look, I've just spoken to Ros—'

'Well that's more than I have! She stood me up on Thursday! She was supposed to text me. I was f—'

'Her father died, Maddy. Last night... two o'clock this morning actually.'

For the briefest moment Madeleine was caught off her stride... but only the briefest moment.

'Oh,... well, she could have rung! When's the funeral? God, I hope it isn't Wednesday. I've got a fitting at twelve. Then I'm going to see Patrick about my hair extensions. We're going to decide on the colour. Something not too bold, just enough to look autumny.'

There was a pause before Nia answered...

'No, it'll be after that, I'm sure.'

Monday, 22nd September, 8.30a.m.

Madeleine was in the sitting room and didn't get up when Hayden announced his imminent departure.

'Oh, if you're taking Ben to school, darling, can you pick up the wallpaper on your way back?' she called. 'Harlow's rang Saturday lunchtime to say it's in. God, if they don't start on the papering this week I'm going to have a nervous breakdown!'

Hayden popped his head around the door. Madeleine was surrounded by cookery books. She didn't look up. He chose not to ask.

***

Friday, 26th September, 12.45p.m.

'Black's definitely not Ros's colour, is it?' Madeleine said to Nia in a half-hearted attempt at a whisper. Hayden sidled along the pew and took his place at her side in the sparsely populated church – he had been talking to someone he knew outside. He looked past Madeleine and gave Nia a brief nod. Madeleine nodded towards a very smartly dressed elderly lady who had just taken her place next to Ros in the front pew, and gave Nia a furtive nudge. 'So who's that? I didn't think Ros had a sister?'

'She hasn't. That's her aunt,' Nia replied in a rather more hushed voice. 'Her father's sister. Noreen, I think? Ros used to stay with her during school summer holidays while her father was working. Gorgeous house in Northumberland, apparently. She never married so Ros'll get it all, of course. '

Next to Madeleine, Hayden waved to a couple who had just parked themselves two pews in front. A man in a long black coat at the front of the church said something to Ros, who gave a sombre nod.

Madeleine nudged Nia again. 'So who's the good-looking guy?'

'The funeral director,' replied Nia without looking round.

In the now half-full church, the organ burst into life. Behind the rows of empty pews, movement in the doorway indicated the arrival of the coffin and as heads turned Ros caught hold of her aunt's frail hand.

***

Tuesday, 30th September, 3.15p.m.

'Right, darling,' said Hayden, giving Madeleine's cheek a passing peck. Stationed at the breakfast bar, studying several pages of a very long list, she raised her cheek but kept her eyes down. 'Just going to get Ben. Saffy's stuck at work. Think I'll take him to the park for half an hour if you don't need me for anything?'

Madeleine ran her pen down the entries, flicking the pages over as she reached the end of each one. Halfway down the third page her pen stopped. She tapped the nib on the paper.

'Could you pop into Millington's and pay the deposit for the catering?'

'Will do. They're at the top of Holburn Street, aren't they? Wheatsheaf logo? Their menu was here somewhere.' He glanced around but the breakfast bar was wheatsheaf-free. 'Looked good.'

This time Madeleine did look up - abject horror etched across her face.

'God, no! After what they suggested as a main course for my vegetarians! No, Millington's are on Hill Street, next to Bar 77. It's double yellows but I always park outside.'

'Yes, I noticed,' Hayden muttered.

'Oh, by the way, darling, I almost forgot,' called Madeleine. Hayden was now on his way to the front door. 'Amrose Street – the agent rang yesterday. We've had an offer.'

Hayden's head reappeared around the door, looking considerably more interested.

'Oh, that's great!' He'd been paying the mortgage since Madeleine moved into Landsmere on the promise that she would repay him as soon as the place was sold. But the asking price and the original purchase price were disappointingly close and unless the house sold soon Hayden was well aware that he was going to be seriously out of pocket. 'How much?'

'Three thousand under the asking,' said Madeleine with a sniff. 'I told the agent he was having a laugh.'

'That's still a profit of five.'

'Well, I told him that I wouldn't accept a drop of more than fifteen hundred,' said Madeleine.

'Fifteen hundred! In this market!' Hayden stepped back into the kitchen. 'It's the only offer you've had, Maddy. How long's that house been on the market? When did he call?'

'Yesterday morning.' Madeleine was studying her list again.

'Well, if I were you,' said Hayden darkly, 'I'd phone him back and tell him that you'll accept an extra grand on what they've offered now and have done.'

His exit was swift and as the front door grated and slammed, Madeleine gave her list another sharp tap.

'Well you're not me, are you?'

Friday, 3rd October, 11.45p.m.

Madeleine lay on her back, head propped up on her pillows. In her hand was her To Do list, which, over the past two months, had been embellished, edited, amended and changed back (sometimes on Hayden's insistence, often not). But she wasn't reading it.

Hayden was in the shower. He was whistling. He'd been doing a lot of whistling lately.

Since Madeleine's return from Spain, Hayden had been treated to what in even his limited experience, he could only rank as phenomenal sex. Of course, Madeleine allowed him the take the credit – how could she not? But the fact was that the vision of Kaz and Justine in flagrante delicto continued to elicit the most magnificent, hip clenching, really tempted to shout out loud and bugger-the-neighbours orgasms that Madeleine had ever encountered. Hayden was, in fact, merely a passenger enjoying the ride. (Sometimes he wasn't even in the saddle!)

Hayden emerged from the shower and, with a yawn, threw his robe over the *re*-reupholstered chaise. Madeleine abandoned her list altogether and let it slide to the floor, while she threw back the duvet, by way of silent invitation for him to clamber aboard. But Hayden's regret-filled grin suggested that she was about to be disappointed.

'Sorry, darling,' he said, climbing in next to her. 'That meeting really took it out of me today. I'm knackered.'

But by now Madeleine was in no mood to be left wanting. She did, for a millisecond, toy with retiring to the bathroom (she had discovered a new and far more satisfying use for her old electric toothbrush) but the bed was warm and the silk sheets against her skin added a certain something. So, shimmying across the king-sized, twelve-turn intuitively sprung, hand-made mattress, she slid her hand slowly down over his thigh while her lips brushed his ear and whispered, 'And I know just how to make sure you get a good night's sleep.'

Monday, 6th October, 3p.m.

Hayden's phone trilled in his briefcase. He had been in a meeting in the City since ten-thirty a.m. with some very unhappy shareholders and was not in the mood for Madeleine and her constant list of errands. 'It'll all be fine once the wedding's over,' he reminded himself while clinging on to a particularly splendid memory of Madeleine, the chaise and the peep-hole basque – guaranteed to persuade him to forgive her for anything. But when he looked at the number it was not the one he was expecting or indeed recognised. With a flick of his finger across the screen he answered the call.

'Hello, Hayden Elliot speaking,' he said, pushing the vision of Madeleine out of his mind with some difficulty.

'Oh, good afternoon, Mr Elliot. It's Christie here, from Country Homes. We've had a revised offer for 14 Amrose Street. I can't contact Miss Edwards and the people are with me now.'

'How much?'

'They've increased their offer by fifteen hundred and can complete as soon as possible – they're cash buyers, Mr Elliot. I did mention this to Miss Edwards. I have to say, it's a good offer, especially in this climate.' The voice on the other end of the phone was professional to the point of cool and in any other circumstance Hayden would have called her bluff. But the house was costing him money every month, and the wedding was costing him a hell of a lot more. Something had to go.

'Right, we'll take it,' he said, nodding needlessly. Then, just to make sure she understood that victory was not all hers, Hayden added, 'As long as they can complete in eight weeks.'

Tuesday, 7th October 10.15a.m.

Madeleine flicked through the post and sauntered into the kitchen.

'Coffee?' said Hayden, pouring anyway (it was a 'Do bears shit…?' question and he knew it).

Madeleine drew the steaming mug across the unit towards her

and exchanged it for a white envelope.

'You might as well open that,' she said, taking the remainder of the post with her to her usual place at the breakfast bar.

The envelope bore the Country Homes logo as part of the postmark.

'It's your house,' said Hayden. He had broken the news about accepting the offer the night before but for some inexplicable reason it had not been well received.

'I thought so. But as you're now obviously acting as my agent, I thought you–'

Hayden's phone rang loudly. It was Saffy. Her voice was trembling.

'Dad, it's Saffy. Look, are you busy at the moment?'

'No, love, what's the matter?'

'It's Ben. The Head's just called. He's banged his head in the playground. He's just been sick, Dad. They want to take him to the infirmary now but I'm on the train to Birmingham.' Fear and frustration choked in her voice. 'I'll get on the return train at the next station, Dad, but I'm already an hour away.'

Hayden was already dragging his jacket over his shoulders.

'Don't worry, Saf. I'm on my way now. I'll call you when I get to the school. Don't worry, love, he'll be fine.'

He tucked the phone in his pocket and patted the fabric. Madeleine threw him a battle-weary glare.

'What's happened now?'

'Ben's fallen over. Hit his head. I've got to take him to the hospital.'

The keys for the Land Rover jangled in his pocket but he remembered that he hadn't used it since the day he and Saffy had taken Morris's body to the crematorium and it had threatened not to start then. He unhooked the dust-coated key for Madeleine's Audi from the key rack and raced out of the kitchen. 'I'll take the

Audi, unless you need it?'

'Oh,' objected Madeleine, her voice loaded with indignation. 'And why can't Saffy go? After all, she's got your car, as usual!'

'For God's sake, Maddy. She's on a train to Birmingham!' barked Hayden, already hauling on the front door.

'Oh, so hasn't she heard of the emergency cord?' spat Madeleine. The sound of the Audi's wheels spinning on the gravel outside seconds later suggested possibly not.

Wednesday, 8th October 11.35a.m.

From the window seat of Horton's, Nia could see Madeleine's troubled face as soon as Brian opened the rear door of the Jaguar. She had seen so little of Madeleine since Ros's father's funeral it was difficult to anticipate the nature of *la catastrophe du moment* in the veritable smorgasbord of petty disasters that were the focus of Madeleine's existence. Today Nia's money was on paint colour – that dining room was turning into Madeleine's nemesis (if you listened to Madeleine anyway); but then Nia remembered a reference to hair extensions…

'So he's alright?' said Nia, when Madeleine had finally finished telling her, very briefly, about Ben and in far more detail about how horrid Hayden had been about borrowing her car.

Madeleine gave a dismissive wave. 'Oh yes! Well, I made him apologise, of course. Honestly, I was in that huge house on my own all night. God knows why it took so long – Hayden didn't get home 'til 4 o'clock. I might have needed my car!'

'And Ben?' said Nia patiently.

'I assume so. Still in hospital. Bump on his head, I think.

Hayden was up and out again this morning before I'd even had a shower and obviously I'm only worthy of scant detail. He's just avoiding having to talk about Amrose Street, I'm sure. God, first he sells my home from under me and then he takes my car! It'll be a pro-nup agreement next! Honestly, Nia, I'm starting to wonder what I'm letting myself in for!'

Thursday, 9th October 8.45p.m.

Hayden gently pushed the door to Ben's bedroom with his index finger. Saffy was sitting on a chair beside her son's bed. She jumped at the sound and Hayden immediately regretted the intrusion – she had obviously been dozing.

'Hi,' he whispered. 'OK to come in?'

Saffy answered with a quick nod and stretched. Hayden ventured quietly into the room and looked down at his sleeping grandson. 'Asleep then?' Madagascar was firmly tucked into the crook of the little boy's arm.

'Yes,' whispered Saffy with a tired smile. 'And after two very long nights in a children's ward I'm not going to be far behind him.'

'Did he go off alright just now?'

'Took him a little while. He's still worried about making Mrs O'Reilly cry. Bless him. I tried to explain she was scared for him, not of him, but I'm not sure he's convinced. Was there a lot of blood?'

'Quite a bit,' said Hayden taking on a dismissive tone. There had been copious amounts of blood but it was all over now and he knew Saffy was already beating herself up for not being there sooner. 'You know head wounds – always bleed like hell. Poor El– Mrs O'Reilly. She was in quite a state when I arrived. The Head was very good though – the ambulance was already there.' He'd told her this before when she had arrived at the hospital while they were waiting for Ben's X-ray results. But now, in the safe quiet of her son's bedroom he knew this time round his words would be heard.

Saffy gently brushed a wayward lock of hair from her son's forehead. Three bloody butterfly stitches decorated the little boy's forehead, almost, but not quite covering a yellowing egg-like lump where the bruise was starting to come out. 'She came back in today but Ben was out for the count.'

Saffy got up and they both stood and watched Ben sleep for a few moments before Saffy spoke again.

'She's nice, isn't she – Mrs O'Reilly? I couldn't believe how long she stayed at the hospital that first night.' She turned to look at her father. 'It was good of you to take her home, Dad... and thanks for looking after us.'

He put his arm around her shoulder and drew her close. A lump in his throat stopped him from speaking but he knew he didn't need to say a word.

Saturday, 11th October, 12.05p.m.

Nia steered her car into the first lay-by she came across, pulled on the handbrake and turned the key to switch off the engine. Silence reigned. And after the unbelievable noise that had suddenly started emanating from somewhere under her car, that silence was golden. After a few moments of frantic rummaging in the depths of her handbag she located her phone and found Madeleine's number.

'Maddy, hi, it's me,' said Nia when Madeleine finally answered.

'Nia, God, where are you? The caterers are already here. Have you got the chair covers?'

'Yes, they're lovely. The problem is, Maddy, my car's started making the most horrendous noise. I don't think I should drive it any further.'

'What? But you've got the covers. That was the whole point of this meeting – to finalise the colours. Oh, God, this is all I need, today of all days!'

'Well, I'm going to have to give the garage a call but– oh, God, it's Saturday, isn't it? I'd better call them now in case they close at one.'

'Great! And Hayden's disappeared – the bloody club, probably. Where are you? I'll send the caterers out. They'll have to get the covers an– …sorry, what? … Oh, great. They won't be able to come back. So I won't see the bloody things before next weekend, which means I've got absolutely no idea if they'll match my outfit… as it is, the tablecloths are only right if we don't put the main lights on in the dining room on. Oh, God, this is turning into a fucking disaster!'

Monday, 13th October, 9.45a.m.

'So why can't Saffy take him? For God's sake, I was labouring under the impression that she was his mother!' was Madeleine's response when Hayden had broken the news that he was going to take Ben to the hospital for a check-up before taking him in to school.

'I'm sorry, darling,' said Hayden, his voice steady. 'But Saffy's only been in that job five weeks. She was up against stiff competition to get it and she's desperate not to mess them about. They've already altered her hours so she can pick Ben up on a Friday.'

'Well, it's nice to see that *someone*'s got spare hours!' Madeleine's eyes flashed. 'In case you've forgotten we are getting married on Saturday. There's a mountain of stuff to do and babysitting is not on my list!'

'Well, I'm sorry that my only grandson's recent head injury is getting in the way of your wedding!' said Hayden, almost, but not quite shouting now. 'And anyway, I wasn't under the impression my services would be needed today or have you changed that fucking list again?'

Monday, 13th October, 5.35p.m.

Madeleine sobbed into her wine glass.

'He was just so horrid, Nia.'

Hayden had returned to the house only briefly that lunchtime and had gone straight to his study, taking with him the soup Mrs B had made for their lunch. A little after two Brian had arrived and, muttering something about a late meeting, Hayden had exited the house as quickly as he'd arrived. At five o'clock there was still no sign of him and Madeleine, having arranged to meet Nia and Ros for a pre-wedding drink at Horton's, had been forced to take her own car. She had just finished recounting this sorry tale and she was clearly not happy.

'I'm just trying to make sure my wedding day is a success – what's wrong with that? How could he be so insensitive?'

Nia trod as carefully as she could while quietly admiring Hayden's staying power.

'Oh, I'm sure he didn't mean it, Maddy. Hayden's such a sweetie. He's probably just been worried about Ben and… well… maybe your… enthusiasm's just adding to the pressure a bit?'

Ros looked suddenly grave.

'Gosh, did you expect to be taking on a ready-made family, Madeleine?' she asked, adding after a pause, 'You are absolutely sure you want to go ahead with all this, aren't you?'

Madeleine looked like she'd been shot. Nia held her breath.

'Of course!' she said, suddenly not a tear in sight. 'This wedding is going to be the best day of my life. I'm going to look absolutely fabulous, the house will look immaculate and I will be Mrs Madeleine Elliot. And once I get back from my honeymoon, I can assure you, I will be making changes!'

Tuesday 14th October, 10.45a.m.

'Hi, Christie, it's Madeleine,' Madeleine announced.

To her enormous irritation Hayden had once again disappeared somewhere with Brian, giving her no other choice than to take her car if she had any hope of getting to the tanning salon by eleven. Exiting Landsmere's potholed driveway, she pushed her foot down on the accelerator and slid the Audi into sixth. With a fifteen-minute drive ahead she felt there was nothing else to do but to catch up on a few calls. Her first, while glancing between the road and her phone to find the number, was to Country Homes.

'Yes,' Madeleine nodded. 'Madeleine Edwards, well, until

Saturday, of course.' She did the wrinkly nose thing and glanced at her reflection in the rear view mirror just to check the effect was as desired. 'I'm just calling to let you know there's been a bit of a change this end and the sale's off.'

'…'

'Yes, I'm sorry too but can't be helped. I don't need to sign anything, do I… No, fab. Right, well thanks for your help. Take care. Bye.'

Her next phone call was to her new hairdresser – luckily she'd stored the number on the weekend.

'Hi, Sonia…? Oh. Is she there? I need to change my Friday appointment to tomorrow, mid-day.'

'…'

'Nine-thirty! Are you sure she can't see me any later?'

'…'

'She might have but I'm getting married on Saturday!'

'…'

'Hm! Well, it'll have to do, but I'm really not impre– Sonia, hi! Madeleine here. I have to change my appointment. Any chance of fitting me mid-day tomorrow?'

'…'

'Eleven? Oh, you're a sweetie… no, the hair extensions, Autumn Palette. They were being ordered for me.'

Madeleine waited for quite a few minutes with her phone tucked under her chin before a voice, not Sonia's, confirmed that the Autumn Palette hair extensions would be in before her appointment the following day. Madeleine rang off, indicated left and pulled across the first two spaces she spotted in the almost full car park. On the passenger seat next to her bag lay a battered business card that she had come across in the drawer of the hall table when she had been searching for a spare pen that morning.

'Right, that bloody driveway,' she muttered and dialled the

number. The phone at the other end was answered almost immediately.

'Hello, this is William H. Bosworth on 07972 1876– '

'Ah, Mr Bosworth,' Madeleine cut in. 'Madeleine Edwards here, Landsm–'

The voice on the other end continued speaking.

'I'm sorry but I'm not available to answer your call at the moment. Please leave a message and I will telephone you back upon my return. Please wait until after the beep.'

Madeleine sighed and started again – slowly.

'Mr Bosworth, Madeleine Edwards here, Landsmere Grange. I need you to come over on Friday to fill the holes in the drive…' She left her number and rang off. Studying the remaining items on her now somewhat frayed To Do list, she put a red line through the entry '*Get drive sorted!!*' Almost all of the entries now bore a similar mark. She allowed herself a smile. 'Well, Ms Edwards, I think we're finally getting somewhere.'

Thursday 16th October, 11.10a.m.

Madeleine admired her reflection in the mirror behind the reception desk. She really was wearing very well for her age… and that tan was just right. Behind her, the salon, small with room for only two sinks and two chairs, looked out over the newest part of the harbour redevelopment, where the reflection of a crane some way off and the sound of not too distant banging reinforced the half-finished nature of the neighbourhood went completely unnoticed by the bride-to-be. Next door the old harbourmaster's building, crumbling after years of neglect, was being lovingly coaxed into the twenty-first century and converted into four luxury apartments (Madeleine had popped her head in to offer interior design services some three weeks previously, but as yet there had been no commissioning phone call – just as well, she had decided; she was far too busy with the wedding).

'Hiya,' said a voice Madeleine didn't recognise.

'Oh,' said Madeleine, looking past the reflection of a young girl. 'I was expecting Sonia.'

'Day off,' replied the girl with an expression that could easily have been construed as not giving a fuck. 'I'm Ellie-Mae. I'm doing your hair extensions.'

Presented with such a rock solid case for Sonia's absence and Ellie-Mae's reason for being, even Madeleine realised the futility of argument and took the seat offered by the young girl.

To Madeleine's relief, Ellie-May had quickly cottoned on to her lack of any desire to strike up conversation. So while the girl separated and glued, Madeleine had got busy. Her list and her phone had rarely left her ear; she had called Mr Bosworth again (he had left a message confirming her request but she just needed him to understand she meant this Friday). Next was the florist; then her beautician, the caterers, the decorators, the chair hire company, the caterers again and the limousine company.

Some three and a half hours later Madeleine's list was considerably redder and she had a lot more hair. She was also pleased. Ellie-May led her back to the reception area and disappeared with a waiting customer. The receptionist gave an empty smile and pushed forward the payment machine. Madeleine entered Hayden's pin number without a pause. Ellie-May reappeared. Madeleine's phone trilled.

'Nia, hi! Just finished at the hairdressers.' Ellie-May was mouthing something and pointing from the sinks to her own head. Madeleine nodded, dropped a pound coin into the tips jar and left the salon with her phone still clamped to her ear. 'Let's meet at Horton's – you can have a sneak preview. It looks fab!'

Thursday 16th October, 3p.m.

'Wow, Maddy! You look amazing!' said Nia, trying not to fix her smile. The hair extensions were certainly dramatic – Kate Bush on acid sprang into Nia's mind. 'I wasn't expecting so much... volume! And those colours! Drink?'

Madeleine glanced at the huge pseudo Victorian clock face on the wall at end of the bar. Her reflection looked back from a nearby window.

'Hmm, three o'clock... oh, go on, I'll have a quickie.' She did that irritating smiley, wrinkly-nose thing again and shrugged her shoulders. 'Only a small one though. Hayden's gone off with Brian so I had to bring the car.'

Nia went to get the drinks, leaving Madeleine to find seats. She claimed one of the leather sofas next to the window. Nia returned with two small glasses of red wine.

'Merlot OK?' She pushed one of the glasses towards Madeleine. 'So how's it going?'

'Oh fab!' said Madeleine, watching herself in the window. 'Hayden's keeping out of the way, and I haven't seen much of Saffy or the brat child either – a situation I would love to get used to.'

'Any mention of a move there?'

Madeleine dragged her eyes from the window and sipped her drink before she answered.

'Not really, but, well... the sale of Amrose Street's just fallen through so I'm really going to press Hayden now. I mean, she is working, for chrissake! If she paid me rent I'd have my own independent income. And it's so close to that school.'

Nia recalled a distant discussion about Hayden paying Madeleine's mortgage but didn't bring it up. Instead she said, 'But I thought Hayden picked Ben up most days. Ben seems very happy by the way, I drove past them the other day. They were talking to a woman – long dark hair, Mediterranean looking?'

'Yes,' said Madeleine, making far more eye contact with the window than with her friend. 'One of the teachers… Mrs O'Brien? O'Leary?… something Scottish. She was with her brother at the County Club a few weeks ago. Good-looking guy. Spanish. Bit know-ally.'

Nia suddenly beamed. 'Talking of Spain,' she said with a gulp of her drink. 'Haven't heard mention of the apartment hunt in ages… or the hen weekend, for that matter!'

'Oh, we're still looking,' said Madeleine. 'No time at the mo, with all the work on the house. The dining room looks fab, by the way.' She paused; Nia waited for mention of the hen weekend but Madeleine suddenly looked troubled. 'God, I just hope those seat covers are alright.'

Nia waited again; this time for Madeleine to enquire about her car. No question came.

'It was my exhaust, by the way. Had to have a new one… and shock absorbers. I stopped them looking in the end in case they found anything else!'

'Oh, that reminds me,' said Madeleine, tearing her eyes from the window to glance down at her nails. 'I need to collect that new nail polish.' She downed the remainder of her wine and moved to leave. 'Found the perfect colour in that tiny pharmacy at the bottom of Bell Street – although I had to order it!'

For the tiniest second Nia wanted to tell Madeleine exactly what she thought about the tireless search for the holy grail of ivory nail polishes but she had something to ask so steered clear.

'Oh, I'll walk down with you. My car's parked opposite.' They headed for the door. 'So everything's set for the big day? Did Kaz get that underwear for you? Ros told me about it. I was in Kaz's shop the other day. Her stuff is gorgeous but my God, the prices!'

'No, Victoria's Secret. Ordered on line. So much easier than traipsing into town and trying on knickers in a chilly changing room.'

'I suppose so... anyway, she said to say hello.' They walked on a few paces before Nia spoke again. 'Actually, Maddy, I was wondering if I could ask a favour?'

'What?' Madeleine stepped out on to the street.

'Well, er... the thing is, do you think it would be possible for me to bring *un ami*?'

'A what?'

'Ooh, I'm so excited, Maddy!' Nia clasped her hands together. 'Peter and I... well, he's left his wife... for good this time. He's moved in and I was wondering... could I bring him on Saturday?' The words tumbled out, almost getting lost in the noise of a bus pulling away from the kerb opposite. Madeleine stopped dead.

'Nia, I can't believe you're asking me this. Have you any idea how long the seating plan took?'

'Oh, well what if he came a bit later?' Nia could feel defeat in the air but was not going to give up without a fight. 'He could come to the do in the evening. Or have you planned the seating for that, too?'

Madeleine pursed her lips and, Nia noticed, flared her nostrils very slightly.

'I'm sorry, Nia, but no. It's far too late to make changes. It would cause chaos for the caterers and God knows they've been a challenge so far! Sorry, Nia, no.'

As she finished speaking, her last word was punctuated by an odd splattering sound. Madeleine crouched as if suddenly struck and put her hand to her head.

Nia spotted the bird poo just before Madeleine's fingers felt it, and for a very brief pre-trickle moment Nia could have been forgiven for thinking it was an egg nestling in an explosion of red, brown and gold. Above, a seagull wheeled; its mocking cry bouncing around the walls of the surrounding buildings. Unable to speak, Nia drew a crumpled hanky from her pocket to offer to Madeleine. But as tears of suppressed laughter washed down her face she closed her fingers and kept it for herself.

Friday, 17th October, 8.50a.m.

Madeleine lay in bed, enjoying the peace. With Saffy at work and Hayden doing the school run the house would be quiet for at least half an hour until Mrs B arrived with the vacuum. It had always irked Madeleine that, despite numerous requests, the housekeeper insisted on doing the bedrooms first – hers and Hayden's specifically. Mrs Bosworth's stock response to Madeleine's regular objections was, 'That was always Mrs Elliot's preference,' leaving little doubt as to which Mrs Elliot the housekeeper was referring.

Hmm! thought Madeleine, *After Saturday, this new Mrs Elliot will be making sure things are done to her preferences!*

Shrouded in the crisp cotton duvet, Madeleine nestled down. Her scalp felt strange with the addition of her new hair extensions. But, she consoled herself, when she walked down that aisle in eighteen hours' time – the product of months of preparation – she would be the perfect bride and all the hard work would be worth it.

Her wedding dress (currently safe at Amrose Street ready for Brian to collect later) was a triumph. Every time she tried it on even she was surprised at just how wonderful she looked – especially now the bruising along her bikini line had faded back (the price you pay for a particularly rigorous waxing). And the evening outfit... well, let's just say, it would be the deal sealer; although the guests wouldn't know the intimate details, of course!

As well as her own perfect look, the interior decorators had finally finished. The new curtains in the dining room had been hung and, following a particularly vocal tantrum, re-hung, and the caterers would be arriving with the crockery and glasses at ten-thirty that morning. All Madeleine needed to do was confirm that it would be Sonia coming to put the finishing touches to her hair the following morning and her list was complete.

She rolled over on to her side. A discarded stocking was draped over the corner of the chaise – its partner lay limp just outside the bathroom door – both evidence not so much of a torrid night of wild sex but of a woman desperate to wash seagull shit out of her hair before anyone came home.

Now, hair clean once more, Madeleine recalled that it had been Kaz who had introduced her to that particular brand of stocking, insisting that silk was definitely the way forward if you wanted to make a lasting impression. Nia's message from Kaz skipped through Madeleine's mind. She did miss the shopping trips, meals out and gallons of champagne (the bills for which Kaz had always paid without even a blink). She missed too the almost inexhaustible supply of designer clothes that Kaz had practically given to Madeleine. Madeleine rolled onto her back and gazed up at the ceiling. There had even been talk of Kaz treating Madeleine to a stay at a very exclusive health spa just outside Canterb– On the pillow something long and dark caught Madeleine's eye. Downstairs the scrape of wood on quarry tiles indicated the arrival of Mrs B. Madeleine moved her head and the thing on her pillow moved too. Madeleine leapt out of bed. Her screams were probably heard at the other end of the potholed drive.

Friday, 17th October, 1.30p.m.

'Three-thirty! But this is an emergency!' snarled Madeleine. In the leather tub chairs opposite, Nia and Ros sat in wide-eyed silence, frothy cappuccinos untouched and wilting in front of them. Madeleine shook her head and another limp length of hair drifted from her head. It landed with a weak '*phat*' on the floor beside her chair. Nia tried hard not to notice and suspected Ros did, too.

'Well, if that's the earliest you can possibly do I suppose it'll have to!' continued Madeleine. Having almost exhausted the supply of hairdressers in the county in the past two years, Madeleine had had to resort to the Yellow Pages and getting an appointment at very short notice on a Friday afternoon was proving a challenge. Under that tan, Nia strongly suspected, was a face white with worry. Madeleine gave a stiff nod. 'Right, three-thirty, yes.' She put the phone back in her bag and then retrieved it. 'Oh, shit, I'd better check Bill Bosworth got my message.'

'You've done that already,' Nia reassured her.

'Twice,' said Ros helpfully. 'If he doesn't come today, do you think he'll have time to do it all tomorrow? Did you say the stuff arrived today?'

'Yes,' said Madeleine, looking like she'd just discovered her two ugly sisters had put her precious pumpkin into a pie. 'It's practically blocking the drive. Barry's going to start spreading it out this afternoon.' She glanced at her reflection in the window,

'Although what's the point now?'

'Oh, come on, Maddy, it's not that bad. The hairdresser'll be able to salvage something,' said Nia.

Ros's eyes roved over Madeleine's moulting head. 'Are you sure that girl didn't say anything about not washing your hair? What did they say when you went in today?'

Madeleine's eyes sparkled with anger.

'Ros, I've told you already. No one told me not to wash my hair for twenty-four hours. I think I would have remembered if they had. I told them this morning. I'm not an idiot! I said that if it's that sodding important they should be issuing handouts!' She reached for her coffee but abandoned before her fingers touched the cup. 'Honestly, they were so rude!'

'Did they actually refuse to do anything?' said Nia, suspecting there might be two sides to this tale.

'Absolutely! I insisted but they said they were already overbooked and tried to fob me off by saying that Sonia would be able to sort it out tomorrow when she came over at seven. Obviously I told them *that* won't be happening now!'

'So, technically,' said Nia carefully, 'they didn't actually refuse.'

'Nonsense!' objected Madeleine. 'They refused point blank to do anything today. So tough luck, Miss Edwards, you'll have to fend for your fucking self!'

'So they did think something could be done?' pressed Ros. 'But not until tomorrow?'

'Well, if that's how you want to view it,' said Madeleine, looking decidedly haughty. 'But *what* they could do is anyone's guess! No, I need something done today! It's my wedding tomorrow. I intend to look absolutely fabulous and I need a good night's sleep – not one filled with worry!'

***

Saturday, 18th October, 7a.m.

Just as Madeleine threw back the duvet the front door scraped open, scuppering her plan for a bath before her entourage arrived. 'Oh, what a surprise – no one sorted out that bloody door!' she muttered, throwing on her robe. 'Honestly, you ask someone to do just one thing!'

She had given the beautician a key just in case she overslept, and was pleased he had decided to use it. From the top of the stairs she called out, 'Hello, I'm up here.'

There was no answer from the hall. She looked over the balustrade. No person either. But then a noise from the kitchen suggested that someone was filling the kettle. She smiled. What amazing service! So, pulling her robe secure she skipped down the stairs and pushed open the kitchen door.

'Hayden! What the..? Fuck! What have you forgotten? Couldn't Brian have come? Honestly, you could have shouted. I would have stayed upstairs!'

Hayden flicked the switch on the kettle and got two mugs from the dishwasher. He spooned a teaspoon of instant coffee into each mug, splashed milk into one and added a heaped spoonful of sugar into one of the cups. As he tipped the spoon Madeleine noticed his hand was shaking.

'Oh, great, you've got a hangover!'

For the first time since Madeleine had entered the kitchen Hayden looked Madeleine in the face. 'Sit down, Maddy. I've got something to tell you.'

Madeleine stood. 'What?' Then a look of abject horror swept over her face. 'It's my dress, isn't it? You've damaged it. Is it ripped? How bad?'

Hayden dragged a stool out from under the breakfast bar, sat and nursed his coffee cup in both hands. 'The dress is fine,

Maddy. So is the house and the seating plan and the place settings and the flowers… The problem is… I'm not.'

'What?'

Madeleine's mind raced. What could she possibly have forgotten? His suit had been delivered to Amrose Street on Wednesday, his shoes had been polished to within an inch of their lives by Mrs B; he had even finally agreed to have that manicure and his hair had been trimmed (together with those annoying little whiskers that had a tendency to poke out from his nostrils). How could he not be fine?

'I'm not going to marry you, Maddy… I… don't love you.'

'But that's—'

'I've met someone. I didn't plan it, it just happened and last night I…' He coughed and took a large gulp of coffee before he finished the sentence. 'I spent the night with her.'

'What? In my house?' said Madeleine, suddenly outraged.

Hayden allowed himself a gentle laugh.

'No, I…we stayed in a hotel.'

'Which one? Oh, not Stradley House? Oh, great! Whenever I suggested it, you always said it was too close to Landsmere!'

'It doesn't matter, Maddy,' said Hayden, his voice steady. 'All I know is that I can't marry you. I feel terrible but I just can't.'

The meaning of Hayden's words finally penetrated her wedding-focused brain.

'So while I've been working my arse off to make sure this wedding is a success… so *you* look great in front of *your* friends, you've been screwing some little bit on the side?' Hayden opened his mouth but Madeleine's had slid into gear. 'So who is it? Some little slut Tranter's brought in? Or a gold-digging divorcee from the club? God, to think I was about to give my life up for someone as shallow as you!'

'It's Ben's teacher actually, Elaina O'Reilly. You met her—'

Madeleine's horror was complete.

'That!' spat Madeleine. 'Fucking hell, Hayden! The Widow Reilly? You couldn't write it!! Mrs Straight-laced, private school teacher! God, after all I've given you – my devotion, my dedication… my body! Well, I hope *she* likes to get her arse out for you in the morning? Tell you what, I'll leave the peephole basque if you like – and the Vaseline! After all, she'll have to get used to it sooner or later!'

She dashed the coffee-filled cup across the breakfast bar, sending a spray of brown liquid up the newly painted wall.

A little voice behind her broke the sudden silence. 'Um, does this mean I won't be needed?'

She turned to see a young man standing in the doorway clad in drainpipe jeans, sporting a pale pink scarf and a Dalmatian-patterned waistcoat, his index finger hooked around the handle of a lime-green vanity case.

Saturday, 18th October, 7.30a.m.

'Where are my fucking keys?' stormed Madeleine. She had thrown together a bag of clothes, with the intention of sending Nia to get the rest of her things at a later date. 'And the keys for Amrose Street? Thank fuck I didn't sell after all!'

'Take the Audi, Maddy. I want you to have it,' said Hayden, his voice calm. The keys for the Beetle were on the end hook under the key for the rarely used potting shed.

'I was planning to!' The notion of taking her old Beetle hadn't entered her head.

She found the keys on the hall table, grabbed her bag and

hauled on the front door. A blur of legs and grey hair flashed past, pursued by a giggling Ben. Ben skidded to a halt and pointed at the panting hound.

'Look, Aunty Madeleine, Ba Ritten bought me a puppy! Her name is Madagascar, but Mummy wants to call her Maddy! She's an Irish Wolfhound!' It suddenly struck Madeleine that Ben had lost his lisp – not that she really cared when, or how. She'd always known the arrival of Hayden's daughter would prove problematic.

Saffy halted in the middle of the courtyard. A young man stood just behind her, his arm on her shoulder – Madeleine had a vague memory of the vet who had nursed Morris but she was in no mood for pleasantries. None of them looked dressed for a wedding.

'And I suppose I'm the last to know?' hissed Madeleine. 'And if that fucking animal has shat in my house, you'll be getting the redecoration bill!'

Saffy glanced at her feet then looked Madeleine in the eye.

'He loves her, you know. He really does.'

'Well, I just hope that one day I'll be able to forgive him,' said Madeleine, throwing Saffy her best hurt look and her bag into the car.

Taking absolutely no notice of the potholes Madeleine accelerated away from the house, leaving Saffy and Paul to dodge the hail of gravel made by her wheel-spinning departure. The to-do list, complete with contact numbers and names was now stuffed deep into Madeleine's bag. The caterers were due at eight a.m. – Hayden might not want a wedding but he was damn well going to have one, even if the star attraction wasn't going to be there!

The thought of all the guests arriving for the non-wedding made Madeleine laugh out loud. All that food, all those flowers; the bill for the dress had appeared on Hayden's gold card statement only that week – although she hadn't had chance to mention it. Oh yes, he'd pay! He would definitely pay!

Coming the other way, Bill Bosworth was singing. The sound of the steamroller almost drowned out Status Quo *Rocking All Over the World* blasting from his iPod fit to burst eardrums, but not quite: Bill was indeed giving it large. Despite the chill air, it was a beautiful morning and with any luck he would be able to sort this little job out before ten and then go off for a bit of fishing later. High tide was at four and there was a good chance he might be bringing Mrs B home a nice sea bass.

With the engine now warm and the morning sun streaming into the roller's cab, Bill started to regret donning an extra layer that morning. He nudged open the side window, took a deep sniff of the autumn morning and… inhaled something straight up his nose.

One explosive sneeze followed another and when he opened his eyes again there, coming at him at speed, was a bright red Audi.

Unable to stop, Bill closed his eyes and waited for the crash. Nothing happened.

He opened his one eye – no car. He looked behind and down at the ground the machine had just flattened – no car. The Audi was nowhere to be seen.

'Blimey,' he muttered, seeing no point at all in turning off his iPod. 'So the nail varnish didn't match after all then!'

At the end of the drive, the Audi skidded to a halt just in time to give way to a police car making for town, blue lights flashing and siren screaming.

But where to go? It occurred to Madeleine, albeit briefly, that she really should probably phone Nia and Ros to tell them about the non-wedding… but nah… Hayden could tell them. Hayden could bloody well tell everyone. After all, most of them were his friends anyway!

Madeleine peered at her reflection in the rear view mirror. The repaired hair extensions really did suit her, and that colour was exactly right. Her eyebrows looked good, too, and yesterday's last minute decision to go for the eyelash tint really did add the perfect finishing touch to the autumn look she'd worked so hard to achieve. Turning her head to admire the gold tints that were now catching the sunlight nicely, she saw again the hastily packed Louis Vuitton bag on the back seat.

Now there was one lesson that Madeleine had learned a long time ago – and that was never delete a phone number. You never knew when you might need it.

With a smile she fished her mobile out from under the driver's seat, where it had slid when she had dodged the steamroller…

As a familiar voice said, 'Hello,' Madeleine's face broke into her best smile.

'Kaz, hi!…'